"You want to get rid of me?"

Dean combed his fingers through his hair. "I can't believe after only one week—"

"Nine days," Elise corrected. "Nine long, horrifying days."

Dean looked down at her, her turquoise eyes flashing with anger. "You're beautiful when you're ticked off."

His husky voice caused her to falter. "Don't try to sweet-talk me, Detective Cornell."

He leaned closer until their mouths were a breath apart. "Doc, I can think of a hell of a lot more things I'd like to do with you than sweet-talking. Wanna hear what they are?"

She'd never thought it physically possible for one's heart to jump into one's throat—until now. "Don't change the subject!"

"You were the one who started it." His warm breath fanned across her lips. "Shall we see what else we can start?"

ABOUT THE AUTHOR

The author of almost thirty novels, Linda Randall Wisdom is well-known to readers of Harlequin American Romance and romance readers everywhere. Her lively stories, filled with sexy heroes, humor and passionate romance, have been delighting us for years—ever since she sold her first book on her wedding anniversary, which, Linda says, proves she was destined to write romances. Like the veterinarian heroine in *Sometimes a Lady,* Linda lives with a houseful of exotic animals, in Southern California.

Books by Linda Randall Wisdom
HARLEQUIN AMERICAN ROMANCE

Don't miss any of our special offers. Write to us at the following address for information on our newest releases.

Harlequin Reader Service
P.O. Box 1397, Buffalo, NY 14240
Canadian address: P.O. Box 603,
Fort Erie, Ont. L2A 5X3

LINDA RANDALL WISDOM

SOMETIMES A LADY

Harlequin Books

TORONTO • NEW YORK • LONDON
AMSTERDAM • PARIS • SYDNEY • HAMBURG
STOCKHOLM • ATHENS • TOKYO • MILAN

For Elaine Chase—
for the laughter, the tears, the shared phone calls.
Most importantly, the friendship.

Published January 1992

ISBN 0-373-16422-X

SOMETIMES A LADY

Chapter One

"If you've come to rob the place, you're too late."

Her voice was pitched low enough not to carry to the wrong set of ears, which made it music to this man's acute hearing. Dean slowly inched up from the belly crawl he'd been performing since sliding through a rear window that was smaller than he'd gauged. He swore his back was scraped raw from his wiggling; he'd almost gotten stuck halfway in. The guys at the station and the six-o'clock news sure would have loved *that*—it was the type of event that haunted a man right up to his retirement dinner.

He raised his head slightly and surveyed the area. The main lobby of the midtown bank was the tension-ridden stage of a robbery gone bad. A guard had already been wounded, and ten people were still being held hostage while the police negotiator tried to deal with three unstable kooks probably sky-high on drugs.

"You're awfully calm for a hostage," he commented sotto voce to the woman watching him with a pair of the most beautiful eyes he'd ever seen. Turquoise eyes, strawberry-blond hair, heart-shaped face. Just the kind of woman he wouldn't mind getting to know better. She smelled real good to a man who'd been crawling along a dusty floor. He crept over to a column where he could crouch down, unseen by the robbers brandishing lethal-looking weapons over a huddled group of men and women.

Her lips barely moved as she kept a wary eye on the armed men. "It doesn't do any good to get upset over a situation I can't resolve by myself."

He grinned. "Good girl."

She arched an eyebrow. "The times are changing, my friend. *Woman* is the appropriate term." She looked back down at the man lying beside her, who moaned, shifting restlessly, his bloodstained gray uniform shirt torn open to reveal a wadded-up half-slip used as a compress.

The one-man rescue team hissed through his teeth. "How bad is he?"

"Bad enough. I was able to stop the bleeding, but he's awfully shocky."

Dean rubbed a hand over his beard. "You a nurse?"

Her lips twitched with what looked like secret amusement. "I'm a doctor." She eyed the dark-haired, dark-eyed man who looked like the answer to any woman's dream. The kind who got the blood stirring and the hormones jumping. The kind she preferred to stay as far away from as possible.

He looked properly rueful. "Guess I blew it with my sexist assumptions, huh?" He wondered what she'd say if he told her that she had the most beautiful eyes he'd ever seen and, by the way, was she free Saturday night?

"So what are *you* here for? To take a census?"

He grinned as he pointed to the gold shield clipped to his shirt pocket. "Detective Dean Cornell. I'm your rescue party."

She rolled her eyes. "God help us."

"Your prayers have been answered."

"I don't think so."

"What's going on back there?" A man wearing dark clothing and a ski mask and cradling an automatic weapon against his chest walked toward the woman and her patient—and Detective Dean Cornell.

The doctor showed no outward sign of fear. She had once vowed she would never be victimized by a man with a gun again, and her firm resolve kept her from backing down in abject terror before this animal. "I'm talking to my patient in hopes of keeping him alive. I didn't think you'd want a murder charge added to your list of misdeeds."

"Lady, if you don't want to see that pretty face roughed up, you won't open your mouth again." His voice was strained, high-pitched with either fear or something even more dangerous.

She didn't flinch. "Sorry, I thought you'd want your question answered."

The man stalked back toward the front where his two accomplices paced restlessly, twitching fingers caressing their guns. She watched him, wondering why he seemed so familiar to her even though she couldn't see his face. She dreaded the idea he might have been in her clinic at one time.

For Elise Carpenter it was the perfect climax to a hellish morning. The minute she'd gotten up and realized it was Friday the thirteenth, she should have climbed back into bed and stayed there.

First the automated teller ate her bankcard, forcing her to go inside to cash a check and request a new card. Before she finished her transactions, three maniacs ran in, waving automatic rifles and yelling, "Hold up." Between customers screaming, a teller hitting the alarm button, the guard getting shot, and panicked robbers seeing no choice but to hold the people hostage while deciding how to get out of there in one piece, she felt as if she were living a nightmare.

She'd fudged her credentials a bit in hopes of helping the wounded guard and told the robbers she was a doctor. And just as she saw her day going to hell in a hand basket, this overgrown adolescent, looking more like a street person than a cop, crawled into the lobby and announced he was going to save her! She only hoped her daughters in Riverside County and sister here in town wouldn't hear her name on the evening news; thank heavens, her parents were on a cruise.

"Detective, if you have an extra weapon on you, I'm a crack shot," she said softly.

"Sorry, I never carry a spare. You think these guys will surrender to that SWAT team or come out shooting?"

"The latter. While I don't claim to be an expert, I'd hazard a guess two of them are coming down from some heavy-duty drugs and growing more unstable by the minute. The leader is just as unbalanced. Probably even more so. He appears to enjoy intimidating anyone who gets in his way. He's the one who shot the guard."

Dean swore under his breath. "Okay, Doc, remain calm, and we'll get you out of here as soon as possible."

She turned her head slightly and ran into a pair of eyes so dark a brown they were almost black. Bittersweet chocolate, she thought illogically. Good thing she was a *milk* chocolate fan. The detective wore a full beard that was just a bit shaggy, as if he hadn't taken the time to trim it lately. His hair, too, was overlong, and had waves most women would kill for. Hadn't the character ever heard of haircuts?

Still she had to admit that this thug with a badge looked as if he could handle any situation that came along. So why didn't she put her trust in him? Easy. He was a cop. Past experience had taught her police weren't all they were cracked up to be. "Ah, yes, the men in blue to the rescue. It's amazing, I feel safer already."

Dean frowned. Her sardonic tone told him she didn't have much faith in law enforcers. The cop in him noted the hectic rose color dotting her creamy complexion and the glitter in her gemstone eyes; he'd hazard a guess both were indicative of a temper most people would probably duck to avoid. Not him; he never backed down from a good fight. He glanced at his watch.

"I need to count on you, Doc. In a minute all hell's going to break loose, and we're gonna have to pray those people up front hit the deck fast."

"What you're talking about is performing your personalized version of *Die Hard* and taking a chance with people's lives."

"*Saving* lives is more like it."

Dean watched the second hand on his watch, slowly counting down. Precisely as it swept past the twelve, he leaped up.

"All right, freeze!" His eyes widened as the three gunmen, automatics ready, spun around, and he realized his backup hadn't yet appeared. "Sh—!" He dove for cover, rolling over and over as the front door crashed open in a storm of glass and men in uniform came running in, guns drawn.

Thanks to quick thinking and near-precision action, gunfire was kept to a minimum. Elise huddled protectively over her patient and fervently prayed it would all be over soon and she would remain in one piece.

"YOU OKAY, ma'am?" A uniformed officer wearing a bullet-proof vest bent over her.

She ignored his outstretched hand and stood up, dusting her hands against her thighs. "Yes, I'm fine, but this man needs immediate medical attention."

"Paramedics!" he bellowed.

"Oh, damn."

Elise turned at the sound of the disgruntled voice. Her "hero" was sprawled on the floor, mumbling curses and holding his right hand against his left shoulder, which was stained a bright red.

"We have another casualty," she announced crisply. "Why am I not surprised?" she added quietly, hoping nonetheless that Detective Cornell was not gravely injured.

Dean looked into Elise's eyes. "I can't stand the sight of blood," he told her just before he keeled to one side and passed out cold.

A tall man in his mid-forties appeared and crouched down next to Dean's prone figure. "Good going, buddy," he said in a gravelly voice. He chuckled, then caught the surprise on Elise's face. "It's just a flesh wound. This guy can handle any situation as long as it doesn't involve his own blood. Then he's a goner."

Elise shook her head. "Some rescuer he turned out to be." She moved away to accompany the paramedics as they wheeled out the wounded bank guard.

WHEN DEAN CAME TO, he found himself strapped to a gurney outside the open doors of an ambulance.

"Hey, Mac," he croaked, trying unsuccessfully to lift his hand out from under restraining straps.

Frank "Mac" McConnell appeared at his side. "Don't worry, buddy, you'll live." He grinned.

"You guys were five seconds late," he accused, closing his eyes to fight the light-headedness overtaking him.

"Your watch was probably fast. That's what happens when you buy cheap merchandise."

Dean turned his head. "Better me shot than you, I guess. If you'd gotten it, Stacy would have skinned me alive."

Mac chuckled. "Yeah, you're right there."

Dean shifted, then winced as white-hot pain tore through his shoulder. "Is the gorgeous doc anywhere around?"

"Yeah, over there."

Dean tried to move, then swore under his breath as shafts of pain whizzed through his shoulder. "Could you ask her if she'd like a new patient? Be sure to tell her what a great guy I am."

Mac shook his head. Trust Dean to use any situation, including a gunshot wound, to get a pretty woman's attention. "I don't know, Dean, she doesn't seem too friendly to cops."

"Oh, come on, she's the best thing I've seen in years. Besides, I don't have a regular doctor. Give me a break. I could be dying here." He hoped he looked suitably pathetic.

"We should be so lucky." Mac sauntered off, catching up with Elise, who was talking to one of the uniformed officers.

With a hopeful gaze, Dean watched Mac talk to her and saw her amused smile as she glanced toward the gurney. She said something else and pulled a card out of her purse, handing it to Mac. Dean didn't like the expression in Mac's eyes when he returned.

"At first she turned you down flat," he said without preamble. "Then she reconsidered and said maybe she *was* the doctor for you." He dropped the business card onto Dean's chest.

Dean craned his neck to decipher the small print on the blue pasteboard. He couldn't. "Meaning what?"

Mac tipped the card. "Read it and weep, my friend."

With the card angled, Dean read: Dr. Elise Carpenter, Doctor of Veterinary Science. Below, in smaller print was her specialty: exotic animals.

"The world is cruel, Mac. Really cruel."

"WERE YOU FRIGHTENED in there?"

"Did you feel as if they would kill you at any time?"

"Please, look this way?"

"Vultures," Elise muttered to the young officer record-ing her words, glaring at the press people buzzing all around them.

He looked confused. "Ma'am?"

She sighed. "Let's just get this over with, all right?" Her brow creased in a puzzled frown as she looked beyond the officer's shoulder to the three handcuffed prisoners being led toward waiting patrol cars. Something about the leader of the deadly trio still jogged her mind. Then he struggled briefly, and the sleeve of his sweatshirt slid back to reveal the tattoo of a grinning skull with a coiled snake emerging from the mouth. A vivid scar was slashed across the skull. The tattoo and a scar.

The officer's words became nothing more than white noise as she stared at the tattoo and the scar while old memories exploded in her brain. She was suddenly blind to her surroundings and deaf to the young man's worried-sounding questions as scenes from five years ago flashed through her mind, renewing pain she thought she'd finally put behind her.

The clinic she and her husband Steve had worked so hard to expand...the night they stayed late to tend an ailing macaw...the two men breaking in, looking for drugs...Steven fighting with them, getting shot during the struggle...one of the intruders slapping her around...the seemingly miraculous sound of a police cruiser's siren. She'd fought back, grabbing a scalpel and slashing at her attacker, cutting open his arm, which left him crazy with pain and determined to do worse to her. It all unfolded be-fore her eyes: the frantic ride to the hospital, only to hear her husband pronounced dead on arrival...two hours later, going into early labor and miscarrying the baby boy they'd hoped for after having their three delightful daughters.

Then came the questions, the investigation, the arrests, finally the lineup. She had identified the two men easily, especially the one with the distinctive tattoo on his left arm, now marred by a diagonal slash. And then, because of police error—a "technicality," the wrong name was typed on the arrest report—the man was freed, leaving a bitter widow with three young children to raise.

From that day on, Elise had had no use for the police.

Elise stared at the man, feeling all the anger and all the pain rise up. All the fury of a woman who had lost too much and never had the chance to see justice served. Justice she felt compelled to carry out herself if no one else would do it.

"You bastard!" she screamed, shoving past the stunned officer and running toward the prisoner, murder on her mind. Just as she reached her prey, a strong arm circled her waist, lifting her off her feet and out of the way. "No! Let me go!" She vainly batted at the arm.

"That I can't do, Doc," Mac murmured, stepping back a few paces. "Now, we know these creeps put you through hell back there, but you can't take the law into your own hands."

The pain bursting through her brain left her blind with fury. "You don't understand! That son of a bitch killed my husband and my baby five years ago, and you idiots let him loose!" The anguish flowing through her made her entire body quiver with rage.

Mac uttered a pungent curse as he noticed the television news cameras hungrily recording the scene. "Look, Doc, I think we should go down to the station and get this straightened out." He ushered her toward his car and away from the hungry press eagerly recording every word.

Elise sat stiffly in the passenger seat. The memories had ripped open old wounds and now she couldn't hold back the pain. She clenched her teeth to keep the moans inside. She turned to stare blankly out the window.

"You okay, Doc?" Mac asked in his quiet, gravelly voice as he turned into the precinct parking lot.

She didn't turn her head. "Never better."

He stopped the car and got out, walking around to assist her. Elise noticed the broad gold band on his left ring finger and a gold chain circling his wrist. The chain looked too delicate for such a masculine guy.

"How long have you been married, Detective?" she asked as he guided her toward a side door into the station.

His craggy features softened. "A little over two years. We're expecting our first child soon."

"I was married almost twelve years when I had to explain to my three children that a crazed drug addict had killed their father and their unborn baby brother," she said in a quiet, deadly monotone. "Then I had to explain to them that the man responsible wouldn't receive the justice he deserved because the police had had to let him go. All because someone couldn't spell."

Careful not to react visibly, Mac winced inside. He didn't have to look hard to see why Dean was attracted to the woman. She was lovely, with strawberry-blond hair pulled back in a French braid, delicate features and bright turquoise eyes that had seen too much horror for any one lifetime. She also had a cool, touch-me-not manner, which probably attracted his partner the most. He made a mental note to call the hospital to check on Dean as soon as he could get away to a phone. First, though, he had some bad news for good ol' Captain Anderson. Tomorrow's glowing headlines featuring the department's neat easy capture of the bank robbers was going to turn into something very messy unless they could contain the secondary story—fast.

"She *WHAT?*" Captain Anderson's face was so red Mac wondered if the man would keel over from shock.

Mac rubbed a hand wearily over his face. Maybe Dean *had* gotten the better deal by being shot. At least he didn't have to sit in on this. Mac doubted his butt would be in one piece once this business was finished. "She's the widow of a veterinarian killed five years ago by one of the prisoners. Seems he got off due to a clerical error, and now she's out for blood—his *and* ours. And not necessarily in that order. The press got an earful when she recognized him." He waited for the explosion.

He didn't have long to wait. The captain paced back and forth, haranguing the world in general, Dean and Mac specifically.

"Where is she now?" the captain asked once he ran out of steam.

"She's at my desk calling her sister." He smiled wryly at his superior's look of fury. "Captain, she's not under arrest. She wanted to assure her sister she was all right, since the woman has probably seen the story on the news."

"I want her in here, now."

Mac pushed himself out of the chair. "You got it." He hoped he could stick around to see Captain Anderson and Dr. Carpenter faced off. Somehow he doubted the doctor would be intimidated.

As soon as Elise entered Captain Anderson's office, it was clear who would dominate the conversation.

"Captain, I've given my statement, identified the robbers and insisted on double-checking your men's paperwork to insure there are no mistakes *this time,*" she began without preamble. "Now I'd like to go home and say a few prayers that you don't screw up the arrest."

The older man's jaw worked furiously. He glanced down at her statement. "Mrs. Carpenter."

"*Dr.* Carpenter."

He took a deep breath. "Doctor. I'm sorry you've had to face your husband's alleged killer more than once."

Her eyes were turquoise chips of ice. "*Alleged?* Captain, I watched the man turn his gun on my husband and shoot him in the head. The overhead lights were on, so there was no mistaking the shooter's identity. His face and that tattoo have been firmly etched in my memory. I only wish I had used my scalpel on his throat instead of his arm. Then we wouldn't be having this conversation right now. You let him get away this time, and I'll tell the press a story that will make your name mud." Her voice was soft and dangerous. "A story that will give your superiors in city hall something to think about."

Captain Anderson's face darkened with fury. "I don't appreciate being threatened, Dr. Carpenter."

She didn't back down. "I never threaten, Captain Anderson. I only state the facts." With that, she spun on her heel and stalked out of the office.

"You!" The captain pointed his finger at Mac, who lounged near the door. "Keep an eye on her and find out when that idiotic partner of yours will be fit to return to work."

Mac straightened up and touched two fingers to his forehead in salute. "Gotcha."

He walked out and found Elise greeting a woman who looked so much like her they had to be related. Elise noticed Mac and quickly strode over to his desk.

"Detective, I know I've been a bit of a bitch, and I apologize for taking it out on you." She stuck out her hand. "Thank you for putting up with me."

"No apology necessary, Doc. I enjoyed watching you make mincemeat out of the captain in there. We don't get to see that happen too often."

Her lips twitched. "You know, with a little effort and some spit and polish, you and your partner might just pass in polite company." With that, she left.

"AH, COME ON, it's only a flesh wound." Dean knew he was whining, but he couldn't help it; he hated hospitals almost as much as he hated the sight of his own blood. "I'll go home and go straight to bed, I promise."

The doctor writing on his chart looked at him with disbelief. "Give me a break, Detective. I know you guys only too well. You're staying here overnight for observation."

Dean groaned with impatience. "But I have a dog to feed!"

"You do not." Stacy McConnell walked into the room—actually, waddled, since she was close to eight months pregnant. "You hate animals."

"Stacy." He winced as he pushed himself up into a sitting position. "How did you know I was here?"

She grinned. "You were on the evening news, my dear. They said you were unconscious from loss of blood, but I knew better. You passed out once you realized the blood was yours, didn't you?" She dropped a stack of comic books onto his bed. "Here, I brought you some reading material." She rested her hands on the chair arms and slowly lowered herself downward, glancing with gratitude at the doctor, who gave her a helping hand. "Thanks. Sitting isn't as easy as it used to be."

"You didn't *drive* down here, did you? Mac'd bust a gut if he thought you drove here by yourself."

"No, Janet dropped me off. I left a message for Mac that he could meet me here." She covered his hand. "How are you feeling?"

He grimaced. "I just want to go home."

"Dean, a five-year-old would be acting more mature than you are right now," Stacy remonstrated, smiling at him with affection.

"I don't care. I want out of here!"

"Wouldn't you rather check out the nurses?" Mac walked in, pausing to kiss his wife before perching on her chair arm.

"The only woman I wanted to check out turned me down flat."

Mac grinned. "Ah, yes, Dr. Carpenter. The lady's something else."

"Watch it, bud." Stacy elbowed him in the midriff. "Remember you're a married man."

He pretended great pain. "I meant for Dean here."

"I should hope so."

"What happened?" Dean demanded, sensing he'd missed something.

Mac quickly filled him in, including the episode in Captain Anderson's office.

"Oh, man, I miss all the good stuff," Dean moaned, trying, without much success, to turn over. He glared at the IV that impeded his movement. "The old man must be having a coronary over all this."

"He was popping antacids like they were candy when I left. We're to keep on top of this, and if anything goes wrong, our heads roll."

Dean wasn't worried. "He's been threatening us with that for years."

"Yeah, but the lady has some pretty nasty ammunition. The public likes nothing better than learning the police screwed up. And this was one big mess. I pulled the file to see what we're in for. It should have been cut-and-dried if it hadn't been for some idiot who typed in the wrong name."

Dean was hopeful. "At least I'll get to see her again."

"Her and her three kids."

"Oh, come on, Kris, you know I've tried to date but each time was a complete disaster."

"You didn't give them a chance!"

"A chance? One guy was allergic to the animals. Another thought a vet would be a great drug connection. And let's not forget that production control manager from your company who got so miffed when Baby insulted him that he informed me my children's emotional growth would be stunted by their bizarre home life."

Kristen waved a hand. "Well, Baby does get pretty insulting if anyone dares to refer to her as a bird. It's your fault for raising her like a child. She's positive she's human and that all the other animals are *her* pets. That bird is strange, Elise. Very strange."

She smiled. "She's not strange, she's special. How many women get a hand-fed blue-and-gold baby macaw for a wedding present?"

Kristen shook her head, used to her sister's preoccupation with exotic animals. "Did you get hold of the girls?"

Elise nodded, her expression sober once more. "They were worried after seeing the news, but I assured them everything was fine. Myrna said she was going to take them out to dinner and the movies tonight and not to cut my time short at the conference. Keri, likewise told me that she'd keep an eye on Lisa and Becky."

"Ten to one those three are ecstatic Myrna is staying with them. I'm sure they're doing everything you don't allow them to and they plan to live it up as long as possible," Kristen teased.

Elise pushed herself up and out of the hot tub, sitting on the edge as she reached for her glass of wine. "Funny, if I hadn't decided to miss the conference's opening speeches, I would have missed seeing that slime caught again." Her features turned grim. "I want to see that bastard behind bars. I'm not going to allow Steve's killer to get away again."

"Elise, don't even think of anything that smacks of vigilantism," Kristen warned. "Let the police do their work."

"Then they'd better not screw up again."

"HEY, LOOK, it's the hero returning from the wars!" came the announcement from the squad room.

Dean bowed several times as he made his way to his desk. "Thank you, thank you, men. But no big deal, obviously, since four days later I'm back in the trenches. Just a flesh wound. Nothing to worry about."

"Is that why you passed out cold the minute you saw the blood?" one uniform joked.

"Once I have full mobility back, I'll take you to task for that remark." Dean tossed his sheepskin-lined denim jacket onto his chair before heading for Mac's desk. After a bit of searching he found what he was looking for: Dr. Elise Carpenter's statement and a bit of personal information.

Too bad she didn't live in the area. Still, Murrieta over in Riverside County would make a nice drive. Thirty-seven, widowed, three daughters, ages sixteen, twelve and seven. Lucky he was pretty good with kids, although most of the kids he dealt with were rough-and-tumble boys.

"Better watch it, Cornell, or you'll end up as soppy as that partner of yours," he muttered to himself.

"Be prepared, old buddy."

Dean looked up, wisecrack ready, but his smile disappeared when he saw his partner's grim expression.

"Something tells me I'm not going to like what you're about to say."

"Heads are going to roll," Mac announced. "And ours will lead the procession."

Cold entered his veins. "What happened?"

"Dr. Carpenter's favorite man walked out of the county jail this morning and hasn't been seen or heard from since."

Chapter Two

"Thank you for giving me a ride, Andrew. I guess that battery I bought for my car wasn't as good as the mechanic said it was." Elise forced a stiff smile to her lips. Standing on her sister's front stoop, she dipped her head, rummaging through her purse for her keys, eager for the safety of the house.

An arm slung itself heavily across her shoulders. "You know, Elise, the evening doesn't have to end." Whiskey-scented breath wafted unpleasantly across her face. "It's still early."

"Yes, it does have to end, and while you think it's early, I don't." She wiggled out of his loose embrace, using what her daughters called her this-is-my-final-warning voice.

When she left the hotel where the veterinarians' conference-closing banquet was held, she didn't expect her car to refuse to start. Tired and ready for a relaxing bath and bed, she'd eagerly accepted Dr. Andrew Marsh's offer of a ride after he'd looked under her car hood and pronounced the battery dead. Still tired from the past few days' events, including the bank robbery, the reporters and the conference, she'd noticed too late that Andrew had drunk too much that evening to be a completely safe driver. It had become especially obvious when one of his hands kept finding its way to his passenger's knee during the short drive from the hotel to Kristen's.

"In fact," she added now, "I think you should seriously consider calling a cab to return you to the hotel."

He swayed forward, his eyes glazed from the alcohol he'd consumed. "Then I'll have to come inside to call, won't I?" He looked at the darkened windows. "Looks real cozy. Your sister out for the evening?"

"She's most definitely home, and she would not appreciate an unexpected visitor." She tried to insert her key in the lock and bat Andrew's hands away at the same time. "Andrew, do you mind!"

"Not at all, sweetie. C'mon, just one little kiss." At almost any other time Elise might have found his pucker laughable. Right now, though, she only thought about slapping it off his face.

"Andrew, get your hands off me this minute or you'll find yourself practicing surgery with both arms in slings," she threatened.

"Aw, come on, Elise, loosen up."

"Hey, buddy, the lady told you to get your hands off her. I suggest you do as she says."

Both Elise and Andrew turned at the unexpected interruption from the shrubbery along the front of the house. The foliage parted to reveal Dean Cornell and Mac McConnell. Both were dressed in faded jeans and denim jackets and looked as if they should be straddling Harleys instead of protecting the public.

"I don't need this," Elise moaned softly, looking skyward.

"Who do you think you are?" Andrew protested, all puffed-up drunken swagger. "We're having a private conversation here."

Dean's chilling smile should have sobered up the inebriated doctor faster than a cold shower and hot coffee would have. He pulled out a leather wallet and flashed a badge. "We're the fuzz, buddy. Maybe you'd better run along before I slap you with a morals charge." He scowled at the man. "Of course, if you get back behind that wheel, a DWI would be impossible to avoid."

Elise lifted her eyes to the sky and silently counted to ten. She was *not* happy about this.

"Elise is going to call me a cab." Andrew moved a step closer to her as if seeking protection from these scruffy-looking men.

Mac spoke up. "There's a 7-Eleven at the corner with three pay phones, friend. I suggest you use one of them. I'll even give you a quarter."

"He can call from here," Elise inserted, not about to let these buffoons take charge. By now she was so angry she could chew nails. Who the hell were they to tell people what to do? Her eyes flashed fury as she first directed her ire on Dean then moved on to Mac.

Andrew scurried down the walk, keeping one eye on the two men still standing there. "No wonder nobody can get close to you, with bodyguards like these macho jerks," he called out, determined to have the last word before practically running down the street.

Hands braced on her hips, Elise spun around and faced the two detectives with all the fury her three daughters prayed they would never incur.

"You idiots, what do you think you were doing just then?" She kept her voice low in deference to the neighbors, although she wanted nothing more than to scream. "That man is a colleague who throws a lot of business my way. You treated him like a common criminal!"

"Yeah, and it appeared he expected to be paid for all that business he sends you, too," Dean replied, unfazed by her temper. In truth, he was dazzled by it, along with seeing her slender body dressed in a bronze silk sheath and cream wool coat. The perfume she wore tonight was heavier than the one he remembered from the bank and packed a powerful wallop. Her reddish blond hair was twisted up in an intricate knot, revealing the slender column of her throat, which was adorned by a tricolor twisted chin. Her high heels matched her dress and did wonderful things for a pair of legs he decided he could look at forever.

Elise eyed the suggestive saying on Dean's T-shirt with faint disgust. "You don't get out often, do you?"

"Down boy," Mac murmured in his gravelly voice before Dean could respond to Elise's comment.

Dean reluctantly pulled himself back to the business at hand. "Dr. Carpenter, we'd like to come in and talk to you."

"Detective, do you know what time it is?"

"Yes, ma'am, we do. We've been waiting for you for the past two hours. We wouldn't be here if we didn't feel it was important."

"Amazing how something so important had you lurking in the bushes," she muttered, pulling the screen door open with such force it almost came off its hinges before she unlocked the inner door and thrust it open. The two men were on her heels as she stormed into the living room.

"We're sorry if we ruined your date," Dean told her without a hint of apology. He privately thought that kind of man wasn't right for someone like this lady.

"It wasn't a date. I was at a conference; I had a dead battery, and Dr. Marsh offered to drive me home." She shrugged off her coat and draped it over the back of a chair. "Let's cut out the small talk, shall we? Exactly why are you here? It's been a long day and an equally long evening. The sooner you tell me why you're here, the sooner you're gone and I'm catching up on some much-needed sleep."

Mac and Dean exchanged a telling look. One Elise didn't like.

She stiffened. What if... "What is it? Is it something about my daughters? Just tell me, dammit!" Her voice was raspy; her stomach rolled. If anything had happened to one of the girls, she doubted she could go on.

It had been decided beforehand that Dean would be the one to break the news. Gently. But after seeing the terror etched on her face as she demanded reassurance her daughters were all right, he knew he had to blurt out the truth and not waste any time. "As far as we know, your daughters are just fine, Dr. Carpenter. The bad news is that Carl Dietrich got loose."

Her face froze, but her brilliant turquoise eyes blazed fire. She swallowed the bitterness that rose in her throat. No, it couldn't happen again! She blinked rapidly to keep back the tears that burned her eyes and firmed a mouth that trembled with emotion. For a moment her hand sought support, but she snatched it back. She refused to lean on anything.

"Who screwed up the paperwork this time?" Her voice was raw with feeling. Her fists were clenched at her sides.

"Nobody, Doc," Mac said. "He escaped from the county jail."

"He escaped?" she hissed. "What happened, did somebody forget to lock his cell? Or did he just say, 'Hey, guys, I don't belong in here. Why don't you let me out, okay?' Naturally, they went along with what he said and escorted him to the front door. Right?"

Dean drew in a deep breath. He'd expected her to be angry. In this situation, anyone would be upset. He didn't expect to hear such deep pain coupled with such vivid bitterness. He felt her pain. For a cop who prided himself on his lack of emotion on his cases, this was highly unusual. He prayed he wasn't losing his edge; that was dangerous for someone in his line of work.

"Dr. Carpenter, we're sorry we have to bring you this kind of news," he said. "We don't know why it happened, only that it did. Somehow Dietrich walked out of the jail. We have an APB out, and we plan to pick him up as soon as possible."

Her harsh laugh held no humor. "Spare me the platitudes, Detective. Because of a clerical error he was freed the last time. Because someone wasn't doing his job, he strolled out of the county jail. And don't try to tell me any different. I read the papers. I know what goes on. And this time a man who beat the system before got a second chance to do it again. Why should I expect anything better? You people haven't done anything right yet. You couldn't even time storming the bank correctly!"

Dean winced at the accusation.

"I can just hear your cop reasoning now!" she fairly shouted, tossing her silk clutch bag onto the couch. "So you lost a prisoner. Hey, no problem. You'll be able to replace him with another in no time, right? What's one prisoner to you?"

"This one is pretty important, not only to us, but to the bank," Mac pointed out. "Banks don't appreciate guys trying to withdraw funds that don't belong to them."

"And I don't appreciate men killing my husband and murdering my unborn child," Elise said quietly. "Two murders he can't even be tried for. Whose husband or wife will he have to kill before he's finally brought to justice?"

Neither man had an answer, but she didn't expect one. She walked around the room, passing her hand over the back of a chair.

"I gather you came here to tell me that my testimony is no longer required?" she said quietly.

"He'll be caught, Doc," Mac assured her.

She raised her head. It wasn't until then, with the lamp backlighting her, that they could see the sheen of tears in her eyes. Tears she didn't want them to know about.

She couldn't look at either of them. But turning away didn't help, either. "Will he? To date, your track record hasn't been very good. I'm sure you'll understand if I don't thank you for your news or offer to show you to the door." Only a stirring in the air told her someone was behind her. The faint scent of soap teased her nostrils. Something in the back of her mind told her it was Dean Cornell standing behind her, not Frank McConnell. The tiny click of the door latch and the silent presence behind her told her she and Dean were now alone.

"Dr. Carpenter, we will find Dietrich, I promise," Dean murmured. "And while I know we're not your favorite people, I want you to know you can call Mac or me if anything comes up. I'll leave you my card." He placed it on the back of the chair.

"You don't understand," she whispered, closing her eyes. "I didn't want to go through this hell a second time, and now, if you do your jobs right—for once—I'll actually have to go through it a *third* time. That's why I'm angry."

Although he knew she couldn't see him, Dean nodded his understanding. He deeply regretted all that had happened. Ironic, that the woman who fascinated him so much was brought into his life in such a tragic way. A part of him wanted to track down Carl Dietrich and lay the man's head at Elise Carpenter's feet. He also wanted to reach out, touch her arm, reassure her. But he sensed if he offered her anything in the way of comfort, she'd probably hit him.

Though Elise continued to face away from the detective she felt a wholly unfamiliar urge to simply lay her head on his shoulder and cry. To let someone else do all the worrying for once. And Dean Cornell had very broad shoulders.

She thrust the betraying thought out of her mind with the stern reminder that, broad shoulders or not, good-looking and all-around sexy or not, the man was a cop. A stupid, bungling, incompetent cop. Still, a tiny voice reminded her, he was pretty brave in that bank. She had to give him credit for that.

"I'm very tired, Detective," she finally murmured, afraid if she turned around she might do something foolish. Like throw herself into his arms. "Please go."

Dean let himself out of the house and walked to the car, where Mac stood waiting.

"She's in a lot of pain over this." Dean pulled open the driver's door and slid behind the wheel. "I just wish I could do something for her."

"I thought you already had that planned."

Dean winced. "Yeah, but that was before I realized there was more to her than just a pretty face. She saw her husband shot in the head and then was beat up so badly she lost her baby. If that patrolman hadn't decided to investigate, she might have been killed, too. Then we let her husband's killer walk, and when we book him on something else, he just ambles out of jail as if he was only visiting. No wonder she hates cops. Right about now I don't like us much, either."

"How about we do something to make us look good in the lady's pretty eyes?" Mac suggested. "Why don't we check out her car at the hotel?"

With the ease of a longtime friend and partner, Dean immediately picked up the line of thought. "You think Mr. Personality had something to do with her dead battery?"

"Could be."

"Then you're right—it might not hurt to check it out."

UNABLE TO SLEEP, Elise stood in the kitchen, nursing a glass of wine she didn't want, when Kristen stumbled in, wincing under the bright overhead light. Her gaze fell on the wineglass.

"I gather the Bobbsey Twins told you about Dietrich." She opened the refrigerator, drew out the wine bottle and poured a glass for herself before sitting down at the table across from her sister. "I invited them to wait inside, but I guess they feel more comfortable lurking around in the dark."

"It was better when they hanged bank robbers without benefit of trial," Elise grumbled, tracing the rim of her glass with her fingertips. She glanced at the manicured nails that had to be kept at a serviceable length because of her work. "Steve always hated guns, but I felt we should keep one at the clinic for nights we worked late. He used to say no one would bother a veterinary clinic. That assumption cost him his life."

"Most people who plan to use a gun against an intruder end up shot with it themselves." Kristen pointed out. "Let it go, Elise. Let the boys in blue do their job."

Her lips tightened. "It appears I have no choice on that point. I have a practice to return to, along with three daughters to look after. But that doesn't mean I have to like it."

Kristen sipped her wine. "I guess this wouldn't be the time to tell you that I think Detective Cornell is quite a man. I never liked beards before, but his suits him—along with that scrumptious hair that hasn't been cut any time recently. A man like him could tempt a woman to dial 911 on a regular basis." Her lips tipped in a leer.

Elise couldn't help smiling. Her sister was well-known for her penchant for clean-shaven men in three-piece suits who would never dirty their hands on mundane tasks. "I'm sure the man in question prefers nubile nineteen-year-olds who don't have one original thought in their heads to a woman who won't see thirty again."

"Thanks for that thought, Elise! Not seeing thirty again is bad enough without you driving the nails in even deeper."

"Well, really, didn't that T-shirt he wore tell you something about the man?"

Kristen only giggled.

Elise shook her head. "Kristen, a man like that would bring a woman nothing but trouble."

"Yes, but that kind of trouble a woman wouldn't mind handling. And if you were the least bit honest with yourself, you would admit the same thing."

Elise pictured Steve. Tawny hair always kept short because he thought that would stave off the early baldness the men in his family suffered. Aqua eyes that readily showed laughter. He loved his wife, his family and his work, though not always in that order. A man who had no enemies. Yet that hadn't stopped him from getting killed. Nor did it stop his widow from having to sell the practice they'd worked so hard to build, when she couldn't bear to enter the offices again. Her move to Riverside County was as much for her own sanity as to try to give her daughters a new life without so many painful reminders. It had worked until now.

"If you don't mind, I think I'll drive home in the morning instead of early afternoon. After Myrna's had my girls for four days, I'm sure she'll be only too happy to return to normal life," she said. Then she groaned as her memory bank kicked in. "As soon as I get my car fixed, that is." She filled her sister in on the evening's events, including Dean's intervention. "I dread to think what story Andrew will tell the others."

Kristen wrinkled her nose. "Detective Cornell was probably right—the man was looking for payment for all the business he's sent your way over the years. I always thought he was kind of sleazy."

"But he has a lot of influence in this field. As for sleaze, I'd say it's a toss-up between Andrew and Detective Cornell as to who's worse."

Kristen finished her wine and stood up, yawning. "The cop's no sleaze. Besides, I think he has his eye on you."

Elise remembered his penetrating gaze. "That's his problem."

Kristen smiled. "No, sister dear, I do believe that's yours."

"COME ON, lazy, you've got to see this!"

Elise groaned, pulling the covers over her head. "Go away," she mumbled, kicking out at the weight on the side of the bed.

"Elise, there's a surprise for you in the driveway."

She rolled over onto her back and pulled the covers down enough to barely open one eye. "What time is it?"

"A little after six."

The comforter covered the eye. "Come back in four hours."

Insistent hands continued the torture of pushing her out of bed. "I swear, Elise, you're as bad about getting up as ever. If you don't get up this minute, I'll pour a pitcher of cold water on your head."

Elise muttered uncomplimentary things about her sister as she slowly unfurled the comforter. She knew Kristen well enough to fear she would follow through on her threat.

"I hope the day will come when you find a man as sadistic as you are." She sat up on the edge of the bed, pushing her hair from her eyes. "What is so important that it can't wait until the sun comes up?"

Kristen grabbed her hand and pulled her to her feet. "This." She practically dragged her to the window.

Elise peered sleepily between the drapes, started to turn away, then turned back for a better look. "That's my car!"

"I know."

"How?"

Kristen's grin threatened to split her face. "I think I have a good idea. There's a piece of paper under the windshield wiper."

"You couldn't have gone out and gotten it?"

Kristen grimaced. "Do you know how cold it is out there right now?"

Sighing, Elise dragged on her robe and walked outside. Her Pathfinder—freshly washed and waxed, judging by the shine on its dark red surface—sat sedately in the driveway as if it had been there all night. She plucked the folded sheet of paper from under the windshield wiper and carried it inside. Kristen was already in the kitchen brewing coffee.

"What does it say?" she asked eagerly.

Elise unfolded the paper and read the dark scrawl aloud.

"No dead battery, only disconnected battery cables, I'm sure courtesy of you know who. From now on, make sure all your doors are locked, and don't keep your spare key in such a logical place. Even if it did keep me from having to hotwire your ignition. P.S. You owe me $12.95 for the wash and wax."

Elise chuckled.

Kristen snatched the paper out of her hand and quickly scanned it. "It's not signed."

"It doesn't have to be. Only a policeman would warn you to lock your car doors to protect against theft after he'd already commandeered it."

Kristen continued studying the paper. "It might prove interesting to have his handwriting analyzed."

"They'd probably say he should be locked away for the good of the public." Elise's eyes didn't leave Kristen's movements as she placed the paper on the table.

Kristen didn't miss her sister's intensity. "You're more interested in the man than you'd like to admit."

"Kris, the man has three strikes against him. He has an adolescent sense of humor, and he looks as if he's just climbed out of a ragbag."

"And the third?"

She looked grim. "The third and worst, he's a cop."

"IT'S AS IF the creep disappeared off the face of the earth." Dean stood in the kitchen doorway watching Mac grab two cans of beer out of the refrigerator. He accepted the one Mac handed him. "One of our sources should have had something for us by now."

Mac nodded before drinking deeply. "Yeah, and it worries me that they don't."

"You thinking what I am—that he left the area?"

"Seems possible." Mac led the way into the living room and gestured to one of the chairs.

Dean settled down, his legs stretched out in front of him. He rested the can on his flat belly. "We should have told her about Dietrich's threats against her."

"And have Anderson on our asses for sure."

"Dietrich said he'd go after her." Dean shifted his weight. "I think he meant it."

"You know the rules. We have to wait for a complaint before we can act on it. Plus, the lady lives out of our jurisdiction. All we can do is concentrate on tracking down Dietrich and make sure he stays put this time." Mac set his beer aside and stretched his arms over his head. "I'm getting too old for this. I should say the hell with it and put in for retirement. They've had more than twenty years of my life. I should be able to do what I want now."

"I've heard that story before."

The two men looked up to find a heavy-eyed Stacy standing in the hallway. She rested her hands on her distended belly. "Do you two realize what time it is?"

Mac held out his arms. "Sorry if we woke you, honey."

Stacy walked slowly. "I'm too heavy for you."

"Nah, you're still a light bundle."

With his help, she arranged herself in his lap, his hand splayed across her belly in a caressing motion. With more than a little envy, Dean watched the love flowing between them. Years ago, he'd decided marriage and family life weren't for him. He knew the divorce statistics among the police force and didn't want to be part of them. But watching Stacy and Mac, he thought more and more about finding a special woman and giving it a try.

Stacy kissed Mac and drew back, her nose wrinkled in disgust. "It's not even light out, and you two are drinking beer?"

"It's made from grain," Dean pointed out.

She shook her head, laughing at his logic. "You guys are hopeless."

"You could always adopt me and turn me into a better person."

"I think we already have. You already eat most of your meals here, and I seem to find more and more of your clothes in the laundry. If this keeps up, you're going to have to take a turn with the washer and dryer, Cornell," she warned in mock threat, relaxing under Mac's massage of her lower back. "I swear, McConnell, this kid of yours is going to be a soccer player." She rested her head against his shoulder.

He lifted his hand, the gold bracelet glinting at his wrist. The bracelet had once graced Stacy's ankle, a visual reminder of her less than perfect past, until the time she let go of the memories. Now Mac wore the bracelet as a reminder of their future together.

"I wish I could help."

"Believe me, you will when you're with me in the delivery room."

Dean was amused to see his partner's face pale. While Mac hadn't said it out loud, Dean sensed his friend wasn't too sure about being there when his child was born. It seemed Mac didn't have such a strong stomach after all.

"If you two are going to get soppy, I'm leaving," he announced.

"Up yours, Cornell," Mac said amiably.

"What time do you guys have to be in to work?" Stacy asked.

Mac glanced at his watch. "About an hour and a half."

"Were you able to talk to Dr. Carpenter?"

Dean nodded. "Something tells me she won't be sending us a Christmas card this year."

Mac and Stacy exchanged a telling look. She slowly climbed off his lap.

"Let me fix you two some breakfast," she offered.

"Pancakes?" Dean asked hopefully. "With plenty of butter and syrup?"

She smiled at him. "All right."

"And bacon, crisp?"

"Who's married to the lady?" Mac demanded.

"You are, but it's me she really loves," Dean confided.

"Your latest batch of clean clothes is in the guest room chest of drawers," Stacy told him. "Why don't both of you take your showers while I start breakfast."

Mac's gaze didn't leave his wife's retreating figure as he watched her make her way slowly into the kitchen. Worry was etched on his face, and along with the worry, such love that Dean felt as if he were intruding on something private.

He's seen a lot of changes in his partner over the past two years. Mac's loner personality had expanded to include a special woman, and he laughed and joked more with the others. He even took Captain Anderson's tantrums better. The two men's friendship hadn't diminished because of Mac's marriage. Stacy treated Dean like a brother and cheerfully bullied him whenever she got the chance. Dean found himself part of a family, which only got him thinking more and more about making one of his own.

"I love that lady so much," Mac breathed. "I don't know what I would do if anything happened to her."

"Nothing's going to happen," Dean was quick to assure him. "The guys at the station have the routine down pat. They should, since seven of them have become new fathers since the first of the year. Nothing's going to interfere with you being at the hospital to see my godson coming into the world." He set his can of beer aside. "You think Dr. Carpenter's going to thank us for returning her truck?"

"After she reads the note you wrote? I doubt it."

"A woman alone at night should lock her car doors!"

"That isn't the part I'm talking about."

Dean nodded in understanding. "I wanted to get her attention."

Mac grinned. "I'm sure you did. I'm just not sure it'll get you the kind of attention you're hoping for."

"Yeah, I should have left off the cost of the wash and wax."

"If you guys want some breakfast, you'd better get your showers taken within the next five minutes," Stacy called out.

"Only if you scrub my back, darlin'," Dean called back.

"In your dreams, Cornell!"

He grinned broadly. "That's where you already are."

"HEY, CORNELL," the desk sergeant sang out, holding an envelope above his head as Dean and Mac entered the station that morning. "Got something for you. A lady just left it. A real looker, too. Nice legs."

Dean grabbed the envelope and walked on by. "You need to get out more, Stan."

"I try to. Thing is, my wife objects," he chortled.

"Comedians, they're all comedians," he muttered, heading for his desk, then stopping short. "You say she just left it?" He looked down at the envelope. The faint hint of something warm and exotic wafted upward to tease his nostrils. The kind of scent that got a man thinking of silk sheets and a roaring fire. His name was written on the front in a neat feminine script. It may have been unfamiliar, but he still knew who'd written it.

Stan nodded. "Not more'n a minute ago."

Dean raced for the door, slapping it open with one hand and descending the steps two at a time. One glance at the adjoining parking lot located his quarry.

"So you didn't forget about me after all, did ya, Doc?" he called out.

Elise was in the process of closing her car door when she heard him. "One thing you should know, Detective, I always pay my debts," she returned sweetly, slamming the door shut. The engine started up with a muted roar, and the window rolled down as she drove past him. "Have a nice day!"

"Would it have hurt her to stop and just talk?" Dean groused, watching the small truck travel down the street.

"Your hormones are showing again, friend," Mac growled, walking up behind him. He spied the envelope Dean clutched. "What did she leave you?"

"I hope her telephone number, but I doubt it." He tore open the envelope, revealing a rectangular piece of pale blue paper. No note, no phone number, just the muted picture of whales crashing the ocean waves, partially obscured by the numbers neatly written across it—$12.95—

and the signature, Elise A. Carpenter. In the corner marked
memo, it read, *for services rendered.* Dean's shoulders
shook with laughter.

"It is a shame I won't see the lady again. I'd say we could
be a perfect match."

Mac shook his head. "Yeah, just like Little Red Riding
Hood and the big bad wolf."

Chapter Three

"It's time to get up. It's time to get up. It's time to get up in the morning!" The raspy voice intruded on what Elise considered the quality sleep she wanted to continue for at least four more days.

"Go 'way," she muttered, pushing at the offender, who merely screeched and hopped away a couple steps before coming back to nip her bare shoulder.

"Fud up."

"Fud up yourself, you mangy kid." She opened her eyes to find the black feather lines decorating the dark eyes of a blue-and-gold macaw peering into her face. "Baby, there are times I hate your alarm-clock routine."

"Mama, Mama," the bird chanted, grabbing several strands of hair with her beak and pulling back on them slightly, intent on grooming her mom to a macaw's high standards.

Elise groaned. "Baby, go find Keri," she told the macaw. "Go get Keri."

"No."

She sighed as she rolled over. "You are so obnoxious." She pushed herself upward.

"Mom?" A tall slender teenager stood in the doorway. "Sorry. Baby got away before I could stop her. She's missed you."

Elise nodded as the macaw huddled closer to her side. "That's okay. I should go in early to the clinic anyway." She pushed wayward strands of hair away from her face, wincing as she heard strident sounds from the front of the house. Ah, home sweet home, she thought to herself. "Hey, you two, give it a rest!" she hollered in their general direction.

Two more girls soon appeared, both wearing murderous expressions.

The taller of the two spoke up first, determined to present her side of the case. "Mom, she wrote all over the front of my notebook!"

The smaller one's face scrunched up in anger. "It's my notebook!"

"No, it's not!"

"You said I could have it."

"Did not!"

"Did so!"

Elise put two fingers in her mouth and released a shrill whistle guaranteed to wake the dead.

"Honestly, Mom..." Keri looked as if her mother had done the unforgivable.

"It's the only thing that works with these two." Elise faced her middle daughter. "Lisa, did you give Becky your notebook?"

The girl shifted uncomfortably under her mother's gaze. "Not exactly."

"Either you did or you didn't. Which is it?"

"Well, I want it back," she wailed.

"That's tough, sweetheart. If you gave it to Becky, it's hers, and she can do anything she wants with it." She turned to her youngest. "And no more quarreling from you either. I didn't come home to listen to you two fight."

Keri urged them out of the room, suggesting they eat their breakfast. "They were upset after they saw that news report," she said quietly. "Since then they've been fighting and obnoxious like this."

Elise gestured Keri closer to the bed until she sat on the edge. A disgruntled Baby was set on the headboard, which already displayed macaw chew marks. Elise wrapped her arms around her eldest daughter.

"It's all over, sweetheart," she assured her, rocking her gently. "I'm back, and it's all over."

"Except the man who killed Daddy is free again."

She released a deep breath. "Yes, but the police will catch him."

"Do you really believe that?"

At that moment, Keri sounded more six than sixteen, the child needing reassurance from the one adult she could trust completely.

"No, honey, I don't," Elise said finally. "But I keep saying it in hopes it will help me feel better. So let's put this all behind us and get on with life, okay? We did it before, we can do it again. Right?" She smiled, kissing her daughter's forehead.

Keri managed a faint smile. "All right." She held on to Elise tightly, as if her touch was crucial. "Florence went into hibernation."

Elise laughed softly. "The same place?"

Keri nodded. "Where else but under the guest room bed? I'm just glad she gave up on the living room fireplace for her winter quarters. We couldn't build a fire for the first two years we were here. Henry's in the coat closet."

"It wouldn't be so bad if we didn't have two tortoises who snore." Elise released her daughter and stood up, reaching for her robe. She glanced at the bedside clock. "Your bus should be here soon."

"If you'd let me use the car, I could drive all of us to school and we wouldn't have to wait for the bus," Keri said slyly.

"We'll discuss it when you can pay for your own car insurance." Elise held out her arm for Baby to step onto.

"Mama, Mama," the macaw crooned, nuzzling her.

"Come on, Baby, let's get some breakfast," Keri offered, holding out her arm.

The macaw glared at her, ruffling her brilliant blue and gold feathers and staying put on Elise's arm. "No. Fud up."

Keri rolled her eyes. "I swear, that's all that bird says. When she's not demanding to be let out, she's telling everyone to shut up. She's so spoiled!"

Elise stroked the bird's feathers in a grooming motion. "She still misses your dad. She loved him a great deal." She recovered. "Come on, Baby, you can take a shower with me."

While Elise showered, Baby sat perched on top of the cubicle, singing a bawdy ditty at the top of her lungs— something she only did in the shower. While Elise stood under the stream of hot water, she thought of the many mornings Steve would bring Baby in to shower with him.

She had been surprised when he presented her with a baby macaw for a wedding present. From the beginning the newly wedded couple had treated the genial bird like one of the family, hand-feeding her, talking to her and, Elise guessed, spoiling her rotten. Now Baby was convinced she was human and got belligerent if anyone tried to tell her differently. The bird bossed the rest of the family and other pets as if she were head of the household.

When Steve died, the macaw grieved right along with the rest of them. Finally, after months of moping and mournful silence, she started to bounce back to her usual bratty self. From then on, Baby joined Elise at the clinic and bossed whoever happened to be in earshot. Elise was grateful for that return to *some* kind of normalcy in their lives as she struggled to rear her sixteen-, twelve- and seven-year-old daughters as best she could.

"Baby, I wish someone had told you you couldn't sing worth a damn," she informed the bird as she toweled off and dressed in jeans and a pale green-and-cream-colored soft flannel shirt. Feeling somewhat restored and more like her old self, she headed for the kitchen.

"Mommy, I can't find my blue jacket," Becky complained, jumping out of her chair and running to her mother. She wound her arms around Elise's legs.

"Since I haven't been here for the past week, I'm not sure I'd know where it is, either," she replied, bending down to kiss the top of her head. "I'd suggest you'd try looking in your closet first."

Becky sniffed, clearly not happy with that idea. "Lisa probably took it."

"Why would I want that crummy old jacket?" Lisa asked.

Elise fixed her middle daughter with a daunting stare. "Tonight, we'll have a talk about attitude."

She grimaced. "She's always accusing me of taking her crummy stuff!"

"Well, honey, you have given her reason to," Elise observed with gentle logic, thinking fleetingly of Kristen's house with its bubbling spa and peace and quiet.

"The bus will be here in five minutes. Off with you." Myrna, the Carpenters' housekeeper and part-time surrogate mother, began distributing lunch bags and book bags and herding the girls out the door. A goose's honks followed the girls' chatter as they left after kissing their mother goodbye.

Elise gratefully accepted the cup of coffee Myrna handed her. "I'd run away from home, but with my luck, the kids would only track me down."

Myrna's back was to Elise as she stood at the stove, whipping up eggs and checking on bacon cooking in the microwave oven.

"You're probably right," the housekeeper chuckled as she slipped a piece of toast to a waiting Baby.

"Thanks for looking after the girls while I was gone. I really appreciate it." Elise dug into the food Myrna set in front of her.

"Nonsense, you know I enjoy it."

"Yes, but lately I feel as if I should offer you combat pay. If it isn't Keri upset over Lisa daring to intrude on her two shelves in the medicine cabinet, Lisa is furious with Becky for entering her room without permission and Becky is angry at Keri for refusing to help her with her homework." She rubbed her forehead. She wasn't surprised that a headache was cropping up. After everything else that had happened over the past few days, a headache was a minor inconvenience. "There are days when I feel as if I were living in a war zone."

"Mama, Mama," Baby croaked, climbing up one of the chairs and eyeing Elise's food with a hungry gleam.

"No," she said firmly.

"Baby, you already had your breakfast," Myrna reminded the bird.

The macaw snapped around and glared at the woman. "Fud up."

Myrna rolled her eyes. "Who had the nerve to teach her that?"

Elise laughed. "She just came up with it one day. The best explanation I can come up with is she heard it from television, since I never said 'shut up' to anyone."

"It's not just that. It's the fact that she doesn't believe she's a *b...i...r...d.*" Even though Myrna spelled out the last word, Baby turned her head to glare suspiciously at her. "See what I mean?"

"She'll be happier back at the clinic, where she has more people and animals to boss." Elise picked up her plate and carried it to the sink. She glanced at the large wall clock. "Where I should have been five minutes ago."

It took Elise another ten minutes before she could leave the house and walk down the driveway to the building just off the main road that held the Carpenter Avian and Exotic Animal Clinic. She looked over the two acres she'd bought five years ago, grateful that she was able to have her home and business on the same piece of property. While the area was far more rural than Pasadena had been, it held a peace she had sought five years ago and enjoyed now.

The house in the rear had been remodeled to suit the family and the house in the front turned into a clinic that did a booming business. Elise marveled that people were willing to drive sometimes an hour and a half to see her. While she knew avian and exotic animal veterinarians were not as plentiful as those dealing with felines and canines, she still couldn't believe her patient load kept increasing.

Because she knew where she was going, Baby hated what she considered the indignity of making the short walk to the clinic encased in a pet carrier. As a result, she threatened Frances, the watch goose, and Herman, Frances's mate, with extra vehemence. The family dogs—Bailey, a harlequin Great Dane, Duke, a tan-and-black German shepherd, and Kola, a malamute husky—greeted Elise with high-pitched barks quickly silenced when she threw them their favorite treats.

"Not nice," Baby informed Elise when she was first put into the carrier.

"I don't care if you don't think I'm nice. You know the rules. No creature with wings leaves this house without being in a carrier," Elise replied, releasing the latch. "Besides, I'm sure Donna has missed you these past few days."

"Hey there, boss." A young technician dressed in surgical greens lifted a hand in greeting as Elise opened the back door. "How was the conference?"

Elise walked into an enclosed aviary off the waiting area, where Baby, along with a few other birds, spent their days. She left Baby preening on top of a tall dome cage and headed for her office. "The usual. How about here?"

"No emergencies, although Mrs. Harper called again." Donna's hazel eyes glinted with laughter.

Elise cursed under her breath. "She's still in a snit?"

"More than ever. As far as she's concerned, her darling little Robin is a girl, not a boy, as you informed her after the surgical sexing."

Elise thought of the Rosy Breasted cockatoo who was more spoiled than Baby, hard as it was to believe. "I told her as long as she wanted to keep Robin as a pet and not put her out for breeding, there was no reason to put the bird through the stress of having it sexed," she muttered. "But, no, she insisted she wanted to know her little girl was really a little girl. You'd think the end of the world had come just because her little girl is a little boy. And a mean one, at that. That beak can nail a person with deadly accuracy."

"She's insisted you made a mistake, and she wants a second opinion."

"A *what?* That procedure is hard enough on a bird once, but for someone to demand it be done a second time..." She shook her head in frustration at the problems some of her clients offered her. "Did you give her some names?"

Donna nodded. "That's why she called. The other doctors all refused to perform the procedure a second time. She was told that if you said she was a male, she was a male. End of discussion."

"What's on the books for today?"

"Cheryl said you're going to love today. First up is a monitor lizard with a nicked tail. He'll be here in about ten minutes. And Althea is coming in. Sean said she has a slight temperature. He's afraid she might have eaten a bad mouse.'' Donna stared up at the ceiling, ticking the list off on her fingertips.

Elise tightened her lips to keep from laughing. "Eaten a bad mouse?" she choked.

Donna nodded, her own lips kept just as tight. "He wondered if snakes can get salmonella from bad mice. I told him I'd ask you."

"Thanks a lot," she muttered. "I could have settled for treating cats' fur balls and giving rabies and distemper shots to dogs, but, no, I wanted to treat exotics. To work in a field that's sparsely populated. What do I get from it? A woman screaming that I can't read the sex of her cockatoo correctly and a man worrying about his python eating a bad mouse. Don't you have anything good to tell me?"

"The electric bill was down fifteen dollars from last month."

ELISE THREW HERSELF into the blessed routine of work as she treated a cockatiel who'd pulled a blood feather and needed his wound packed before he bled to death, and examined a little boy's rabbit who'd supposedly swallowed the child's nickel. She went from one examination room to another, pleased to be back where she felt most comfortable and where the hours passed most easily. By the time the day wound down, she felt tired but happy with herself.

"Long day," Donna commented from her slouched position against the hallway wall.

Elise nodded. "Anyone else out there?"

Donna shook her head. "So far, so good. Some man called for you when you were with a patient but wouldn't leave his name. He said he'd call back."

Elise shrugged, her thoughts elsewhere. "Then let's lock up for the night. Is the answering machine on?"

"Cheryl turned it on before she left." Donna ran her fingers through black spiky hair. After she made sure all the instruments had been sterilized and put away, she grabbed a sweatshirt, which she pulled on over her surgical greens.

Elise chuckled. "You really don't mind leaving here looking like that?"

"Hey," Donna intoned dramatically, "we get animal blood, bird poop and other disgusting stuff all over us. Why not wear something easy to clean? I prefer these to jeans." Her dark eyes twinkled. "Besides, Gary says they're kinda sexy."

For a brief moment, a dark-bearded man came into Elise's mind's eye. He'd probably consider them sexy, too, her brain told her. She ruthlessly pushed Detective Cornell from her thoughts, glad she'd never have to see him again.

As Elise walked back to the house with a grumbling Baby in her carrier, she felt a faint prickling of unease lodge between her shoulder blades. The sense was so strong, so thick, she had to forcibly resist the urge to turn around. If she didn't know better, she'd swear she was being watched, but she told herself it was nothing more than her imagination. Why would anyone be watching her? Still, the feeling refused to go away. In fact, it intensified. She tightened her grip on Baby's carrier and forced herself to keep her stride normal even though the impulse to run for the house and lock the door behind her was so strong she almost shook with it.

She didn't breathe a sigh of relief until she reached her front door. When she closed it behind her, she made sure to secure the dead bolt. Even if it was nothing more than an attack of nerves, she wasn't going to take any chances. While Frances and Herman were excellent watch geese and the dogs were semitrained, they weren't infallible. She even peeked out between the folds of the curtains, as if she might find the reason for her unease in the middle of the yard.

"Myrna left a chicken-noodle casserole in the oven," Keri informed her from her post on the couch, books spread out in front of her on the coffee table. The television set blared, making Elise wonder how her daughter got anything accomplished with the noise level so loud.

She walked over and turned down the volume. "Didn't I say no MTV until the homework was done?"

"It is done. I'm just getting ahead in a couple of my classes."

"I think I used that excuse when I was in school. Where's Lisa and Becky?"

"Lisa's working on her science project, and Becky's in her room." Keri marked the page and closed the book lying in her lap. "Someone called for you."

Elise remained still. She told herself to act normal, act as if nothing were wrong, as she opened the carrier and released Baby, who promptly waddled toward her cage and climbed inside. "Oh? Who?"

Keri shrugged. "He didn't say. He just said he'd call back. He's probably selling something, although he did ask for you by name."

Elise wanted to believe that but couldn't bring herself to agree with her daughter. Two calls for her in one day, one at the office and the other at her home, both times from a man refusing to leave his name. She didn't like it. She felt the lump in her throat grow.

"Why don't you set the table while I freshen up." She forced herself to speak normally. Nothing was wrong, her brain insisted. So why this feeling? Why calls for her with the caller refusing to leave his name? And why did she feel as if she were waiting for the other shoe to drop?

"It's Lisa's turn to set the table this week."

"Fine, then ask her to do so."

Elise quickly washed up and changed her clothes, then stopped to check the locks on all the bedroom windows on her way back to the living room. She tried to tell herself she was being paranoid, but it didn't work. She glanced out a window. "If you don't watch yourself, next thing you know you'll be looking under the bed for the boogeyman," she chided herself.

Elise ate little of her dinner and concentrated so hard on a reassuring appearance of normalcy for the girls that she had a headache by the time she checked on her sleeping children before practically crawling to her own bedroom. No matter what, she couldn't shake the feeling that something *was* wrong. She felt uneasy that the man with no name hadn't called back. Unless, as Keri suggested, he was nothing more than a phone solicitor selling carpeting or performing a telephone survey on what brand of coffee she drank. She resisted the urge to turn on all the lights to banish even faint shadows in room corners and to turn on the floodlights outside to keep away unseen enemies. Instead, she assured herself that if trouble came to her door, she'd give trouble back in spades.

By the time she dropped into bed, she felt ready to stay there for several days. Sleep didn't come easy, but eventually her weary body overtook her worried mind and she sank into blissful oblivion.

"MOM! MOM!"

Her oldest daughter's frantic whisper slowly made its way through her sleep-fogged brain.

"What?" She reached out to turn on her lamp, but Keri's hand stayed her action.

"Don't turn it on," she whispered. "There's someone walking around outside."

Elise shot upward, her earlier fears back with a vengeance. "Are you sure?"

Keri nodded, then whispered again when she realized her mother couldn't see her. "Something woke me up, and when I looked toward my window, I saw a figure walk past." Her voice trembled. "Mom, I don't hear Frances and Herman or the dogs. What if something happened to them?"

Elise reached for the phone. When no dial tone greeted her, she cursed under her breath.

"Are Lisa and Becky still asleep?"

"Yes."

She silently blessed the Fates for giving her a daughter who didn't panic easily. "Keri, the phone's dead." She could feel her hand crushed in the young girl's grip. "I'm going to go to the gun cabinet and get out the rifle. I want you to wake Lisa and Becky, take them into your room and make sure they remain quiet. Lock the bedroom door, and don't let anyone in but me. If you hear anything, take your keys, go out your window and run for the clinic. Hopefully, that phone line hasn't been cut, also. Lock that door behind you and call the sheriff's office. Tell them what's going on and remain there until help comes."

"I'm not going to leave you," Keri insisted.

"Yes, you are," Elise said firmly. "I need you to look after the girls for me. Do this for me, Keri. I'm counting on you."

In the dim light she could see the girl's downcast head.

"All right." The words were barely audible.

Elise gave her a quick hug and jumped out of bed. "All right, go now."

Elise took several deep breaths before she made her way down the hall. She had just reached the living room when she heard Keri hushing Lisa and Becky's frightened whispers. Elise reached the locked wooden cabinet, quickly unlocked the door and pulled out a rifle, which she easily loaded in the dark. She didn't have any doubts about her ability. She had practiced many times with her eyes closed.

She wasn't about to allow anything as mundane as darkness to hamper her.

When something thumped against her front door, she jumped, then quickly regained her senses. Someone had climbed the fence surrounding the property, silenced the geese and dogs and cut her telephone lines. She wasn't going to allow that person to get away with it.

Then, just as suddenly, an explosion of light flared in the front yard, and she heard the roar of a motorcycle.

Deafening herself to her daughters' screams, Elise kept the rifle close to her body as she cautiously eased the front door open. What she found on the doormat turned her stomach.

"Mom?" Keri ventured from nearby.

"Get back, Keri," she ordered hoarsely, scanning the yard but seeing nothing other than the shadowed figures of the geese and the dogs lying in the middle of the yard.

"But, Mom . . ."

"Get back!"

Her daughter's gasp sent her spinning around.

"Keri, go back to your sisters."

"What is it?" the girl cried out from behind the protective mask of her hands over her mouth.

"A squirrel. I'll take care of it."

"But Frances and Herman? The dogs? Are they . . . ?"

"I don't know yet. Go back to Lisa and Becky. I'll check on Frances and Herman."

"What if someone's still out there?"

"No, whoever it was is gone now," Elise could say with conviction. The unease she'd felt all evening had dissipated. As she stepped over the slaughtered rodent, she noticed a sheet of paper underneath. Two words were written—in red. She dreaded to think what had been used for ink. And a blurred thumbprint was the signature. A name wasn't necessary. She stared at the words, seeing the threat.

I'm back.

Chapter Four

"Are you sure this note was written by Carl Dietrich, Dr. Carpenter?" the deputy asked as he continued jotting down his report.

She silently counted to ten. How many times would she be asked the same ridiculous questions!

"If you sent that print to the Pasadena police department, I'm sure they could verify it," she replied. Why weren't they doing more than just looking around the grounds? The formerly locked gate now lay in the road, two groggy geese were recovering from drugged "treats," and three dogs had been felled by tranquilizer darts. Fear and anger warred within her. "Talk to Detectives Dean Cornell and Frank McConnell in Pasadena. They can tell you all you want to know about the situation."

The deputy didn't look up from his writing. "Do you feel you might be in any danger, Doctor?"

"My phone lines were cut, my animals drugged, this disgusting 'message' was left on my doorstep and my children were terrorized. Oh, no, I don't feel threatened. Why on earth would I?" Sarcasm dripped from every word. "The man who killed my husband and unborn child is running around loose after leisurely walking out of the county jail where he was being held for armed bank robbery. He also knows I'd like nothing better than to see him strung up by his . . ." She paused to take a calming breath, reading the expression in the deputy's eyes. "Don't you dare think I'm hysterical, Deputy. That's one luxury I never allow myself. Now, I do intend to do everything possible to protect my daughters, with or without your assistance." The expression on her face told him loud and clear what she thought of his assistance.

"Dr. Carpenter, don't try anything foolish," he warned.

"Then get the bastard who's terrorizing me!"

"It could have been a bunch of kids. Some of the wilder gangs have been known to pull stunts like this."

"You talk to Detectives Cornell and McConnell. I don't think they'll agree with you." She wondered what the two men would think if they could hear her basically begging for their help. "And if you won't contact them, I will."

"They have no jurisdiction in Riverside County."

"I don't give a damn if they're from Mars," she said through gritted teeth. "Don't mess with me, Deputy. Just do what I suggest or I'll talk to someone who will."

The man's features turned to stone. He clearly didn't like being told what to do by this or any woman. "Lady, I'm only trying to do my job."

"Then make sure you do it right."

By the time the deputy sheriff and crime lab team left the property, it was dawn, and Elise felt as if she'd been up for days. She fixed a pot of hot chocolate and sat the girls at the kitchen table.

"We have some new rules," she began without preamble. "From now on, you will be driven to school by either Myrna or myself. You are not to go to a friend's house after school without one of us taking you there and picking you up, and you are not to answer the phone here at the house. Let the answering machine pick up the calls. Don't go off anywhere, even with a friend. I know you won't like these restrictions, but for the time being, they're necessary.''

Becky climbed into Elise's lap and wrapped her arms around her. "Is Frances and Herman dead, Mommy?"

She hugged her youngest. "No, darling, they're just sleeping. They'll be fine in a few hours. And the dogs will be waking up soon, too."

"I wish you'd shot the creep who did it," Lisa said with bloodthirsty glee.

Keri looked at her mother with a wisdom beyond her years. "What else are we going to do?"

Elise drew in a deep breath. "We're going to watch out for ourselves, because the way the police are treating the situation, I doubt they're going to be much help. I'll look into having a security system installed in the house. I really should have done so a long time ago." Her face settled into grim lines. "And if that creature dares to step foot on this property again, I will shoot him down like the madman he is."

"HEY, CORNELL, Captain Anderson wants to see you," one of the men shouted. "He's about to have a coronary, so I suggest you don't waste any time."

Dean groaned. "Oh, man! I just got in. Does he have to ruin my day first thing?" He threw some papers onto his desk.

"Better you than me."

"Yeah, yeah." He looked around. "Mac in yet?"

"No, his wife had a doctor's appointment. With her being so close to her due date, he wanted to take her. Besides, Anderson asked for you."

Dean sighed. "I should have read my horoscope this morning. It probably would have told me to stay in bed." He headed for the frosted glass door and knocked.

"Come in, Cornell." Captain Anderson's usual sour expression appeared to have soured even more overnight.

"You wanted to see me, sir?"

"I talked to a Detective Lieutenant Santee over at the Riverside County Sheriff's station in Lake Elsinore earlier today. It appears Dr. Elise Carpenter told them to call either you or McConnell. Since you two weren't in, I took the call."

Dean seethed inside. How many other calls had Anderson intercepted in the past just to make him or Mac look incompetent? He wouldn't put it past the man.

"Considering everything, I'm surprised Dr. Carpenter would suggest we be contacted."

"I doubt she would have if it hadn't been for an attack on her home last night." Captain Anderson shook his head. "The sheriff's office feels it was just some kids playing one of their sick jokes, and I tend to agree."

"What happened?"

He looked down at the paper in front of him. "Someone cut her phone lines, drugged her watchdogs and left a slaughtered squirrel on her front porch. Probably kids high on drugs doing their thing. There was also a note left there, written in the squirrel's blood, saying 'I'm back.' A bloody thumbprint on the paper turned out to be smeared too much to get a match."

The back of Dean's neck tingled madly. "Has this kind of thing ever happened in her neighborhood before?" Dean questioned tautly.

"I didn't ask, and Santee didn't say."

Dean leaned forward, planting his hands on the desk. "Dietrich made some pretty nasty threats against the lady, and from what we've seen of his record, this could be something he'd pull just to give her a good scare before moving in for the kill."

"If Dietrich had any brains, he'd be in Mexico by now."

"If you and this Santee feel it has nothing to do Dietrich, why are you bothering to tell me about it?"

The older man looked at him as if he were a bothersome insect. "Because I told Santee I would pass it on to you, and I don't want you saying you don't receive your messages." Hostility radiated outward.

"I'd like to go down there and talk to Dr. Carpenter."

"It's out of our jurisdiction."

"It could have something to do with our case," he argued. "What's wrong with going down there to check things out?"

"Waste of time. If you have any questions, talk to Santee on the phone. There's no need to talk to the woman."

Dean bit back the hot words that threatened to erupt. The last thing he needed right now was to be bumped down to pounding a beat. "Fine, I'll do that."

He wasted no time in putting through the call, grateful he could talk to the man immediately. Detective Santee filled him in with excerpts from the deputy's report and a later telephone call from Dr. Carpenter.

"The lady was very insistent on our contacting you, even though we still feel the work was nothing more than a bunch of kids out to stir up some havoc," he explained. "I checked into this Carl Dietrich, and I can see why she's worried, but it still doesn't check out."

"This creep is capable of anything," Dean replied. "Especially from the sounds of the note left with the squirrel and the bloody thumbprint. Too bad it was too smeared to help out. While he was an unwilling resident in our local jail, he made some pretty nasty threats against the doctor, so I believe he'd do it. What kind of protection are you giving her?"

"Detective, what happened isn't serious enough to offer her anything more than a few more drive-bys during the night. And she's lucky to get that. We just don't have the manpower."

Dean ground his teeth in frustration. "That's not enough."

"If Dr. Carpenter wants anything more in the way of protection, she'll have to arrange for it herself."

"Have you met the lady?"

"No, but my deputy said she met him at the door with a nasty-looking shotgun that she looked prepared to use if necessary."

A pair of hot-tempered turquoise eyes seared Dean's memory. He thought quickly as he scanned the calendar. "If it was Dietrich out there that night, and I seriously think it was, would you be amenable to our sending someone down to kinda look after her? If we work together on this, we might be able to catch Dietrich and keep him put away."

"I don't see much problem on my end, but between you and me, I don't think your captain will go for it."

Dean grinned. "Are you kidding? If I volunteer for this special duty, he'll run home and pack my bags for me!"

"ARE YOU SURE about this?" Mac slumped in a chair, watching Dean sort through a jumble of clothing.

"Sure, why not?" He held up a wrinkled chambray shirt. "Does this look clean to you?"

Mac shook his head. "Ol' buddy, you've turned into a slob in your old age."

"My cleaning lady quit."

"What number was she?"

"I lost count after thirty-six. Stacy promised to find someone for me, but she said I'm too well-known." He stuffed some T-shirts into a duffel bag.

Mac brushed the top of his Coke can against his mustache. "Does the doc know you're going out there to protect her from whatever goes bump in the night?"

"Nope, I figured it would be better if I just show up on her doorstep. That way she can't do anything about it."

"She can throw you out on your ass."

Dean hesitated. "Not after I explain I'm there to catch Carl Dietrich for her."

"So far the police haven't done too good a job of keeping the guy on ice," he drawled. "I don't think the lady will exactly welcome you with open arms."

Dean pushed his duffel bag off the chair and dropped down into the seat. "I've got a feeling about this, Mac," he said quietly. "A bad feeling. Dietrich is out there with the idea of scaring the hell out of the lady until he's got her so unhinged it will be a snap to finish the job. He's playing with her now, but it won't be long before he makes his final move. I plan to be there when he does."

"And leave me without a partner. With my luck, Anderson will stick me with Carlton." Mac grimaced.

Dean shook his head. "You're taking your vacation time soon so you'll be home when Stacy's baby comes, and with the way Anderson feels about us, it's better if I'm not around. Although I must admit, driving him crazy always makes my day." He grinned, his teeth flashing white between his beard. "You should have seen his face when I gave him my suggestion. He still doesn't believe it's Dietrich down there, but he's seen too many of our hunches come through, and he doesn't want me to be right and have it come out that he ignored my suggestions. Besides, I think he was happy to know we'd both be out of his thinning hair for a while." He gathered up some equipment while Mac grabbed his duffel bag. "I'm just sorry it took a week for me to catch up on my work before I could leave."

Mac helped him carry his things out to his truck. "Still, you know my number, and I'm always available for backup." He tossed the duffel bag into the back.

Dean nodded. "Yeah, I know. But for now, you just concentrate on keeping Stacy happy," he said quietly, sticking out his hand. "And call me the minute my god-child enters the world."

The two men shook hands, then embraced, as if both friends sensed that life was changing for all of them.

"MOM, YOU HAVEN'T SIGNED the permission slip yet!" Lisa waved the sheet of paper in front of Elise's nose. "If I don't take it in tomorrow, I won't be able to go to the zoo."

Elise hesitated. While things had been quiet the past few days, she still felt uneasy every time she or one of the girls left the house. "Lisa, I don't know."

"But everyone else is going!" she wailed. "You can't not sign it."

She pressed her fingers against her forehead in hopes of stopping the headache that had been lurking there all day. "Lisa, I am the mother here. I can do anything I darn well please."

"It's been over a week, and nothing more has happened. Plus, I'll be with my class and two others. I won't go off by myself, I promise," she whined, clasping her hands in front of her. "Please, Mom."

"Mom, if you don't let her go, she'll just make our lives miserable," Keri told her. "You know she will."

"If she tries, *I'll* be the one to make *her* life miserable," Elise stated emphatically, glaring at her middle daughter. "All right, I'll sign, but you remember what you've promised. No wandering off by yourself." She scribbled her name and the date at the bottom of the slip before she could change her mind. As if sensing her mother's thoughts, Lisa swiftly buried the paper in her book bag.

Elise knew she couldn't wrap her daughters in cotton for the rest of their lives even if she wanted to. "I realize you think I'm being unduly paranoid, but for now I feel more comfortable taking precautions," she said quietly.

"The sheriff seems to think we're okay," Keri said, more to reassure herself than to reassure her mother.

"The sheriff's deputy also thought I was nothing more than a hysterical woman." Her head snapped up when she heard the sound of a truck engine getting closer to the house and the dogs' excited barking. "Don't tell me Cheryl forgot to lock the gate when she left," she muttered, running for the gun cabinet.

"Mom, it might not be anything." Keri's eyes were large.

"Yes, and then again, it might be." She pulled the rifle out. She halted in the midst of loading it when she heard a familiar voice cursing Frances and Herman's frenzied honks.

"Hey! Damn! Ow, cut that out! Hey, Doc, come here and rescue me!"

She lowered the rifle. "After everything else that's happened, why am I not surprised?" She walked over to the door and pulled it open. The floodlights illuminating the front yard brought Dean Cornell into sharp relief. She noticed he had one hand on his rear, with an agitated Frances standing behind him. "Detective Cornell, fancy meeting you here." A tiny part of her wanted to laugh out loud at the picture before her. Another part wanted to say how happy she was to see him. Still another part wanted to escort him off the property. Right about now, she wasn't sure what part to listen to.

"Call off the goose, please," he growled. "Between that beaked monster going for my butt and the dogs heading for my b...crotch, I could end up as a chewed-up soprano here."

"They don't appreciate uninvited visitors."

Dean eyed her rifle. He wasn't sure if it was loaded and didn't want to chance finding out the hard way. "Detective Santee didn't call you about me?"

"Was he supposed to?"

"The coward," he muttered. "I'm here to offer you police protection."

"Police protection. How interesting." She raised an eyebrow. "You're out of your jurisdiction, Detective. Pasadena is seventy miles away from here."

"Is he the guy from the bank who fainted when he got shot?" Lisa whispered, peering around Elise's back. "Is he really a cop, Mom?"

Keri sniffed with disdain. "He looks more like someone off the streets." She walked away, clearly uninterested.

"Sometimes it helps to blend in." Dean looked at Elise. "Look, Doc, it's simple. You had a nasty incident. You were smart enough to tell the authorities here to call us about that note you received. While they might not have believed you, Mac and I did. And we figure Dietrich is going to strike again. When he does, I want to be here."

"I can't believe your captain allowed you to come down here, even if the sheriff's department allowed you to cross lines." She didn't budge from her post in the doorway. She was having enough trouble dealing with the fact that the first man in years to catch her attention was with the police force. Even as scruffy as Dean Cornell looked, with a goose hovering behind him and a German shepherd guarding him from the front, he still looked good enough to pounce on. No wonder people told her she needed to get out more!

"Are you kidding? He was ecstatic to see me go. Mac is taking some vacation time to be with his wife before their baby is born, so he didn't mind my being gone, too. Can't say I mind being here." His dark eyes swept over her from head to toe, the midnight gleam telling her he didn't mind what he saw one bit.

Elise still had trouble taking it all in. "So why didn't Detective Santee contact me about this?"

"Probably because he's a chicken at heart. Considering your previous dealings, he wouldn't have any trouble figuring out what your response would be."

"And he's right, you can just climb back into that rattletrap you call a truck and head on home, because I'm more than capable of protecting my children," she informed him, aware she was grasping at thin air. No one knew how much that night had shaken her up, how difficult it had been for her to sleep because she feared the next time there would be more than a note written in animal blood. It didn't take an expert to tell her Carl Dietrich wasn't sane and that she might not be able to protect the girls next time around. Still, a stubborn part of her refused to admit it to this cocky guy standing before her.

In the wink of an eye, Dean was on the porch and had snatched Elise's rifle out of her hands and backed her against the doorjamb, with the gun muzzle nestled neatly against her throat. He ignored the frightened cries behind him and the goose honking its agitation. Finally he lowered the gun and stepped back.

"Yeah, you're protecting them real good. Just like you protected yourself just now." His eyes bored into hers. Compassion warred with realism in the dark depths. "Next time it might not be me taking away that gun, and the next person just might decide to use it instead of teaching you a lesson."

Elise's face could have been carved from white marble. "You've made your point, Detective." She refused to show him how his graphic lesson had unsettled her. "I'm just a helpless mother of three children who can be wrestled to the ground by anyone bigger."

"Kick him where it counts, Mom!" Lisa shouted.

Elise didn't turn her head. "Lisa, if I hear one more word from you, I will dig out that permission slip and burn it. All of you, back inside."

"Mom, what if he's right?" Keri spoke up. "We don't want you hurt. And he looks as if he can handle anything that comes along."

Dean didn't look away from Keri. "Face it, Doc, you've got me as a houseguest whether you want me or not."

She nearly ground her teeth in frustration. "For how long?"

"For however long it takes."

For a split second, Elise felt as if there were two meanings to his words... and she wasn't sure she was ready for the second one. Then she pulled herself together with the only defense remaining to her: sarcasm. "Where *do* you buy your clothes, Detective Cornell? At one of those trendy little boutiques called Bikers R Us?"

He glanced down at the death's head outlined in glittering paint against the black fabric. "You really have a problem with my wardrobe, don't you? I'll have you know my mother bought this for me."

Elise didn't dare look at the jeans that fit him so tightly she wondered how he could even breath. She didn't want to look at him at all. He brought back feelings she preferred to keep repressed. She did some rapid thinking. The guest room wasn't exactly quiet during this time of year, thanks to Florence's snoring. In fact, her entire household had never been known for its peace and quiet. As far as she knew, this man was the consummate bachelor. Twenty-four hours in a household of squabbling girls and snoring turtles and loudmouthed macaws should be more than enough to do the trick. Yes, she'd just sit back and see what kind of man he was.

"Since I can't get rid of you, I suppose I'll have to show you to the guest room," she said finally.

Dean looked wary at her too-easy capitulation. "Yeah?"

She gestured inside. "Come on."

He hopped off the porch and ran to the truck, pulling his bags out of the back.

"Girls, it's past your bedtime," Elise announced once she stepped inside.

Keri gaped at her. "Now?"

"Now."

Sensing this was no time to argue, they hurried to their rooms.

Elise turned to Dean, who had paused on the threshold and was warily gazing around as if expecting to be attacked again. "I'll show you to your room." She took the rifle and replaced it in the cabinet, locking the door and palming the key.

He watched her with a nod of approval. "The lock on your front gate was a snap to pick. You need something a lot more heavy-duty."

She found her jaw tightening again and concentrated on relaxing it. "It's nice to know our police officers have the same skills as the crooks they're paid to catch."

Dean grabbed her arm and spun her around. "Hey, that's how we stay alive," he tautly informed her. His grip on her arm tightened as the light scent of her perfume reached his nostrils. He took a moment to compose himself. "Look, Doc, you've got some cute kids, and I don't want to see them crying because I have to tell them they don't have a mother anymore."

Elise could feel his fingers burning into her skin. Why did he have to be so damned attractive? she silently railed at herself. "Let go of me," she said, her lips barely moving.

He released her, one finger at a time. "I've had a long drive on top of a long day. I'd like to get some sleep," he said quietly.

She inclined her head and led him down the hallway. She opened the door and flipped the light switch to turn on the bedside lamp.

Dean entered the room and looked around, pausing once to check the windows. "Good locks, but they could be better" was all he said. He stopped in the middle of the room, a frown creasing his brow. "Am I overtired, or do I hear someone snoring?"

She resisted the urge to smile with satisfaction. "Under the bed."

Dean bent down and flipped up the covers. "What the hell?" His head snapped back up. "There's a turtle under here!"

"To be precise, Florence is a tortoise, and she's just gone into hibernation," she explained coolly.

"How am I supposed to sleep in here with this?" His eyes narrowed. "Oh, I see. I'm *not* supposed to. It's a good thing I can sleep through anything when I'm tired enough, because this critter sounds like a freight train." He dropped his duffel bag onto the bedspread.

"The bathroom is next door," Elise went on in her touch-me-not voice. "All I ask is you stay out of the way between seven and eight-thirty when the girls are getting ready for school."

"What about you?"

"I have my own bathroom." She realized her mistake the moment she said it.

Devilment danced in his eyes. "Perhaps I should share yours, so the girls and I won't have to worry about running into each other."

"I don't think so." Behind her back her fingers gripped the doorknob with frantic desperation. "And another thing, Detective. I have three girls who aren't used to men being around the house at all hours. I would appreciate your watching your language and manners. I've tried to teach them not all men are Neanderthals. Please don't show them differently.'' She turned to leave.

Dean dropped down onto the bed. "I can live with that. Oh, Doc?"

She turned her head, her eyes snapping the question before she voiced it. "What?"

"Did anyone ever tell you you smell so sexy it wouldn't be difficult to hustle you off to a dark corner for some heavy-duty necking? And that those jeans of yours show off a great butt? I'm talking world-class here."

Elise's fingers tightened on the doorknob. She looked furious, ready to slam the door if it hadn't been for her daughter.

Dean grinned, fully aware of the waves of fury rolling in his direction. "There, I've gotten it all out of my system." He held up his hands. "Good night."

"Good night," she spat.

"Oh, and, Doc, if you hear anything suspicious, feel free to wake me up. After all, that's what I'm here for." His words followed her out into the hallway.

A seething Elise followed her usual routine of checking all the doors and windows before heading for her bedroom. She checked the impulse to lock her door. She never knew if one of the girls might wake up and need her. Right after her father's death, Becky had suffered serious nightmares, and for the past week they had begun to recur. When that happened, she would come into her mother's bedroom and climb into bed with her. Plus, Elise felt Dean's words were more teasing than serious.

"At least I hope so," she murmured, standing in the bathroom and turning on the shower.

Dean cocked his head when he heard a shower running. For a moment, he visualized the very proper Elise A. Carpenter standing naked under running water. The picture sent interesting impulses to his libido.

He whistled between his teeth. "Damn, and here I told Mac this would be a breeze."

With the idea of Elise in the shower still running through his mind, he took the time to check out the rest of the house. He noted the new locks on the doors and windows, the precise location of the gun cabinet, even the book bags lying on the coffee table waiting for their owners to snatch them up in the morning and dash off to school. The house wasn't fancy but comfortable, the furniture well suited for a household with children. The kind of place a man could put his feet up and not be yelled at for doing so. At the same time, he knew he wouldn't find a speck of dust anywhere.

"Fud up," a raspy voice grumbled from one corner.

Dean spun around, crouched in a defensive position. Then the shadowy outline of a tall dome cage caught his attention. He walked over and carefully lifted one corner of the covers. He could swear the macaw he faced was glaring at him.

"Fud up," the macaw informed him, snapping her beak at him.

He dropped the cover. "You got it, bird."

He stepped back a pace as the macaw screeched, then called him a name he didn't think a bird in this all-female family would know. Deciding retreat would be a good idea, he returned to the room to gather up his toothbrush and toothpaste, more than ready for bed.

In no time he was lying in one of the most uncomfortable beds he'd ever known. Dean preferred extra-firm mattresses, and this one was more like a featherbed.

"She did this on purpose," he muttered, punching his pillow and turning onto his side. His eyes had started to drift shut when a light but steady droning sound vibrated into his head. He uttered a pungent curse and rolled over onto his other side.

"Geese that think a person's rear is fair game, dogs that go for the other side, birds that insult you and a tortoise that sounds like a jet engine." He punched the pillow even harder. "The woman is a sadist."

"YOU STAY OUT of my stuff!"

"You said I could use it!"

"Did not!"

"Did so!"

"Give it back before I punch you good!"

"Will not, it's mine!"

"Becky, give it back to me right now or else!"

"Mom, they're at it again!"

Dean's eyes flew open and he stalked into the hallway to find out who was waging war just outside his room.

"What the hell is going on here?" he roared, not in the best of moods after having only two hours of what he might call decent sleep.

Lisa and Becky turned their heads and lifted them at the dark-visaged image of wrath standing over them.

"Wow," Lisa breathed, her mouth dropped open.

"Mom said you have to—" Keri skidded to a stop, her own mouth dropping open in shock. Elise was right on her heels. Luckily she was able to maintain her composure. Which wasn't easy. Dean Cornell stood there wearing nothing more than a scanty pair of bright red briefs that barely covered the essentials.

"Mom, she took my glue!" Lisa wailed.

"Kitchen," she said tersely.

"Mom!"

She stared them down. "Both of you. Now."

Grumbling, the girls headed toward the front of the house.

"Detective Cornell, just last night I explained about your being careful in this house." Elise concentrated on looking only at his face—a challenging task, considering how good the rest of him looked . . . and how much of it was bare. "That means I not only want you to watch your language, but please don't leave your room until you're properly dressed."

He crossed his arms over his chest and leaned against the doorjamb, looking all too relaxed. "I am properly dressed."

Before she could help it, her eyes flickered downward and lingered a scant second longer than they should have. "I wouldn't call that properly dressed."

His grin did strange things to her insides. "It is when I normally sleep in the raw. I wore the underwear as a concession to this all-female household."

Elise could feel her face growing hot. "Breakfast is in ten minutes. Don't be late." She turned on her heel and walked away, her back so stiff a steel rod couldn't have competed.

"I doubt this is anything they haven't seen before," he called after her. "Hell, even the Disney Channel shows men in their underwear."

Elise was prepared to commit homicide.

"Wow, he looks better than some of those guys on TV," she could hear Lisa enthusing in the kitchen. "I thought most cops had beer bellies, but he sure doesn't."

"He's crude," Keri sniffed, lifting her juice glass to her lips.

"Enough," Elise ordered, walking into the room. "Detective Cornell is here to do a job." She poured herself a cup of coffee. Right about now she was in need of a shot of caffeine. The sight of the obviously virile Detective Cornell felt embedded in her brain.

"It's amazing how one pair of red briefs can leave such a lasting impression on some people's minds," Myrna said under her breath, then looked the essence of innocence when Elise glared at her. It was a well-known fact that the older woman, like Kristen, felt it was time for Elise to add a man to her life.

"Hopefully, he won't be here long enough for us to find out," she said stiffly, downing the hot coffee without a whimper and pouring herself another cup. "The last thing we need is an unwanted guest who acts like the typical heavy-handed cop."

Dean appeared five minutes later, looking incredibly sexy in rumpled jeans and a dark red sweat shirt with the sleeves hacked off. For a split second Elise wondered what color his underwear was this time.

"I'm Myrna, the housekeeper," the woman standing at the stove introduced herself. Tall, thin, with salt-and-pepper hair curled around her face, she looked like the kind of grandmother who baked cookies every weekend. Dean instantly liked her forthright manner. "Hope your appetite is better than most of these kids with their eternal diets."

He grinned. "I eat anything that's not moving."

"Then we'll get along fine."

Elise rolled her eyes, then glanced at her watch. "Hurry up, girls." She turned a cool gaze on Dean. "Either Myrna or I drive the girls to school."

"I'll do it from now on." He gulped the cup of coffee Myrna handed him.

"We haven't had any problems so far."

"No, but if you are the target, you might feel better if you aren't with them if anything happens," he explained, grabbing a piece of bacon and chomping on it. One look at

Elise's stiff features told him she didn't appreciate his obvious logic. Nor that she would have to admit he was right.

Keri looked from one adult to the other. She didn't like the way this conversation was going.

"Mom, he drives a truck that should have been junked fifty years ago. I can't be seen in that thing."

Elise sighed. She didn't bother arguing with him, because she knew she'd lose. "Go with him."

"All *right!*" Lisa shouted, jumping up.

Becky was more cautious. "He's not going to yell at us again, is he?"

Dean dropped a hand on top of her head. "No, princess, and I'm sorry I yelled this morning. After listening to a tortoise snore all night, I wasn't ready for the Civil War to be fought outside my bedroom door. I promise it won't happen again."

She flashed him a smile that resembled her mother's. "Okay."

Keri stood up and walked into the other room for her books. "If any of my friends see me in that—that piece of junk, I'll just die."

"She's at that age when life itself is traumatic," Elise explained.

"I'll fix you breakfast when you get back," Myrna offered.

He grinned. "I won't turn it down."

Dean soon discovered chauffeuring three girls was an experience in itself.

"This is so embarrassing," Keri grumbled, huddling near the door since she would be dropped off first. "If you don't mind, I'd prefer you leave me at the corner." *Where no one can see me getting out of this* was left unspoken.

"I do mind." He was unperturbed. "Your safety is my business, sweetheart."

She turned her head and glared at him. "I am not your sweetheart."

Dean grinned. "I see you take after your mother."

"Do you have your gun with you?" Lisa asked. "If someone stopped us, would you shoot it? Have you killed anyone?"

"You've got a bloodthirsty imagination," he chuckled.

She looked him up and down. "You sure don't look like the cops on TV."

"That's because he's a real one, Lisa," Keri informed her with her bored, lady-of-the manor tone, as Dean privately dubbed it.

The one who captivated him the most was little Becky, with her big eyes, more aquamarine than turquoise, and her short strawberry-blond curls. Right now, she looked up at him as if he were a type of being she'd never encountered before.

"And what about you, Becky?" he asked. "What question do you have to ask me?"

The tip of her tongue appeared for a moment as she thought long and hard. "How come your underwear has lumps in it?"

Dean was grateful to be at a stop light, because he found himself almost choking. When he looked at the innocent face of the little one who'd voiced the provocative question, he found himself the subject of Lisa's curious gaze and Keri's smirk that said *Get yourself out of this one!* Yep, she was like her mother, all right. He fell back on that time-honored reply all men give when asked dangerous questions by small girls.

"Ask your mother."

Chapter Five

"I see you survived driving the girls to school." Myrna set a filled plate in front of him.

Dean hungrily eyed the food and dug in immediately. "Keri crept out of the truck, afraid someone might see her." He picked up a warm blueberry muffin and buttered it liberally. "Lisa ran out of the truck shouting at the top of her lungs that she knows a real cop, and Becky still isn't sure of me."

"Poor little thing," Myrna clucked as she sat down across from him with a cup of coffee in her hand. "She's not used to having men around here."

Meaning the lady doesn't have overnight guests, he decided. He liked that idea.

"I understand Dr. Carpenter's clinic is the front house on the property."

Myrna nodded. "Elise was lucky enough to find a house where she could work close by. She concentrated on settling the girls in first before she opened her clinic."

"How long have you been with her?"

"Four years and ten months." She studied him closely as he mopped up egg with a bit of his muffin. "Ready for seconds? Are all your appetites this hearty?"

Dean couldn't remember the last time he'd blushed, if ever, but this woman appeared to have the capacity to bring that trait out in him. "I tend to burn a lot of calories in my business," he muttered, ducking his head. "It depends on who you talk to about the others."

Myrna laughed loudly and slapped his arm as she got up. "Honey, I'm just happy to see someone enjoy his food. I love cooking, and I love to watch people eat the results." Within moments, Dean had two more muffins in front of him and four more strips of bacon. "Now, you continue with your interrogation. This is fun." Her hazel eyes sparkled.

Dean chuckled. "Nothing throws you, does it?"

"Not much."

He sobered. "She could be in a lot of trouble, Myrna. This guy is not working with a sane mind, and he's targeted the doc as his next victim."

She nodded. "What can I do to help?"

"Give me the information she's going to be too hard-headed to give me," he urged. "That's the only way I can protect her and the girls."

Myrna smiled. "The girls are just as pigheaded as their mama."

"Yeah, I already found that out." He silently wondered what Elise was going to think of him if Becky remembered to ask her about his lumpy underwear. Not accustomed to dealing with members of the opposite sex under the age of consent, he had been thrown for a loop by Becky's innocent question.

"Keri's a good girl—she's just at that age where everything is a major production and appearances are all-important. And Lisa's coming to the age when she's going to have to decide whether she wants to continue being a tomboy or take that next step to being a girl. And Becky, well, she's a little doll." She beamed, for all the world like a proud grandmother. "She can sit there obstinate like her mama and sisters, then give you this glowing smile that makes you forget why you're angry at her.''

"And the doc?" he asked casually. But his inflection didn't get past the keen-minded housekeeper. "What about her?"

"Elise is stubborn, feels the need to do everything herself and not have to depend on others. She works entirely too hard, but she feels she's doing it for the girls. And she doesn't feel too guilty since her clinic is on the property and they have access to her any time they need her. Considering her husband's violent death, they've all managed very well." She released a soft sigh. "Until now. Having to be reminded that that horrible man is in the area waiting to—" She shook her head. "It isn't fair."

Dean popped the last bit of muffin into his mouth. "That's why I'm here."

A smile touched her lips. "'Pears to me you're here more to shake up the family then to protect them."

"Yeah, well, in my line of duty, I'm not used to having to watch my language because of three impressionable girls," he said ruefully.

"They'll keep you on your toes, all right." She chuckled, standing up and snagging his plate to carry it to the sink. "What will you do today? Other than make yourself a nuisance under my feet?"

Taking the more than subtle hint, he likewise stood up and stretched his arms above his head. "Look over the clinic, talk to the staff and see if they've noticed anything out of the ordinary."

"Elise won't like that. She considers the clinic her kingdom, and none dare try anything she doesn't like. And it's already obvious she doesn't appreciate your being here."

"She doesn't have to appreciate my being here. She only has to understand it's for a good reason. Besides, I can be just as stubborn as she is."

Myrna turned around to lean back against the counter, her arms crossed over her chest. "I have an idea things are going to turn pretty interesting around here. I'm glad I'll be around to watch the fireworks."

Dean recalled his first impression of Elise: instant attraction, then amusement at her imperious manner, and now, well, now he wasn't too sure what he thought about her. Except that she was still a lovely woman, even if she did tend to treat him with queenly disdain.

"She doesn't want you here, and she'll fight you every step of the way." Myrna didn't mean it unkindly as she easily read his thoughts. "But she does need you here, and somewhere inside her, that bothers her a lot."

Dean nodded in agreement. "I've been treated worse. I have to admit it will be a challenge to prove to her just how necessary I am. Not to mention that I'm an all-around nice guy."

"Cheryl's the receptionist, and Donna's the head AHT down there—animal health technician, to the layman," she clarified.

"Gotcha." He paused at the back door. "Uh, would you be able to keep that homicidal goose away from me?"

"I thought cops weren't afraid of anything."

"We're not, but no one I've known has come up against a butt-biting goose, either."

Myrna followed him onto the back steps, holding a bowl of grain in her arms. "When she and Herman head for the bowl, you head for the clinic. Frances, Herman, breakfast!" she called out.

To Dean's surprise, the two geese ran toward the steps, their wings outstretched, honking merrily at the sight of food. One goose eyed him suspiciously, and he quickly backed up against the post, much to the housekeeper's amusement.

"Go on," she urged. "You're safe for the moment."

He quickly made his escape. While he walked across the lawn and down the driveway to the front building, he scanned the surroundings. Houses were sparse in this area, and the mountains looked closer than he knew they really were. His senses told him there was nothing to worry about, but he also knew that could be temporary. He made a mental note to call Detective Santee and make an appointment to stop by the sheriff's station that afternoon. And to give Mac a call to see if he'd learned anything new. Even though he'd taken time off until Stacy had the baby, Mac had promised to continue tracking down any promising leads.

When Dean pushed open the heavy glass outer door to the clinic, he felt as if he had stepped into another world, one with an incredible noise level. Several people sat in the chairs ringing the waiting room, some holding cages in their laps. One woman was reading a magazine while a large tortoise rested on a skateboard in front of her. A boy in his late teens sat in a corner holding a narrow leash with a large iguana on the other end. One end of the waiting area boasted a glassed enclosure with several cages that barely contained several screaming tropical birds. He recognized the blue-and-gold macaw who'd told him off the night before.

"May I help you, sir?" A spritely woman stood at a waist-high counter, her eyes questioning since he'd walked in without an animal.

He quickly skirted the clients and their "pets," aware he was under their scrutiny as he flashed his badge. "Uh, yeah, I'm Detective Cornell. I'd like to see Dr. Carpenter."

She hesitated. "She's with a patient right now." She lowered her voice. "I understand why you're here, Detective, but you have to understand she has a very full schedule."

His smile indicated he understood—and he wasn't about to back off. "I want to see her now. I don't think her patient would object."

Another woman appeared. This one was dressed in surgical greens and sported a short, spiky haircut. "So you're the one who's got her eating nails." She grinned. "I'm Donna. It's okay, Cheryl, I'll take him back." She turned and gestured over her shoulder. "Come through the side door there."

The first thing Dean noticed was that the examination rooms he passed didn't look at all that different than the ones in a regular doctor's office, except that the "patients" waiting there were rabbits, reptiles and exotic birds.

"The doc doesn't seem to lack for patients," he commented.

"The ownership of exotic pets is increasing every year," Donna replied, leading him to the rear of the building. "Elise also has an excellent reputation in the field. Word of mouth is better than advertising." She eyed him consideringly. "You don't seem too comfortable."

He shrugged. "I'm not used to being around so many animals."

"Donna!" Elise's voice sounded strained. "Donna!"

Both took off on a run, Dean drawing his gun from under his sweatshirt, where he kept it nestled against his back. Donna pushed open the swinging door and stopped short.

"Althea!"

Dean skidded to a stop. He didn't expect to find a python wrapped snugly around Elise's upper body. Her face was bright red as she gasped for air.

"Get her loose," she panted.

Donna immediately headed for Elise, working her fingers around the large snake, and, with a bit of grunting and heaving, she soon freed her boss.

"What got into her?" Donna placed the coiled snake on the examination table.

"Beats me," Elise rasped, collapsing against the counter. "She got it into her head to hug me, and I couldn't get my hands free to work her loose. Luckily, she wasn't squeezing too hard. The last time she tried this I ended up with two broken ribs."

"I knew I shouldn't have left you alone with her." Donna shook her head with self-disgust.

Elise watched Dean's defensive stance. "Althea isn't armed, Detective. You can put the gun away."

"I'm not so sure." He eyed the now-placid reptile with suspicion and kept a healthy distance.

"Don't tell me you're afraid of a simple python?" A faint hint of amusement laced her voice.

"I wouldn't exactly call anything that could crush a person as easily as a grape 'simple.'" He glared at her. "That thing broke your ribs once and you still try to handle it by yourself? You're nuts!"

"I think I'll check on your next patient." Sensing the hostile vibrations coming from both parties, Donna hurriedly exited the room.

"Surely you had white mice or a lizard or two when you were a child," Elise commented.

He shook his head. "Not even a dog or cat." He didn't tell her that where he grew up pets were a luxury one didn't even dare to consider. That was something he didn't talk about to anyone. Only Mac knew, and even he'd never heard the entire story of Dean's less-than-ideal childhood.

Elise draped the python over her arm and stroked the head, smiling at the tongue flickering out. "Althea was just showing her affection the only way she knows how."

"I thought that's how pythons captured their prey."

She nodded. "They do, and instinct causes Althea to squeeze us a bit too much at times. She's been domestically bred, but that hasn't hampered her abilities one bit. Actually, she's a sweetheart most of the time.'' She looked up at him. ''Now, do you care to tell me why you've burst into my place of business?''

''I want to talk to your staff.''

Her lovely features hardened. ''No.''

''I'm not asking, Doc. I'm telling.''

''They have nothing to tell you.''

''The day of your unwanted visitor, your receptionist received a call from a man who wouldn't leave his name.''

Elise took several calming breaths, so as not to transfer her agitation to the python. ''Which she already told the sheriff. There's nothing more she can tell you than she's already told them.''

''They might not have asked the right questions.''

Bright turquoise eyes warred with dark brown. In the end, neither gave an inch or looked away. It was a standoff.

''You can talk to them at the end of the day and not before. As you can see, I have a great many patients to attend to, and I don't like to keep them waiting too long. It creates undue stress on the animals.''

''Why don't you have another doctor in here to take off some of the strain?''

She had been thinking about that for the past year, when it appeared her practice was growing faster than she'd expected. ''You have to find the right person first.''

''I'll be back a few minutes before five,'' he stated.

''We close at six.''

Dean silently counted to ten. ''Whatever.'' He turned toward the swinging door.

''Detective, there's a rear door you can use.'' She gestured behind her.

Dean noticed the cages and kennels obviously used for animals kept overnight, as well as a lot of unfamiliar equipment whose use he couldn't fathom. Beyond that was a door. He tried the knob and discovered it turned easily. He flashed Elise an accusing look.

"It's unlocked."

"I come in that door in the mornings. I usually don't re-lock it because no one other than staff uses it."

He stalked over to her until they stood toe to toe. "Listen carefully so I won't have to repeat myself. This door is to be locked at all times. You are not to let anyone in— I don't care if it's the president of the United States. In fact, I'll arrange to have a peephole installed in it."

Elise's neck was bent back so far she could feel the slight strain on her muscles. Her flaring nostrils picked up a hint of soap and clean male skin. The cop didn't need any of those men's colognes advertised so heavily; he was potent enough on his own, she thought irrationally. She schooled her features to remain cool and composed but found it more difficult than usual. Darn this man! He'd already caused her enough mental anguish, and he hadn't even been there for twenty-four hours!

"You're disturbing my work, Detective." She silently damned the husky catch in her voice.

He couldn't miss the faint rose flush to her skin, the slight fog in her eyes and the voice that brought to mind a darkened bedroom. His own respiration turned rough with reaction. She wasn't wearing any perfume today, but then again, she didn't need any. Not when her own fresh scent was so evocative. He wanted to find out if that lush mouth tasted as good as it looked and if her skin was really as soft as it appeared, but some rational part of him told him this wasn't the time.

"Goodbye, Detective," she whispered.

"I have a name, you know."

"Yes, but this is a professional situation we're in."

"Is it?" He moved closer until she could feel the heat of his body. "Why don't you try my name? It's easy to say. I'll even make a deal with you— I'll say yours, and then you can say mine."

She didn't consider it that great a deal, and her expression told him so.

"Elise." He waited. "Your turn."

"No." She couldn't. She wasn't about to allow this dark-haired hellion to intrude on her well-ordered life any more than was strictly necessary. And she certainly wasn't going to allow him into her equally well-ordered sanity.

"Elise," he murmured again. His eyes tracked several strands of hair curled along her cheek to her lips. His fingers itched to move it, but he dared not. He was here on business, dammit!

"Dean." It came out huskier than she wanted.

He showed no satisfaction at her capitulation. He merely stepped back and turned to walk out the rear door. "Lock it," he tossed over his shoulder.

Out of his potent range, Elise could only collapse against the examination table. She brushed a stray hair from her face and saw that her hand was trembling. Quickly straightening her shoulders, she marched out of the room. Work had always soothed her mind before; she could only hope it would now, too.

She glanced out the window and noticed Dean standing in the crisp air. His chest rose and fell with deep breaths. She was perversely pleased to note he appeared as affected by the encounter as she.

"So this is what they call protective custody," she murmured, turning away.

"AS YOU CAN SEE, you have more information about Dietrich than we do." Detective Santee, a man in his late forties, gestured toward the sheaf of papers in Dean's hand.

Dean had arranged to meet with him that afternoon before he picked the Carpenter girls up from school. "All we have is Deputy Webster's report and what he just told you."

Dean nodded, thinking about the young man he had just unmercifully grilled. He knew he'd acted like the tough city cop, and after Webster's crack about women who tended to imagine things, he hadn't been able to help himself.

"You were a little rough on the kid," Detective Santee commented.

"He deserved it," he said. "We have a major witness whose life was threatened, and when she tells him what happened, he acts as if she's the type to look under her bed every night. She must have been uneasy that night, probably even frightened, and he didn't offer her one shred of compassion. Hell, he even tried to pass it off as a PMS attack!"

Santee held up his hands in surrender. "Hey, I'm on your side," he assured Dean. "And I agree with you. Webster's a good cop, has good instincts, but he needs work on his bedside manner, so to speak. Public relations isn't his forte."

"No kidding." Dean tossed the papers onto the desk. "Dietrich must be in the area. I can't understand why your men haven't been able to rout him."

"We checked every hotel from the five-stars down to the dives. He could be hiding out with friends, even camping somewhere. CHP—" he named the California Highway Patrol "—has been on the lookout for him and his motorcycle, too. Nothing."

Dean exhaled a sigh of frustration. "With all our resources you'd think we could come up with one lousy creep," he muttered. "Something's not right here."

"He could have left the area," Santee suggested.

Dean shook his head. "No, he's around. I feel it in my bones."

"I didn't think you knew all that much about him."

"I have his file, and I know his type. He's getting his kicks out of outwitting us. I'm sure he knows who I am and exactly why I'm here. My captain wanted me to act like the doc and I were 'old friends,' if you know what I mean, but I knew she wouldn't go for that. We don't exactly get along." Now there was an understatement, his brain jeered. "Course, the captain tends to forget that Dietrich saw me crash his little party in the bank, and I doubt he'd forget my face all that easily."

"Yeah, I know what you mean. And we've all heard stories of that kind of bastard deciding to get even."

The two men traded a few stories and parted as friends. Santee even gave Dean his home number in case he needed to get hold of him after-hours.

"By the way, what's your first name? Or is it a state secret?" Dean asked.

The man smiled. "Nothing I care to divulge to the public."

"Not even a fellow cop?"

"Especially a fellow cop. Stories like that tend to remain with you until the end."

Dean stuck out his hand. "I'll be in touch."

"And I'll let you know if I hear anything."

DEAN REACHED Becky's school just as classes were released for the day and found the little girl waiting in the building's doorway, as he'd instructed her when he dropped her off that morning. Presenting him with a shy smile, she climbed into the truck and they headed down the street to pick up Lisa and Keri. Lisa was easy to find. Keri wasn't. He finally tracked her down at the football field, where she was watching the team practice. By then his temper was not at its best.

"You were told to wait in front," he grumbled, guiding her to the truck with a none-too-gentle hand.

She jerked her arm away, only to have it captured again. "I am not a child to be scolded, Detective Cornell," she snapped.

"Hey, Keri, are you okay?" A boy about her age stepped in front of them.

Dean had to respect the kid for having the courage to go up against a clearly cranky adult male. "Everything is just fine," he growled.

The boy looked suspicious. "Who are you?"

Dean pulled out his badge. "Good enough for you, kid?"

The boy reddened and stepped back. By then, Keri looked mortified.

"It's all right, Brian," she muttered.

"Are you sure, Keri?" he asked.

She nodded, her cheeks by now flaming red. "Yes, I disobeyed the detective's instructions." She clutched her books against her chest and walked swiftly toward the waiting truck, where Lisa and Becky had been avidly watching the entire scene.

"Hey, kid." Dean stopped the boy. "You've got guts. I'm proud of you."

He looked puzzled. "For what?"

"For seeing a friend who might be in trouble and being willing to step in and make sure she was all right. A lot of people would probably just look the other way. You're all right." He held out his hand.

Brian reddened as he grasped the older man's hand. "Well, it's just that Keri's so pretty, and things do happen," he mumbled, staring down at his feet. "We know her mom has been having problems with some bank robber."

Dean caught on immediately. The young rescuer had a crush on the cool Keri!

"I'll put a good word in for you," he assured the boy. He paused. "Do you see her a lot during the school day?"

He nodded. "We have three classes together, and we both belong to the language club."

"Then do me a favor? Keep an eye on her. Make sure no man, other than a teacher, ever approaches her or tries to take her off school grounds. If you see anyone suspicious hanging around her, call me at Keri's house, and if you can't reach me, call a Detective Santee with the sheriff's department."

Brian's eyes widened. "No one's going to hurt her around here, Detective," he fervently assured him.

Certain he had an ally, Dean smiled and headed for the truck.

"Are you through with your macho act now?" Keri demanded as he climbed into the truck. "After that display I'll never be able to hold my head up in school again. They probably think you were arresting me for something."

He chose to ignore her tantrum. As much as he hated to admit it, she had a point. His anger had pushed him to be a little too hard on her, but he doubted she was in the mood for an apology just now. He certainly wasn't. He tried the next best thing. "Hey, that Brian has a good head on his shoulders. And it was pretty cool of him to stand up to me like that." He turned on the ignition. "A real brave kid. You should feel honored he tried to save you from what he thought was suspicious activity."

Keri lifted her chin higher, her expression icy enough to turn Dean into a Popsicle.

Used to the cold shoulder from half the Carpenter women, Dean merely shrugged and pulled away from the curb.

"You know what sounds good to me?" he said casually as he scanned the shopping areas on either side of the busy main street. "An ice-cream sundae."

Becky's eyes widened. "Really? I didn't think grown-ups liked them very much. 'Cept Mom, and that's only every few weeks when she says she's going through her chocolate-or-die phase."

Dean swallowed a chuckle at Becky's description.

"Well, I might not feel like chocolate-or-die, but there's times I like good old-fashioned hot-fudge sundae. Any decent places around here?"

"Not a lot, but there is one," Lisa drawled.

"My treat." Dean pressed home his advantage as he took in Lisa and Becky's excited expression. "I gather Keri isn't fond of hot fudge."

She didn't turn from her studied pose of looking out the window as if the scenery were vastly entertaining and the company equally boring. "Chocolate isn't good for you. It causes nasty blemishes, not to mention that it rots your teeth," she said haughtily.

Dean wasn't about to give up now. "No problem. You can have strawberry."

Chapter Six

"Do you have any idea what you've done?"

Dean puffed out his cheeks and exhaled noisily. He spun on his heel to face a furious Elise bearing down on him.

"No, but I have an idea you're going to tell me."

She looked at him as if the idea of murder were very appealing. "Where shall I start? Your telling Becky to ask me about your damn lumpy underwear?"

"I figured you would prefer the answer came from you rather than from me."

"And your manhandling Keri on the school campus? Was that something I would also prefer?" she angrily demanded, furious because he was right. She *would* prefer answering Becky's question herself. Who knew what *he* might say? So she launched her next missile. "According to Keri, you acted like a Neanderthal with her. For all we know, she'll have bruises on her arm tomorrow!"

His features turned to granite. "Look, Doc, I didn't ask much, only that those kids be waiting for me just inside the front door. I didn't want them wandering off. But your little Miss Keri decided those rules didn't apply to her and was out in the back drooling over the football team. There's a maniac on the loose who might decide to get to you through your kids, and she would have been a perfect target. She's going to have to learn that if she doesn't follow my rules, she'll have to pay the piper. Just because she wants to act cool doesn't mean she has to act stupid, too.''

His cold, matter-of-fact words deflated Elise's anger. "Keri may be a little headstrong, but she isn't stupid."

"If you can't drum into her head what we're up against, I'll play the heavy each and every time, and her precious feelings be damned," he said softly but firmly, starting to turn away.

"Wait a minute, Detective, there's one more thing." Elise's voice was sweetness over acid.

He closed his eyes. Something warned him this was the killer. "Now what? Did they say I drove too fast? Ran a stop light? What?"

"You took the girls out for ice cream."

"It was early enough that I didn't think it would spoil their dinner," he defended himself. "If you're pissed because I didn't ask your permission, I'm sorry. I was just trying to get to know them better in a more relaxing atmosphere."

"Maybe so," she said quietly. "The thing is, you allowed Becky to order the super-duper hot-fudge sundae."

"Yeah, and she ate every bite. Frankly, I was surprised a little kid like her could handle something that large."

Elise shook her head. "That's just it. She couldn't. Becky's super-duper hot-fudge sundae left her with a super-duper stomachache. Right now, she's in bed convinced she'll die at any moment. Actually, I think she's hoping she will."

Dean winced. "Look, I'm sorry. I should have realized that much sugar could put away an adult, much less a little girl."

"Lisa goaded her into it?" Elise guessed.

He grimaced, remembering the exchange in the ice-cream parlor. "She told her she couldn't handle one, and Becky said she could."

Elise's face softened in a tiny smile. "Lisa is good at that kind of thing. She loves to challenge Becky because she knows her darling little sister is the perfect victim for a dare."

Dean shifted uneasily. "Look, Elise, I'm sorry. I guess I blew it. I'm afraid my past experience didn't cover this type of situation."

By now all of her anger had dissipated. "You didn't know." She shifted from one foot to the other, gnawing on her lower lip. "I'm sorry for jumping down your throat like that. It's just that..." She took a deep breath. "All of a sudden my life is turned upside down, and I can't seem to control anything anymore. I'm more worried about my children being in danger than I am about any harm coming to me. They're all I have left," she finished quietly.

Dean swore silently. He could see the naked pain in her eyes. She had already lost her husband and unborn child to this maniac. And after that trauma, she had somehow found the courage to go on to make a new life for herself and her children. If something happened to one of them because of this animal, he knew she would never be the same again.

"Next time I won't let Becky order the super-duper hot-fudge sundae," he vowed.

Elise allowed herself a little smile. "Fine." She turned away.

"Hey, Doc." Dean's voice stopped her. She looked at him over her shoulder. "Thanks for not peeling a strip off my hide."

She smiled. "You do it again and I'll do more than peel a strip off." She headed to her bedroom.

Dean watched her until the door closed after her. "It must be in the genes," he muttered. "Only a mother can have a grown-up man quaking in his boots."

"Boots you shouldn't be wearing in a house where I've just vacuumed the carpets," Myrna scolded, walking out of the bathroom with an armload of laundry. "Tell me something, does your whole apartment look like the same kind of war zone you've left the guest bedroom looking?"

He flushed. "I guess I'm not real big on neatness," he admitted.

She snorted. "Son, you have clothes strewn all over that room, and I don't intend to pick them up for you. I put a basket in a corner for your dirty clothes, but the clean ones should be put away." She directed a glare at him. "Around here, everyone keeps their room clean or is punished appropriately."

"No dessert?"

"No food."

"Mac arranged this, I just know it," he muttered, heading for his room. He had an idea if his room wasn't picked up pronto, there would be no place set for him at dinner. Of course, if Elise Carpenter had anything to do with it, he wouldn't even have a room! The moment he entered he winced at the steady snoring coming from under the bed. "Yep, Mac arranged this and is having himself a good laugh."

DEAN LEARNED a lot about the Carpenters during dinner. Elise patiently listened to each girl talk about her day at school, and if there were homework problems, she promised to help them after dinner. He noticed that while Keri didn't act like his best friend, she'd ceased her obvious cold-shoulder treatment. Now she just acted as if he didn't exist. Lisa still pushed for police stories, the bloodier and gorier the better. Becky stayed in her room with a bowl of soup for her upset stomach.

"Lisa, if you ask about shoot-outs one more time, you will leave this table and figure out your history homework yourself," Elise said finally. "One, it is not appropriate dinner conversation, and two, Detective Cornell might not care to discuss people he's had to shoot during his career."

Dean sent her a look of gratitude, impressed with her sensitivity. He didn't like talking—or even thinking—about the people he'd had to shoot, even if it was in self-defense.

"Luckily, movies and TV are finally showing that a cop's life isn't all that glamorous," he said slowly, staring down at his roast beef and mashed potatoes swimming in rich brown gravy. Myrna sure knew the way to a man's heart. "Most of the time it's a lot of legwork, phone calls and talking to countless people just to chase down one lousy lead. It's a lot of all-nighters drinking cold coffee and eating greasy hamburgers. I'd have an ulcer right now if it wasn't for the fact that I have a cast-iron stomach. Or maybe have no taste buds left."

"You can say that while eating my roast beef?" Myrna asked tartly.

He flashed her a smile. "No, I sure can't. If I keep on eating like this while I'm here, I'll probably gain fifty pounds."

Elise's gaze dropped, taking in the sweatshirt fitting snugly over broad shoulders and a washboard-flat stomach. She doubted there was once ounce of fat on his entire body. When she raised her eyes she found Dean gazing at her, a hint of laughter in the dark depths. Embarrassment threatening to flood her, she quickly glanced away. By now she knew better than to silently dare him to say anything. With his outrageous personality, he would probably do more than just say something. Deciding that cowardice was for once the best tactic, she quickly applied herself to her meal.

"Lisa, you'll help with the dishes tonight," she announced once dinner was finished.

"It's Becky's week!" the girl protested.

"Since she's sick due to your little game, you'll take her place. In fact, you can finish out her week." Elise rose from the table. "Feel free to watch television or listen to the stereo, Detective."

"Actually, I have some homework of my own," he admitted. "Captain Anderson expects daily reports."

"Give him my regards." Her smile indicated the opposite.

"Yeah, I can imagine he'd like that." Dean headed for his room to pick up the notebook where he kept his summary of what he'd learned so far. Which wasn't very much. As far as he was concerned, writing reports was on a par with having teeth drilled. And having a captain who insisted on seeing every *t* crossed and *i* dotted, along with each report handed in on time or else, didn't help.

"I have a typewriter you can use if you'd like," Elise offered.

His eyes lit up. "I'd like."

Elise led him into a small home office where a typewriter stand was arranged next to the desk that held a personal computer. "It has a correcting feature," she explained, whipping off the typewriter cover. "And there's typing paper in the bottom drawer if you need any."

Dean looked at the miraculous electric typewriter with relief. His typing skills weren't the best. "Great, thank you." He sat at the desk, then looked up, cocking his head to one side. "You're great with those girls."

His praise warmed her. "It probably helps that I was a girl once upon a time."

"No, it's more than that," he said quietly. "You really listen to them. So many parents nowadays don't bother to listen to their kids, to find out what they're feeling and show genuine interest in what they do, but you do. You really care, and it shows."

She lingered by the desk, trailing her fingers across the top. No dust married the brightly polished surface, thanks to Myrna. "A single parent has to try harder, and I've always taken my family seriously."

"How come you never remarried?" He inwardly winced, fearing his question might be too indelicate. "A pretty lady like you must have men knocking down her door."

"Most men are leery of a woman with children," she said frankly. "Not to mention I have a career that's very demanding and I haven't met a man I felt was the right one. I'm happy with my life."

Dean looked around the room, taking in the pictures of the girls and a framed photo of a younger Elise standing next to a lanky blond man with a broad smile. Behind them was a large sign proclaiming the building Carpenters' Exotic Animal Clinic. Privately Dean thought the man looked a little too easygoing for a firebrand like Elise. Perhaps that side of her personality hadn't been prominent then. He liked the idea of his being the only one to see the lady's temper.

He also wanted to keep her there as long as possible. "One other thing. What is it with that bird out there? It acts like it's the boss here or something. If I even look at it, it tells me to 'fud up.' "

Elise smiled. "If I were you, I wouldn't refer to Baby as an 'it' or as a bird, because *she* doesn't think she is one."

"Excuse me?"

"She was a wedding gift from my husband. We raised her from infancy. And now she believes she's human and that all the animals are under her jurisdiction. We have no idea where 'fud up' came from, but it's her favorite phrase when things don't go her way."

A bird that thinks it's a person? Dean couldn't comprehend the notion. But then again, until recently he hadn't known tortoises snored, either. "Sounds more like a spoiled brat."

"She's that, too, but she's also a sweetheart when she wants to be."

"And the tortoise that's disturbing my sleep?"

"That's Florence. Henry's in the coat closet."

"You have two?"

She nodded. "They're both desert tortoises, about twenty years old and very intelligent. They both know what the refrigerator is for, and they love to have their heads rubbed. With the weather getting colder, they decided it was time to bed down for the winter, so we won't be seeing much of them until spring. The geese, Frances and Herman, were given to us by a neighbor when we moved in. As for the dogs, one was abandoned as a puppy at our gate, and the other two were dropped off at the clinic late one night. Most vets end up with a menagerie at home, and I'm no exception." Her lips curved. "But surely you grew up with *some* kind of pet? Something tells me you were the type to scare little girls with frogs."

Dean shook his head. "No, my mother wasn't into pets" was all he said.

Elise's eyes softened, but she said nothing, having a pretty good idea Dean wouldn't appreciate sympathy. But her softening also had to do with the boneless grace he displayed, settled in her desk chair, and the way he looked at her as if something other than polite conversation were on his mind.

He leaned back in the chair. "Nice quiet room."

What made her think he was saying something sexy? "It helps when I need to do paperwork."

"Good place for privacy."

Again she read something in his simple words, and her flesh tingled under his intense regard.

"With three girls in the house, privacy isn't the norm," she murmured.

"There are times when people need privacy. Desire it." His gaze dropped to her mouth.

For one improbable moment Elise thought about locking the door. The dark arousal in Dean's eyes told her he would recognize the gesture for what it was. Perhaps he was hypnotizing her to do just that! Her fingers hovered over the doorknob. Then the idea of three girls pounding on the door demanding to know why Mom had locked it burst into her mind.

"Do what you feel is right," Dean said quietly, as if reading her thoughts.

She flushed to realize he might know exactly where her thoughts were heading. Her usual acerbic response was stilled as she mentally groped for a reply. She was saved by the bell, literally. For a moment she stared stupidly at the phone until she roused herself sufficiently to walk toward the desk and place her hand on the receiver.

Dean's hand swiftly covered hers while the other gestured for her to walk around the desk to him. Not until her leg gently bumped his thigh did he release his grip so she could pick up the receiver.

"Hello?" Elise said quietly. Her body stiffened. "How did you get this number?"

The moment Dean realized it wasn't a run-of-the-mill call, he jerked her down into his lap so he could listen in.

"Hey, sweet baby." The taunting whisper slithered over the line. "We didn't get to finish our party five years ago— maybe we can this time."

She was stiff as a board, her eyes boring into Dean's as he carefully wedged the phone a little away from her ear so he could hear.

"If not," he went on, "there's always your cute little daughter. I bet we could have real fun," he went on. Elise felt sick and slammed the phone down in the cradle, narrowly missing cracking Dean's fingers in the process.

"That pig!" she choked. "That filthy pig!"

Elise watched Dean pick up the phone and punch out numbers. "What are you doing?"

"I'm calling Santee about having a tap put on your phone. Although it probably won't do any good." When his connection was made he spoke rapid-fire, detailing the call while casting quick glances at a white-faced Elise, who had gotten off his knee and stood away a short distance.

"Why do you think it won't do any good?" she asked when he finished his call.

"Because there's a good chance he won't call again. This time, he called to shake you up. He knows he's done that, so he'll probably hold off for a while. He's playing a sick game with you as the target," he explained. "Santee's going to arrange a tap as soon as possible. He's also having one put on your clinic phone."

Feeling the presence of others, Elise looked over at the now-open doorway to find Lisa and Keri standing there, wide-eyed and frightened. They were looking to their mother for protection, and she was finally realizing she couldn't provide it on her own. For the first time, she was grateful Dean was there to take charge.

"Girls, why don't you go on to bed," she suggested quietly with a facsimile of a smile. "Everything will be all right."

Lisa looked up at Dean. "If that slime comes to the house, you're going to blow him away with your gun, aren't you?"

"How about if I take him into custody and send him away to prison for a long time?" he suggested.

She shook her head. "That's what was supposed to happen before, and it didn't. And it won't this time, either."

With bowed shoulders, Lisa trudged down the hallway on her sister's heels.

Dean left the office and headed for the kitchen. Mission accomplished, he went to find Elise. She was in the living room, looking dazed. He handed her a glass of wine and toasted her with a glass bearing an inch of amber liquid.

"I didn't think you looked like the Jack Daniel's type." He downed the whiskey, sighing happily when the liquor hit his stomach with a warm glow. "Perfect," he pronounced.

Elise settled herself on the couch, tucking her legs under her. "He's playing a game with me, you said?"

Dean took the chair beside the couch, stretching his legs out in front of him. He eyed her closely, noting her pale features and shadowed eyes, and wished he could give her more than a glass of liquid courage. "Yeah, I'm afraid so." He rolled his glass between his palms, staring down at the residue in the bottom. "It might be a good idea to send the girls somewhere else for the time being."

"No!" She downed the rest of her wine in one gulp and set the glass on the table in front of her. "No, they stay here. What if he decided to make them a target to get back at me? They're better off here, with you." Her voice came out muffled.

He glanced sharply at her. "Does this mean you're finally going to trust me? Go along with me? No matter how much you disagree with my methods?"

She met his gaze squarely. "I'll trust your methods as long as my daughters are kept safe. But if harm comes to any of them, I will go after that man and I will shoot him down like a mad dog."

"Elise, you'd only be stooping to his level," he reminded her. "Not to mention getting sent to jail."

Her smile held no warmth. "All I'll need is a police officer who can't spell, and I'll be out just the way he was."

Dean shook his head. "Revenge only makes things worse, Elise. It won't let you sleep at night, and it won't make life easier."

"If he was dead, I'd sleep just fine."

"That's what you think." He set his glass on the table with a thud, leaning forward to rest his elbows on his thighs, his laced fingers hanging loosely between his spread knees.

Elise's eyes lowered for a fraction of a second to notice the way the soft denim stretched in important places. She quickly raised her glance.

"Killing isn't like in the movies. There's real blood, real gore, people screaming in pain. What you encountered in that bank is nothing compared to..." He trailed off, finally adding, "And a gunshot wound is usually pretty messy."

"I'm well aware of the consequences a bullet can have, Detective. Not only did I stop that bank guard from bleeding to death, but I saw my husband die from a gunshot wound to the head. Steve's death was brutal and senseless, and I will see it in my dreams for the rest of my life." She stood up. "As I said before, if you don't get Dietrich, I will."

Dean grabbed her hand to halt her leave-taking, holding it in a viselike grip. "You go after him and you'll be playing right into his hands," he warned. "You'll be doing just what he wants. And once he has you, he won't let you go until you're dead and no longer a threat to him." When she tried to jerk back her hand, he only tightened his hold. "Get smart, Elise. You might not like us cops, but we know how to handle types like him. You don't. Don't talk to me about senseless killings. In my line of work I've seen a hell of a lot more than I care to think about."

Her eyes flashed fire. "Then *you* bring me his head on a platter!"

His jaw tightened. "Let me do my job, Elise."

Elise looked down at his fingers encircling her wrist. The man was causing feelings long buried to surface, and the sensation was painful. She didn't want to feel again. Especially not with this man. She feared Dean could drag out emotions she'd never even experienced before.

"I don't want this," she said in a low voice, aware she was giving away her feelings but sensing this was a time to tell the truth. "If you don't mind, I'd like to go to bed. I have to get up earlier than usual tomorrow because it's my surgery day."

He didn't loosen his hold. On the contrary, he sat there as if they had all the time in the world. "On one condition."

She could feel the heat of his skin permeate hers and travel up her arm, providing a warmth the wine hadn't given her. "What?"

"Say my name from now on."

She refused to look at him. "I do use your name."

He shook his head. "No, you're real good at my title, but you don't say my name unless I force you to. You said it in the clinic this morning, and it sounded damn good. I want to hear it again."

Her voice had a slight tremble to it. "Dean."

He released her without hesitation. "I told you it wasn't so hard."

This time she did look at him, noting the shaggy black hair with a few streaks of silver running faintly through it. The heavy beard framed a well-shaped face. The deep brown eyes looked deep into her soul. He had a rugged face—not handsome but honest. Faint lines fanned out from his eyes, attesting to years of hard living. But it was those all-seeing eyes she feared the most. She feared that she wouldn't be able to hide anything from him if she didn't watch herself. And that, she knew, was dangerous.

"There's only one problem," she said. "If I stop using your title, I might forget your true reason for being here. I don't want to do that."

AFTER ELISE RETREATED to her bedroom, Dean returned to the kitchen for the Jack Daniel's bottle. As he sat sprawled in the chair, sipping the fiery liquid, he thought about the woman with the strawberry-blond hair and eyes the color of polished turquoise. It had been a long time since a woman had so completely snared his attention the way she had. He hadn't missed the fear in her eyes as Dietrich threatened her over the phone and he'd wanted nothing more than to take her in his arms and assure her no harm would come to her or her children. As a man, he wanted to make that promise. As a cop, he knew better than to make any kind of promise that couldn't be guaranteed. He stretched out an arm, snagging the telephone receiver. Setting the phone in his lap, he punched out a series of numbers.

"Yeah?" Mac's distinctive growl sounded in his ear.

"You a dad yet?"

"Not yet, and the waiting's driving me crazy. Stacy, on the other hand, looks so calm you'd think she was an old hand at this. I already told you you'd be the second to know, right after Amanda," he told him. "What's up?"

Dean filled Mac in on the day's happenings.

"What do you need from this end?" Mac asked.

"I wouldn't know where to begin." Dean took a hearty swallow from his drink. "Santee is going to put a tap on the home and office phones, but this guy isn't playing by the rules. He's going to make her life hell before he makes his major move."

"How about I talk to his accomplices?"

"They didn't make bail?"

"No way they could."

"You're on leave though," he warned. The meaning was clear. Mac wouldn't have any power to perform police activities.

"That hasn't stopped me before. I'll talk to them in the morning and get back to you if there's anything important to report," he promised.

"Thanks buddy."

"Dean?"

"Yeah?"

"Is she getting to you already?"

His laughter held no mirth. "My friend, the lady got to me the first moment I saw her."

BY HABIT, Dean did not awaken easily unless the phone was ringing, which usually meant a work call. Even an alarm clock couldn't galvanize him into action the way work could. Now he lay sprawled in bed, still foggy with sleep, as he dreamed of voices whispering near his ear and something cold circling his wrist. Then his nostrils twitched as he thought he smelled coffee. Yep, that was the smell, all right.

Ah, the smell of coffee brewing, mingled with the snores of the reptile hibernating under his bed. What more could a man want first thing in the morning?

Then something prompted him to finish waking up as he rolled over onto his side. *Tried* to roll over. He soon discovered he couldn't go far, and his eyes flew open. A quick scan of the area told him why. His handcuffs had been used to shackle his wrist to the brass headboard. He jerked up so violently he was almost thrown back to the mattress.

"Dammit!" he roared. "Elise, get the hell in here! Elise!"

Pounding feet sounded down the hallway before his bedroom door swung open, revealing Elise, the three girls and a fascinated Myrna. Dean closed his eyes. The last thing he wanted was an audience.

"I only recall asking for one particular person." His thunderous expression boded ill.

"You didn't ask. You shouted," Elise pointed out. "I guess the others were curious."

Her gaze took in the scene, and she had to bite down hard on her lower lip to keep from bursting into laughter. Funny, she hadn't had much to laugh about lately, and the man sprawled before her wasn't exactly laughable even if the situation was. A magnificent specimen of masculinity lay handcuffed to the bed with the covers tossed every which way, allowing a view of a muscled chest coated with coarse dark hair and a pair of bright teal briefs that barely hid anything. She wished he wore boxer shorts. No, she wished she could stop looking at him so hungrily.

"Why Detective Cornell, I had no idea you went in for the kinky stuff," she drawled. "What kind of man did your department send to protect me?"

"Just get me out of this." He bit out each word as he scowled darkly at her—as if it were all her fault!

"You said he would laugh!" Becky attacked Lisa, pushing her sister away from her. "You said he'd know it was a joke!"

Elise grabbed her two younger daughters before they could escape and pasted on her tell-me-the-truth-or-else expression.

"We wanted to play a joke on him, that's all," Becky blurted out. "Lisa said he'd think it was funny if we handcuffed him to the bed. But he doesn't. He's really mad." She glared at her older sister before hitting her with a tiny fist.

"None of that!" Elise grabbed her hand. "Both of you go to the living room and wait for me."

"Hey, if you don't mind, I'd like to get out of here," Dean called out. Patience was not one of his virtues.

"Where's the key?"

"On the dresser next to my wallet."

Elise gave the two girls one more look. "Didn't I just tell you to go to the living room?"

"Yes."

"Yes," Becky's voice was more subdued than her sister's.

"Then I suggest you do as I say or you'll be without television for a month instead of a week."

"A week? *Mom!*"

"But she made me do it!"

"A week," she repeated. "Lisa, your idea of a joke isn't funny. And, Becky, no one can make you do anything you don't want to. Now go."

"Ladies, can't you continue your discussion later? I'd really like to get out of these handcuffs," Dean said plaintively.

"Now that's the way to keep a man around the house," Myrna chuckled, walking away.

"I think it's sick" was Keri's disgusted comment as she followed the housekeeper.

Elise found Dean's keys and selected the proper one. She unlocked the cuff around his wrist and dropped the keys onto the bed, all the while attempting not to look at his barely clad body. Lisa was right. He most definitely didn't have a beer belly. In fact, his abdomen looked so flat she could probably bounce a quarter off it. His body looked all too good to a woman who hadn't really given the opposite sex much thought over the past five years.

"Now that you've given us another show, I suggest you keep your door locked to discourage unwanted visitors," she said crisply, making sure to keep her gaze fastened firmly on his face. "Yesterday's explanation about your lumpy underwear was quite enough, thank you."

"I figured she'd forget all about it."

"Children never forget."

"So what did you tell her?" Dean's husky voice was music to a starving woman's ears.

She frowned. "Tell her?"

"About my lumpy underwear."

She looked everywhere but at him. "It was just a talk between mother and daughter."

"Come on, give me a hint," he coaxed. "I'm real curious."

"Detective, you're on duty," she hedged.

"I'm not on duty until my badge is pinned on, and as you can see, there aren't too many places to pin it right now." His eyes danced with wicked lights.

Elise walked to the dresser, picked up his leather badge case and tossed it onto the bed. "I'm sure I can find an appropriate place."

"What worries you more, Elise? That you looked at me more closely than you feel you should have, or that you liked what you saw?"

Elise knew when silence was golden, and this was definitely one of those times. She beat a hasty retreat without another word.

DEAN MADE ARRANGEMENTS to meet with Detective Santee again that morning. While he drove into town, he felt the tingling sensation that told him his prey was nearby. A careful scan of the traffic on the freeway revealed nothing. No motorcycle, anyway.

"He ditched it," Dean murmured, pulling into the sheriff's station parking lot. "He got rid of the bike and has a car now."

As he climbed out of his truck, he swept the area but saw nothing amiss. "Come on, you son of a bitch, show yourself." But he knew the challenge wouldn't be answered. Not this soon. He walked into the sheriff's station, furious with himself for being unable to do a damn thing.

HE SAT behind the wheel of the aging Chevy he'd picked up in a honky-tonk parking lot. A quick change of license plates and it was all his. He'd ditched the bike the morning after his raid on the bitch's property. He grinned. That, and his phone call had scared the hell out of her. And he wanted her that way, wanted her to know he'd get to her no matter how she tried to hide. Even that cop living there wouldn't be able to help her. Oh, yeah, he knew the guy was a cop. He remembered seeing him play hero at the bank. After all, he was the one who shot the bastard. Too bad he'd only winged him. No, not even Mr. Hero was going to be able to protect her.

Carl Dietrich rubbed the scar slashed across his arm. The dame had a debt to pay, and eventually he'd make sure she paid it in full. For now he would concentrate on the cop. He watched Dean across the street, visualizing a target painted on the man's forehead. He smiled, then pointed his forefinger at Dean, the thumb cocked.

"Bang, you're dead."

Chapter Seven

"If you barge into my clinic like the proverbial bull in a china shop one more time, I will sic Althea on you." Elise had to rise on tiptoe to do it, but standing nose to nose with the stubborn Detective Cornell was more than worth it. Her eyes spat fire while her mouth issued threats that would have made most men think twice about entering her inner sanctum.

Undeterred, Dean glared back. "Cheryl said you had three new patients today. I wanted to check them out for myself."

She nearly shrieked. "They were referrals from a colleague!"

"Oh, really? Who? The nimble-fingered idiot who drove you home that night?" he sneered. "Lady, you really should check out your colleagues more thoroughly."

Elise fleetingly considered what horrible torture would best suit this insufferable man.

"Detective Cornell, you are turning my clinic into a circus, and I don't appreciate it," she said, furious. "I run on a very tight schedule, and when you barge in here giving my clients that big-nasty-cop routine, as if they might be serial killers, you tend to scare them off. I would prefer they not know you're here, much less why. Your dentist must love you, considering how much you grind your teeth," she added sweetly.

"Only since I've had to deal with you," he growled. "In case you've forgotten, I'm here to save your butt. If you don't like it, you know what you can do." He turned to stalk out the rear door.

"I tried. Your captain refused to give me anyone else."

That stopped Dean in his tracks. He spun around. "You asked for a replacement?"

She wasn't about to tell him the reason behind her request—her growing attraction to him. "Yes, I did. But he told me you were the best. He also said he was glad to have you out of his hair—what's left of it. It wasn't difficult to figure out he doesn't like me any more than he likes you, so he devised the perfect punishment by putting us together. I wouldn't be surprised if he's hoping I'll go completely insane and murder you."

Dean looked at her, mouth open.

"My life has been turned upside down since the night you showed up," she went on. "I've already had my staff tell me we're better to watch than a sitcom."

He combed his fingers through his hair, sending the shaggy strands curving around his fingers. "I can't believe after only one week . . ."

"Nine days," she corrected. "Nine long, horrifying days."

Dean looked down at her, her turquoise eyes flashing with anger.

"You're beautiful when you're ticked off."

His husky voice caused her to falter. "Don't try to sweet-talk me, Detective Cornell."

He leaned closer until their mouths were a breath apart. "Doc, I can think of a hell of a lot more things I'd like to do with you than sweet talking. Wanna hear what they are?"

She'd never thought it physically possible for one's heart to jump into one's throat—until now. "Don't change the subject!" *Wimp!* she castigated herself. How come she couldn't come across as authoritative as she'd like?

"You were the one who started it." His warm breath fanned across her lips. "Shall we see what else we can start?"

She was tempted. Very tempted. But reason reared its cooler head. For a brief moment, she wasn't sure whether to be thankful or not. "Right now, I have to treat an iguana with an eye infection. Would you care to help?"

Dean backed off immediately. Now *he* was the one to call himself a wimp. He hated reptiles. "I think I'll look for someone to interrogate. But—" he visually sliced through her clothing "—once you rid this place of green, scaly things, I'll be back to continue our conversation."

For the next hour all Elise could think of was exactly what Dean's ideas beyond sweet talking would be.

"Come on, Elise, the guy is a hunk. Let loose," Donna told her boss as they grabbed cups of coffee during a blissful free five minutes.

Elise looked at her sharply. "Why are you suddenly trying to drum up a love life for me? Surely *you* don't need to live vicariously. Gary keeps you happy enough, doesn't he?"

Donna's lips thinned. "That jerk! That snake in the grass! That—"

"What did he do?"

"He decided one woman wasn't enough for him. He just didn't expect me to find out. I told him if he ever came near me again, I'd slice him into tiny pieces." Her dark eyes glittered with venom.

Elise chuckled at such a bloodthirsty description coming from her perky technician. "And yet you're still in favor of men and romance?"

Donna's face turned dreamy. "Only because I met Will. He's not as cute as Gary, but he has a way of making a woman feel special. Know what I mean?"

Not exactly, Elise wanted to say. Although, if she cared to admit it, Dean had a way of making her feel special— even if sometimes only a special case for the funny farm!

"Where did you meet Will?" she asked idly as she poured herself a second cup of coffee.

"At Rick's Corral, that new country-western bar in Temecula. It was fate," she said with a sigh.

Elise smiled. If a night of twangy tunes at Rick's Corral qualified as kismet, surely a Pasadena bank robbery would fit the bill. "Yes, it sounds like it."

ELISE'S THOUGHTS about Dean hadn't dissipated as the day went on. How had she ended up with the sexiest man next to Mel Gibson in her house as her protector? And, she wryly wondered, who would protect *him?*

That evening, she ate her dinner quickly, ignoring her own rule of chewing each bite carefully before swallowing. All she knew was that she needed to spend as little time as possible around this man. The fact that Dean's eyes were on her every second didn't help her digestion one bit.

"I don't think any of this is fair," Keri announced as Lisa picked up the dirty dishes and carried them to the sink.

"What?" Elise asked absently.

"Our having *him* take us to school every morning and pick us up." She turned accusing eyes on Dean, who was finishing his third helping of beef stew. "It's bad enough Brian watches my every move. He acts as if he's been specially chosen to protect me."

"He was."

Keri looked horrified. "Do you realize how embarrassing that is to me and my friends? He hangs around me at lunch and during breaks. I swear he isn't more than three

feet away from me at any time. He even follows me between classes!''

"He seems like a nice kid. You should give him a
chance," Dean advised.

She rolled her eyes. "*Him?* Detective Cornell, Brian is a
major geek.''

"So was I at that age," he freely admitted. "I don't think
I turned out so badly.''

Four pairs of feminine eyes turned in his direction.

"You could never have been a geek," Lisa declared.

"Are geeks bad?" Becky asked, mulling over the word.

"No, Becky, they aren't. But for the detective, I imagine
he might be telling us a tall tale. In reality, he was probably
one of those rebels who wore black T-shirts and rode a
motorcycle to school. The type of boy no self-respecting
mother would allow near her darling daughter.''

"Not me! I was one of those guys who made decent
grades and pretty well kept to myself. I was the shy type.''
He tried for the demure look and failed miserably.

Elise shook her head. "That I can't believe. Who needs
help with their homework?" Receiving blessed silence, she
sighed with relief. "Then I'm off to catch up on some paperwork. Make sure the kitchen is straightened up for
Myrna in the morning.''

Dean watched her leave the kitchen. It was a good thing
she couldn't read his mind. If she knew what he was considering about her right now, she'd probably flee the house.

After studying the patient chart in front of her, Elise
headed for her bookcase in search of a particular text.
Somehow the lab results didn't check out. She grabbed a
large volume and began leafing through the pages in search
of an answer.

"You didn't ask me if I needed help with *my* homework.''

She closed her eyes for a brief second, then opened them and turned around. Dean leaned against the doorjamb, waving several sheets of paper in front of him.

She gestured toward one corner of the room. "If you need to use the typewriter, you can take it into the living room or into your room. I won't need it this evening."

He straightened up and walked into the room. "That isn't what I need."

Elise silently vowed she'd bite her tongue off before she'd venture into that territory. "In case you didn't hear me at the table, I'm very busy catching up on my work. I have charts to review and reports to write. I don't have time to play games with egocentric rogue detectives."

His lips curved. "Egocentric rogue? I like the sound of that." He kept moving forward until he stood in front of her, one hand braced against the bookcase. Unless she ducked under the blocking forearm, Elise was effectively trapped. "You like me because I'm an egocentric rogue and not like all those other wimpy guys you feel safe with. You like me because I'm not in the least bit safe," he said huskily.

Her eyes snapped dazzling fires. "Let's get something straight, shall we? I'm not one of your little bimbo police groupies who would be only too happy to jump into bed with a cop. For one thing, my IQ is higher than my shoe size, I can form words of more than two syllables and I never drink anything that has a cute little umbrella in it. So if you're lonely for female company, why don't you try some of the bars in town? I'm sure there will be someone more than suitable for you there."

Dean looked more amused than angry at her insulting remarks. "Tell me something, Doc, what worries you more—the fact that you see my choice in women as brainless idiots, or that you're furious with yourself for actually being attracted to me?" He dipped his head until their faces were mere inches apart.

She tipped her head back. Laughter bubbled up her throat. "Egocentric? I understated the case, Detective. Actually, you're living in a fantasy world to think I would be interested in *you*."

His teeth gleamed white against his dark beard. "You can try pissing me off all you want, Ellie," he said with quiet intimacy, "but it won't work. I can see past that touch-me-not act of yours. I've seen you watch me when you think I don't notice what you're doing. In fact, you tend to study my jeans just as much as you study my mouth. I'm wondering which interests you most."

"Now I know you're suffering from delusions!" She ordered herself not to blush. Did the man have eyes in the back of his head? Still, what could he expect, wearing jeans so tight she didn't understand how he could even breathe?

He leaned even closer, bringing the scent of coffee and warm male skin—suddenly a very erotic combination—to her nostrils. "But I don't mind. You see, there's times when I watch you, too. Did you know your charming tush wiggles when you walk?" His voice turned husky, flowing over her senses.

Now her face did flame with hectic color. "It does not!"

His wicked grin did strange things to her insides. "Does so."

Her eyes grew round as saucers. "I have never wiggled in my life!"

"Maybe I should take a video to prove it to you." He dipped his head, brushing his mouth against the sensitive skin behind her ear, causing her to jump in reaction. "Mmm, you smell really good."

Why had she taken the time to spritz on cologne before dinner? "It's hospital disinfectant," she lied.

"Must be a French manufacturer then." He nuzzled the graceful arc of her throat. "I never knew vets could smell so good."

Elise closed her eyes, vainly trying to recall the Latin names for every bone in a parrot's body. Instead, her mind catalogued other items. His lips were warm, his beard soft as it brushed against her skin, and his hands did marvelous things as they smoothed their way across her waist. She was sinking fast without any hope of rescue. Did she want to be rescued? She wasn't sure.

"This..." She cleared her throat; her voice sounded much too husky. "This isn't a good idea."

"Hmm?" His tongue lapped the area just behind her ear. He chuckled when she jumped. "I'm just doing my job, ma'am."

When the tip of his tongue dipped into the hollow of her throat, Elise doubted she could remember her own name. "Dean, please." She wasn't sure if she was pleading with him to stop or to continue. She was too busy concentrating on not melting to the floor. Slowly she lifted her arms. Her hands didn't need any direction as they tunneled through his thick dark hair, her fingers tangling among the silky strands that curled with a life of their own. His kiss came next, sending flashes of fire through her veins and leaving her short of breath. When his hand covered her breast, she trembled.

"Don't pull away, Elise," he muttered just before his mouth covered hers again.

Elise moaned at the intimate contact. Dean's tongue plunged between her parted lips, taking any remaining starch out of her knees. If he hadn't been holding her so tightly, she surely would have collapsed to the floor and pulled him down with her.

Her fingers tightened their grip in his hair, but Dean was feeling no pain. Not when he had the most delectable woman he'd ever known in his arms and she was kissing him back with more fire than he'd imagined. He closed his arms around her, bringing her up flush against his aroused body, cradling her hips against his. He rubbed his tongue against hers, twisting and turning in a fashion he wanted their bodies to follow as soon as possible. He pulled her shirt out of her jeans, moving his hand upward to the lace covering her breast. He slid his fingers under the lacy cup, unerringly finding the nipple, which grew taut under his caress. He swallowed her soft moan, then moaned deep in his own throat when he felt her fingers hovering over his zipper.

"Touch me, Ellie," he ordered in a raw voice. "Let me feel your hands on me."

She gingerly started to stroke the straining denim fabric, her fingers lingering at the zipper pull. One tug was all it would take.

"Mom, I can't find Billy Bear!"

Becky's wail was better than a cold shower in the middle of a self-generated heat wave. Elise's eyes flew open. She braced her palms against Dean's chest and pushed him away.

"It's…" She breathed deeply, trying to regain her voice. Oh, Lord, if Becky walked in now, she'd have questions about Dean's lumpy jeans Elise wasn't ready to answer! "It's…"

"If it's that bear wearing the red-and-white sweater, it's by the bird cage," Dean called out.

Elise wanted to ask him how he could sound so normal, but her vocal chords still weren't working properly.

"Thank you," she whispered, stepping out of his embrace.

"My pleasure."

She shot him a suspicious glance, refusing to dignify his double entendre and unwilling to admit she had just acted like a hormone-crazed teenager. She vowed, then and there, if Keri ever tried anything like this before she was twenty-one, she would personally lock her in a convent until she was thirty.

"This…" She cleared her throat. She found she couldn't look at him, but looking down didn't help her peace of mind, either. "This was not a good idea. After all, you're here on police business, and as soon as it's settled, we won't be seeing each other again."

Dean didn't like the fact that she could so easily brush him off. "You didn't think about that a couple of minutes ago."

"You caught me at a weak moment."

"You weren't so weak when you dug your fingers into my hair. You wanted me just as much as I wanted you."

"Stop it!" she choked, furious at hearing the truth. "I'd like to be left alone now."

Dean frowned. What happened to the fiery woman he'd just held in his arms? "Elise?"

She held up a hand, palm out. "Dean, please."

He told himself it was a good sign that she used his first name. "We can't sweep this under the rug, Elise, as if it didn't happen."

She refused to look at him. "Do us both a favor and get out."

"We can't just ignore it. I'll let it slide for now, but we'll have to talk about this later," he promised as he walked out of the room. He made a point of closing the door after him.

Elise stumbled to her chair and collapsed in the leather seat. When she covered her face with her hands, she wasn't surprised to find her skin hot to the touch. Right now, she was nothing more than a mass of trembling nerves. A mass of trembling erotic nerves.

"Oh, no," she moaned, dropping her head to her crossed arms on her desktop.

DEAN WASN'T DOING much better. After lying in bed thinking about Elise just down the hall, he decided he wasn't going to get any sleep for a while. He pulled on a pair of jeans and crept out of his room, hoping there would be something boring on television to lull him to sleep.

He rummaged in the kitchen, fixing himself two thick sandwiches and pouring a glass of milk. He took his late-night snack into the living room and snapped on the television. Settled on the couch, his legs propped on the coffee table, he concentrated on classic reruns on the Nickelodeon channel.

"Ah, *Donna Reed*. Better than a sleeping pill." He bit into his sandwich and sipped his milk.

Except with each program, showing picture-perfect mothers of the fifties and sixties, Dean kept thinking about a mother of the nineties. By the time he switched to Bugs Bunny cartoons, he knew he was well on his way to being a lost cause. He may have kissed the woman first, but her hooks were already in him good and deep.

"Well, Carl Dietrich, you scuzzball, at least you did one thing right in your crummy life," he muttered. "You introduced me to Elise."

"MOM? MOM!"

Elise groaned and rolled over. "What are the rules in this household?"

"If your bedroom door is closed, we're not supposed to disturb you unless it's an emergency," Lisa recited.

The last thing she wanted to do was open her eyes. "Is this an emergency?"

"I'm not sure."

She opened one eye at that. It was still dark. "Explain."

Lisa stood at the side of the bed in her nightgown. "Dean's asleep on the couch, and the TV's on."

It took a moment for the statement to settle in Elise's sleep-fogged mind. "Is the house on fire?"

"No."

"Are any of you girls bleeding?"

"No."

"Is Detective Cornell bleeding?"

"No."

Now she opened the other eye. "Then I don't think we have an emergency, do we?"

"He looks awfully uncomfortable, and I thought you could wake him up so he could go to bed."

"I know I'm going to hate asking this, but what time is it?"

"Four-thirty."

"And why are you up?"

"I had to go to the bathroom. Are you gonna wake him up?"

It appeared she had no choice. After all, she couldn't allow the poor man to lie out there and freeze, could she? She flipped back her covers and groped for her robe. Shivering in the chilly predawn air, she wrapped the robe around her body. "Go back to bed. I'll take care of it."

She knew it was a mistake the minute she reached the living room. Only the glowing television screen highlighted Dean, who lay slumped on the couch. An empty plate and glass sat on the coffee table. She walked cautiously over to him. Was it safe to wake a police officer, or would he jump up and catch her in a hammerlock?

She stared at him for a long moment, noting his mouth was slightly open and a soft snore erupted from his chest. She couldn't hold back her smile at the big bad man looking like a harmless little boy with tousled hair and a boneless posture. That comparison ended rapidly, however, when her eyes lowered from his sleeping features to his bare chest. Dark hair blanketed his chest in a blatantly adult masculine way. Her fingers itched to discover if it was as soft as his beard. She shivered—and not from the cold.

"Dean," she whispered. She tried again, louder. "Dean."

"Fud up," a sleepy Baby grumbled from her covered cage in the corner.

"Dean." Elise touched his shoulder lightly, then snatched her fingers back.

"Hmm?" He blinked several times and looked up, slowly focusing. "Elise?"

She nodded. "Lisa found you out here and was afraid you'd get too cold or uncomfortable."

By now he noticed the late-night chill in the air and shivered. He stumbled to his feet and raised his arms over his head in a bone-cracking stretch. "Donna Reed didn't put me to sleep, but Bugs sure did," he mumbled, lazily scratching his chest as he picked up the remote control gadget and switched the television off.

Elise's mouth felt as dry as the desert as her eyes tracked every one of his movements. She knew not just any man could start this volcanic reaction in her the way Dean did. Desperate for distraction, she bent down and picked up the plate and glass.

"If I go to bed like a good little boy, will you tuck me in?"

She walked deliberately, putting one foot firmly in front of the other, toward the kitchen. "I think you're old enough to do that by yourself."

"Maybe so, but it's not as much fun." His husky tone cloaked her like a warm blanket. Not a description she wanted to consider. Blankets meant bed. Thinking about beds now was a very bad idea. "As they say, the night is still young, the moon is full..."

She turned around. "You seem to have a one-track mind, Detective." Her tone came out more amused than angry.

He grinned. "Yeah, well, there's something about you that just causes my mind to wander in that direction."

"Yes, I've noticed." And noticed that washboard belly and thick mat of chest hair swirling around copper-brown nipples rigid from the chilly night air.

"And you're not running off?"

She didn't look away. "Would it do me any good?"

He stared at her a long time. "No."

Silence surrounded them as they watched each other, as if looking for the right answer. Dean was the first to speak.

"Thanks for waking me up, Elise. I would have ended up with a horrendous crick in my neck if I'd stayed there much longer."

She nodded before finishing her walk into the kitchen. "You're welcome. Good night."

Elise took her time rinsing the plate and glass, setting them in the dishwasher and puttering around until she heard Dean's door close with a loud click she was certain was deliberate. Not until then did she walk softly down the hallway to her own room.

For the first time she didn't find it the relaxing retreat it used to be for her. It was too easy now to visualize Dean in her room, in her bed. Only knowing that he probably wasn't having an easy time of sleeping either, what with Florence's loud snores, finally allowed her to drop off into slumber.

"YOU DON'T get fed today."

Dean looked up at Myrna's unsmiling features. "Excuse me?" His mouth salivated at the sight of lightly browned French toast and crispy bacon slices placed on the plates.

She held his plate out of his reach. "I told you in the beginning, those who don't keep up their rooms don't eat

And I got a good look at your room this morning while you were showering. It looked like World War III had struck."

He winced. He couldn't believe one woman could make him feel ten years old again. "Myrna, I promise, right after breakfast, I'll pick everything up." He reached for his plate, but she didn't budge. "Honest."

She was unmoved. "Clean first, then eat."

Dean ignored the giggles revolving around the table.

"Give it up, Dean. Myrna's rules stand for all of us," Elise advised, smiling broadly.

He stood up, pushing his chair back. "This is not fair."

Myrna placed the plate in front of Elise, who promptly reached for the syrup bottle. "Anyone who has underwear hanging from the bedposts shouldn't talk about fair. The faster you straighten things up, the faster you'll get breakfast."

He glared at the housekeeper. "Just don't try driving in *my* part of town, lady." As he walked past Elise's chair, he leaned over and quickly snitched a slice of bacon.

"I'm quaking in my shoes," Myrna said dryly, reaching for the phone as it pealed its second ring. "Carpenter residence. Yes, he's here, but don't keep him long. He has to clean his room before he can eat his breakfast," she concluded.

Dean frantically grabbed for the receiver. "Cornell."

"You mean somebody finally got smart and is making you clean up your own messes?" Mac hooted. "This is one lady I'd like to meet."

"Yeah, you just wait until you have to change dirty diapers," he growled, scowling at the giggling females in his line of sight, none of whom seemed intimidated by his darkest glare. "So what's up, old buddy?"

"Got a bit of info for you," Mac went on, now all business. "I talked to a few contacts who're familiar with Dietrich, and so far, news isn't good."

Why wasn't he surprised? Dean groped for a piece of paper and pencil, which Myrna dug out of a nearby drawer for him. "Okay, go ahead."

"Dietrich has an old buddy from San Quentin days who just got out of Chino about a week ago," he said, naming a minimum-security prison outside of Los Angeles. "According to parole records, the guy is living in Corona. He's got a job working as a mechanic in a car dealership there and is supposedly keeping his nose clean, but that's doubtful, considering his past record. The two go back a long way, so ten to one Dietrich's still around, hiding out with his pal's help, waiting for his next chance to get at the lady."

Dean hid his worry. Corona wasn't all that far from here. And things had been too quiet lately. Dietrich might strike at any time.

"Anything else?" he clipped.

"Yeah, one of his cronies still in the county jail has been talking a mile a minute. It appears Dietrich has a nasty temper and is pretty brutal with those he has a grudge against."

Dean casually turned away from the kitchen crowd. "I don't like this," he muttered into the receiver.

"You be careful, Dean. I don't think he'll stop to consider your badge if you get in his way with the doc. This guy has more than a few screws loose."

The idea of anything happening to Elise or the girls turned his earlier appetite to acid.

"He can try, but he'll end up the loser."

Chapter Eight

"You're going to *what?*" Dean roared.

Elise looked pained as she faced his incredulous features. "I'm sure you heard me correctly the first time."

He closed his eyes. He'd hoped his usually perfect hearing was wrong. "I don't think it would be a good idea."

"But Mom promised we could!" Lisa wailed. "She said there was no reason we couldn't still go." She glared daggers at the man she usually idolized.

Elise knew it was time to step in with the voice of reason. "It's only a trip to the Wild Animal Park, Dean," she soothed. "It's become something of an annual tradition with us. The girls each take a friend and we spend the day at a place of their choice. This year is the park. I doubt anything could happen there. Of course, knowing your feelings about animals, I would understand if you don't care to go."

Her smirk disappeared with his reply. "It appears I'll have to tag along."

"No!" Keri cried out. She turned on Dean. "What can happen to us there? It's not as if this man will even know where we'll be. If you're with us, you'll just ruin the entire day."

"Keri!" Elise admonished. "There's no reason to be rude. After all, Dean is here to protect us, even if nothing has happened for a while." She turned to Dean. "Actually, I'd say Dietrich has probably forgotten all about us by now, and it would be safe for you to return home."

He still hadn't told her about his talk with Mac a week ago regarding Dietrich's friend fresh out of Chino prison and living in Corona. And this wouldn't be the time to do so. While he didn't mind alarming Elise to keep her alert to danger, he didn't want to frighten the girls. He leaned back, tipping the chair onto its rear legs.

"I can't remember the last time I attended the Wild Animal Park," he said casually. "Sounds like a fun day."

Becky looked wary. "You're going to take your gun with you, aren't you?"

Dean paused. "Honey, I'm a policeman. I have to carry it, especially since my job is to keep you and your mom safe."

With the tip of her tongue sticking out, she pondered his explanation with all the seriousness of the young. "Okay," she said finally. "Just make sure you shoot the right person."

"Wonderful, now my youngest is getting bloodthirsty," Elise muttered into her salad. She wondered how much more she was going to have to take. Dean visited the sheriff's station a couple of times a week, continued driving the girls to school and kept a close eye on her clinic. She gleefully noticed he stayed out of there anytime she had reptile patients and made a mental note to schedule as many scaly creatures as she could find.

She tried to forget that night in her office, but she learned it wasn't easy to forget the kind of kiss that traveled down to one's toes and swept back up again. The man had kissing down to an erotic art, and if she didn't keep her wits about her, she would be happily seeking more of it. And she suspected she'd end up with a lot more than a few kisses! Fighting that now-familiar softening inside her, she fixed

WOW!

THE MOST GENEROUS
FREE OFFER EVER!

From the Harlequin Reader Service®

GET 4 FREE BOOKS WORTH MORE THAN $13.00

Affix peel-off stickers to reply card

FOUR FREE BOOKS

4 · 4 · 4 · 4

FOUR FREE BOOKS

PLUS A FREE VICTORIAN PICTURE FRAME

AND A FREE MYSTERY GIFT!

NO COST! NO OBLIGATION TO BUY!
NO PURCHASE NECESSARY!

Because you're a reader of Harlequin romances, the publishers would like you to accept four brand-new Harlequin American Romance® novels, with their compliments. Accepting this offer places you under no obligation to purchase any books, ever!

ACCEPT FOUR BRAND-NEW

YOURS

We'd like to send you four free Harlequin novels,
worth more than $13.00, to introduce you to the benefits of
the Harlequin Reader Service®. We hope your free books
will convince you to subscribe, but that's up to you.
Accepting them places you under no obligation to buy
anything, but we hope you'll want to continue with the
Reader Service.

So unless we hear from you, once a month, we'll send you 4
additional Harlequin American Romance® novels to read
and enjoy. If you choose to keep them, you'll pay just $2.96*
per volume—a saving of 33¢ each off the cover price. There
is no charge for shipping and handling. There are no hidden
extras! And you may cancel at any time, for any reason, just
by sending us a note or a shipping statement marked
"cancel." You can even return any shipment to us at our
expense. Either way, the free books and gifts are yours to
keep!

ALSO FREE!
VICTORIAN PICTURE FRAME

This lovely Victorian pewter-finish miniature is perfect for
displaying a treasured photograph—and it's yours *absolutely
free*—when you accept our no-risk offer.

Perfect for a treasured Photograph

Plus a FREE mystery Gift follow instructions at right.

HARLEQUIN AMERICAN ROMANCE® NOVELS

FREE!

Harlequin Reader Service®

AFFIX
FOUR FREE BOOKS
STICKER HERE

YES, send me my four free books and gifts as explained on the opposite page. I have affixed my "free books" sticker above and my two "free gift" stickers below. I understand that accepting these books and gifts places me under no obligation ever to buy any books; I may cancel at any time, for any reason, and the free books and gifts will be mine to keep!

154 CIH ADNG
(U-H-AR-1/92)

NAME _____
(PLEASE PRINT)

ADDRESS _____ APT. _____

CITY _____

STATE _____ ZIP _____

Offer limited to one per household and not valid to current Harlequin American Romance® subscribers. All orders subject to approval.

AFFIX FREE
VICTORIAN
PICTURE
FRAME
STICKER HERE

AFFIX FREE
MYSTERY GIFT
STICKER HERE

PRINTED IN U.S.A.

DETACH AND RETURN TODAY

BUSINESS REPLY MAIL

FIRST CLASS MAIL   PERMIT NO. 717   BUFFALO, NY

POSTAGE WILL BE PAID BY ADDRESSEE

HARLEQUIN READER SERVICE
3010 WALDEN AVE
PO BOX 1867
BUFFALO NY 14240-9952

NO POSTAGE
NECESSARY
IF MAILED
IN THE
UNITED STATES

him with a warning glare. "Does this mean you have no more protests to our going this Sunday?"

His choirboy-innocent smile sent unholy tingles down her spine. "Nope."

"That's what I was afraid of."

Keri wasn't appeased. "If he's going, I'm *not*."

"Oh, yes, you will," Elise said grimly. "I'm not going to be the only one to suffer that day."

THE MINUTE DEAN WOKE UP the morning of the trip to the Wild Animal Park, he knew something was about to happen. And it wasn't going to be Dietrich's rearrest. The back of his neck started tingling when he woke up, continued while he showered and dressed and didn't abate during breakfast. He tried his best not to appear edgy, but, judging from the wary looks he received, he wasn't hiding it very well. Keri glared at him, Lisa looked disgruntled, Becky unhappy and Elise looked just plain grim.

"You can drive." She tossed him the keys to the Pathfinder. The girls climbed into the back, martyred expressions on their faces.

He spared a glance to the rear. "You're really letting Keri leave the house like that?"

Elise's back went up at anyone casting aspersions on her firstborn. "Like what?"

He jerked his thumb in Keri's direction. "She's wearing enough makeup for three people. Isn't that too much for a sixteen-year-old?"

Elise silently counted to ten, twice. "I don't think blush, lipstick and mascara is too much. And I don't believe it's your business how much or how little she wears."

"Okay, but if some sailor tries to pick her up, don't come running to me."

"So help me, if you ruin this day, I will draw and quarter you myself, and believe me, I have the instruments to do it," she threatened.

He held up his hands in surrender. "Hey, I'm only trying to help."

"No wonder your captain wanted you out of his hair for a while." She climbed into the passenger seat, pulling the belt across her chest. From then on, she only spoke to give directions to the girls' friends' houses. Pretty soon they were on the freeway heading for San Marcos.

During the drive, Dean heard bits and pieces of whispered conversations about policemen, guns and killers. He sighed. So much for keeping a low profile. Still, the cold shoulder Elise was giving him wouldn't easily lend itself to the charade of their being "close friends" either.

After he parked in one of the small lots alongside the main road leading to the park, Elise recited her usual set of rules. The older girls were on their own once inside, but they would have to check in at certain times, no eating too much junk food please, and they would set a time to meet back at the main gate at the end of the day.

Dean's nape tingled madly. "I don't think that's a good idea."

Elise looked as if she were spoiling for a battle. "Why not?"

His hands tightened on the steering wheel. "I think you know why."

She lowered her voice. "Dean, the girls need a simple good time for a change. Besides, the man is after me, not them. And how would he even know what they look like? It's not as if they won't be around a lot of people. They understand not to talk to strangers, and you've warned them so many times that they're almost afraid to talk to their own friends. What could possibly happen to them here?"

How could he explain that when the back of his neck tingled this way, it usually meant that trouble was close by? It wasn't something that could be documented, but he never ignored his internal warning device, since nine times out of ten it was accurate. Still, it wasn't something he could easily explain to the logical Dr. Carpenter, and he didn't feel right discussing the matter in front of the girls.

"They should stick with us," he stated.

"Oh, pu-leeze!" Keri wailed, looking as if he had just suggested they dance naked through the parking lot.

Elise sent her a warning look. She hadn't missed Dean's white-knuckled grip on the steering wheel. Finally she'd realized something was bothering him, and for some reason he wasn't going to go into it now.

"Maybe it *would* be a good idea to at least remain in sight of each other," she said quietly. "After all, Detective Cornell didn't think we should take this trip to begin with. He's been kind enough to travel with us, so the least we can do is go along with his suggestions."

Dean turned his head. She wasn't going to fight him on this! His expression was pure appreciation. They stared at each other, oblivious to the girls climbing out of the back of the truck.

"You know something, don't you?" she said quietly. "Something you can't, or won't, tell us."

He glanced at the girls milling around the truck, the back door now closed. "Word has it Dietrich has a friend in the area who was recently released from Chino. We'd hoped Dietrich might have left the state, but it looks like he's only gone underground. There's days when I feel as if someone is watching the property."

"And you think it's either Dietrich or his friend?" It was more a statement than a question.

His nod was firm.

Elise looked down at her hands, now laced tightly in her lap. "I don't care so much for myself," she murmured. "But if anything happened to my babies..."

He gripped her hands with one of his, feeling the chill of her fear invade his skin. "Nothing is going to happen to anyone as long as I'm around," he vowed fiercely. "He's not going to win this round."

"I can't let them know any of this," she said more to herself than to him. "They've looked forward to this day for a long time. My work keeps me so busy, we rarely have days out like this."

"Hey, are we going in or what?" Lisa knocked on Dean's window.

He opened the door. "Going in," he replied, tugging one of her short curls. He looked over her head at Keri. "You've got two choices. You stick with us, or you and Susan keep an eye on Lisa and Ginger."

"What?" Keri looked dismayed. "That's like glorified baby-sitting!"

"Those are your choices," he said firmly.

Keri nodded grudgingly. "I guess we should be grateful we don't have to have Becky and Kim tagging along, too," she grumbled.

Susan, a spritely brunette, looked up in awe, along with a bit of admiration, for the dark-haired man. "Wow, Keri, how many kids have their own bodyguard? And he's so cute for an older man" she could be heard to say as Keri dragged her up the road with Lisa and Ginger following at a slower pace.

Elise chuckled as she took Dean's arm. "Come on, old man," she crooned. "We'll take it easy up the hill."

"I'm hardly old enough to be that kid's father, and she just made me feel like her grandfather," he muttered, not lost far enough in self-pity to miss the advantage of grasping Elise's hand in a firm grip. Elise looked down at their clasped hands. "I'm old, not dead," he explained.

When they reached the ticket booth, Elise insisted on paying Dean's way.

"It could have gone on my expense report," he told her.

She shook her head. "Amazing what our taxes pay for. Besides, this is our treat. Just relax and enjoy." Before handing out the tickets, she led the girls to a secluded spot. "One last warning. I don't want any of you to say anything out loud as to why Detective Cornell is with us," she said in a low voice. "Call him Dean and leave it at that. Hear me?"

"So he's your boyfriend for the day?" Lisa asked.

Elise paused. She deliberately didn't look at Dean, although she couldn't miss him standing so close behind her. "Yes, I guess so."

"Sounds good to me," he murmured for her ears only.

She resisted giving him a good kick.

Lisa grinned broadly. Dean should have known that, if anyone would get into the act, Lisa would be the one to give it her all.

Once inside the enclosure, the small group headed for the tram that would take them on a tour of the large safari park. Dean soon learned that going somewhere with teenagers meant you didn't sit just anywhere. You sat where you couldn't miss *anything,* which meant frequent sliding from one side of the tram benches to the other. Keri and Susan also insisted on sitting some distance from the others.

"They're afraid someone might automatically assume they're with us adults," Elise explained matter-of-factly.

Dean watched the three teenage boys eyeing the girls in a way he remembered from his younger days. He sent them a male glare that warned them to back off. The boys immediately wilted and rushed to take other seats before the tram left.

Keri turned around and caught Dean looking his fiercest. She immediately stared at her mother. "Mom, make him stop," she hissed, looking horrified.

Elise poked him none too gently in the side with her elbow. "Dean, behave yourself."

"I am. I'm acting like a man who knows exactly what those punks had on their minds," he groused, not in the least apologetic for his heavy-handed tactics.

"It's starting!" Becky squealed, looking out the window as the tram slowly left the station.

Dean wasn't as interested in viewing the wild animals as he was in Elise's sitting so close to him he could smell the light floral fragrance she wore. He also enjoyed the view of her faded jeans cupping her slender body and the oversize mint-green sweater skimming the curves his hands itched to explore. With her hair pulled up in a saucy ponytail and minimum makeup emphasizing her beautiful turquoise eyes, she looked as young as her oldest daughter. Gauging the admiring looks she received from some of the other men on the tram, he was glad he was with her to keep those jerks away from her. After all, he *was* there to protect her delectable rear, right? But deep down he knew it was more than that. He settled back in his seat, arms crossed over his chest, determined to enjoy this day to its fullest. If only his neck would stop its damn tingling!

Elise watched Dean under the cover of conveniently lowered lashes. She sensed something was bothering him and wished he would confide his worries to her. Not that she could do much, but sharing a problem generally helped.

Of course, she had only to look at him to know he wasn't the type to share worries or fears. If anything, he was the kind of man her mother would insist she stay away from. Scuffed boots, faded jeans and a black T-shirt that stretched lovingly across his chest. With the dark beard and shaggy hair, he needed only a motorcycle to complete the picture of the eternal rebel.

Hair that was thick and silky to the touch, she remembered. A beard that brushed tantalizingly across her tender skin...

"Watch it, Doc," Dean muttered out of the side of his mouth. "Your eyes are kinda glazed, and your face is a little too flushed for someone just watching the lions sprawl around out there."

Her gaze flew upward to catch a wicked sparkle in his brown eyes. She didn't even need to feel the heat in her cheeks to know he'd somehow read her thoughts. "You think you're hot stuff, don't you?"

He grinned. "You did, too, not all that long ago."

Aware she didn't have a prayer of having the last word in this conversation, she deliberately turned her back on him as she stared out the window. She could have been looking at a blank wall for all she cared; it was the message her position conveyed that was important to her.

Dean didn't mind looking at Elise's back. He'd already decided he liked all the parts that made up the woman she was. Wouldn't his buddies love to know he'd fallen for this frosty piece of womanhood? Dean, the eternal bachelor—probably because no sane woman would put up with him. At least, that was what one ex-girlfriend had told him. He hadn't minded playing the field in the past. Besides, in his line of business, he didn't know if it was a good idea to have someone else to worry about other than his own skin. And he'd seen the high divorce rate in his department, much less the entire L.A. County police force. It took a special woman to put up with his kind of life. Look how long it took Mac to find the right woman after one disastrous marriage. And now he was beginning a family.

Dean watched the three Carpenter girls. While they shared family similarities, each had her own personality.

Keri, who tried to be so grown-up, was still a young girl dealing with a nasty problem she shouldn't even have to worry about. With her mother's composure and cool, touch-me-not manner, she must already drive the boys crazy. Lisa, who was just leaving her tomboy phase and preparing to enter that sacred teenage world, energetic and curious as hell. She'd make a great cop, he decided. And Becky, sweet little Becky, who entered true school life this year. Poor thing still allowed her older sister to drag her into trouble, but those big turquoise eyes could melt the coldest heart in no time.

He suddenly found himself wanting to be around when these girls grew up. To see what they would be like. Then there was Elise. In his eyes, she was the most important part of the package. Her potential wasn't too hard to visualize, either, since he'd already held her in his arms, kissed her and had the pleasure of her kissing him back.

He shifted uneasily in his seat. Good going, Cornell, he told himself. You're supposed to be thinking about catching bad guys, not about kissing Elise again.

Yeah, but kissing her was good, wasn't it? his libido asked in a taunting whisper. And you would like to kiss her again, wouldn't you? And touch her and find out about those interesting curves. Come on, Cornell, admit it, you're falling for the lady. And you're falling hard.

He glanced around, thinking about a cigarette for the first time in three years. It hadn't been easy to break his four-pack-a-day habit, but with his stubborn nature, he'd kicked it good. Now, all because of a sexy broad, he wanted to fill his lungs with nicotine again!

Hearing him shift around, Elise looked over her shoulder. "What's wrong? Do you want to trade seats?"

He shook his head. "Just got a cramp in my leg," he muttered, crossing his arms over his chest, then uncrossing them.

Elise frowned at him. "If you didn't want to take the tram, you could have waited for us at the station," she told him. "Unless you think the tram might be hijacked during the trip."

He half turned his body. "Look, I just want a smoke, okay?"

Her forehead creased in a puzzled frown. "I've never seen you smoke. And your clothing doesn't smell like a smoker's." Whoops! She'd just given away the fact that she noticed such things. Such as he always smelled of soap instead of stale smoke.

"I quit a few years go, but right now, I would kill for a cigarette," he bit out.

Elise knew better than to ask what had brought on the attack. Instead, she rummaged in her leather shoulder bag and tossed him a stick of gum. "Try that. I've heard it helps."

He unwrapped the foil and popped the rectangle into his mouth. "Mmm, spearmint." He chewed reflectively. "Thanks."

Now Elise had another sensory memory to battle—clean male skin with a hint of spearmint. Her sister and close friends had battled with her for years about getting out and dating; now she almost wished she had. Then she might not be well on her way to having a nervous breakdown right now just because a man's scent did incredible things to her.

"All right, girls, what next?" Elise made a show of studying the pamphlet detailing the special events for the day.

"Petting zoo!"

"Animal nursery."

"Watching the gorillas."

Elise held up her hand, forestalling the inevitable arguments. "You four older girls fight it out among yourselves. We'll meet at the snack bar in two hours for lunch, all right? Dean and I will take Becky and Kim to the petting zoo.''

Dean looked undecided. ''Maybe we should tag along with them.''

''Mom, he's going to ruin our day,'' Keri insisted.

''Dean, they'll be fine,'' Elise assured him. ''They'll be fine.''

She nodded at Keri, silently telling her to escape while the getting was good. She took Dean's arm and steered him in the opposite direction, Becky and Kim racing ahead of them. ''Slow down, girls!'' she called out. ''We oldsters can't keep up with you. And you, stop acting so heavy-handed.'' She looped her arm through his. ''Come on, relax and have fun. After all, how often do you get a cushy assignment like this?''

''Robbery doesn't give us too many. My last one was while I worked vice. I had a prostitution ring convinced I was a well-connected pimp from Chicago.'' Getting caught up in the game, he draped an arm around her shoulders in a possessive manner. ''My partner, who played the part of my main lady, complained she'd never be able to walk again after wearing spike heels for six weeks.''

Elise had an idea it wasn't at all like it was portrayed on television. ''What was your complaint?''

His voice hardened. ''Having to act like the slime I dealt with.''

Elise was glad they'd reached the petting zoo. This wasn't the time to talk about Dean's work. She laughed as Becky and Kim ran around petting the goats and llamas wandering the enclosed area looking for cupped palms filled with grain. She laughed even harder when a daring young goat caught hold of the back of Dean's shirt and started chewing on it.

"Hey, this isn't edible," he informed the goat, trying to free his shirt from the stubborn animal who bleated his refusal to relinquish his prize. "Elise, help!"

"Big brave man afraid of a little goat," she chided, finally pushing the horned animal to one side.

"I told you, I never had pets." He sidestepped a llama hanging its head over his shoulder.

"Maybe not, but they sure seem to like you. Come on, girls, let's find Dean a safer place." She herded Becky and Kim out of the enclosure and guided them to the elephant show.

Elise shared Dean's worries about the other four girls being out of their sight, but she didn't want to ruin their day, and she knew she had to trust them to have the sense to stay out of trouble. She had to think that way or go crazy. While Keri and Lisa's friends didn't understand the need for caution, Keri and Lisa did. She was just glad the two youngest were happy wandering around, watching the gorillas and walking to the lookout points to see the animals scattered in the park closest to the main area. Still, no matter how much she smiled, she couldn't keep from feeling relieved when the time came to meet the others at the snack bar. She only began to panic when the girls were five minutes late and she couldn't ignore Dean glancing at his watch every fifteen seconds.

"Sorry," Lisa panted when they ran up to the waiting adults. "Keri and Susan saw a boy they knew from school and had to stop to talk." She rolled her eyes.

Dean opened his mouth to remind Keri she wasn't to talk to *anyone,* then quickly snapped it shut.

"Let's get something to eat," he said abruptly.

After ordering hamburgers, fries and Cokes, they found two tables off in a corner where the four older girls could sit by themselves with the adults at an adjoining table.

"How do you handle this on a daily basis?" Dean asked, admiration for Elise's calm manner etched on his features. "I mean, all of this would drive a normally sane person to the funny farm in no time."

Elise shrugged. "You just try not to let the little things get on your nerves." She swirled a French fry in catsup and popped it into her mouth. "That way you're not a nervous wreck when the big stuff comes up. I won't get upset over Keri not keeping her room immaculate, but I will have a fit if she doesn't keep up her grades because she's decided the opposite sex or making junior varsity cheerleader is more important."

"You should be proud of yourself. You've done a great job with them."

"Mom, can we go through the gift shops?" Lisa stood by her mother's chair.

She looked around. "Where's Keri and Susan?"

She wrinkled her nose. "In the bathroom, where else? I think they're afraid someone might not think they have enough mascara on or something."

Elise sighed. "All right, but stay there until we show up, all right?"

Lisa and Ginger nodded, clearly eager to be off. "We will."

"Between your practice and the girls, you really don't have a lot of free time," Dean commented, gathering up empty food containers and dropping them onto the plastic tray.

Elise tipped her head to the side. "Oh, please, Cornell, you've never been coy before. Spit it out."

He stared her straight in the eye. "Men."

She stared right back. "Are you asking about my sex life, Detective?"

"Yeah."

"Fine, I'll tell you if you'll tell me."

Dean winced. "All right, let's try something else."

Elise flashed him a smug smile. "Chicken."

"No, just smart. A man in my position doesn't have a lot of chances to meet appropriate members of the opposite sex."

"You mean the ones you can take home to meet mother."

"Right. We mostly meet the ones you take home when mother isn't home."

She nodded. She silently admitted she was very curious about the women Dean had seen in the past. The only thing she felt certain of was that he hadn't dated a woman with children before. "We're thrown together under special circumstances, Dean," she said softly. "Did you ever stop to think that, otherwise, you probably wouldn't have given me a second glance?"

He reached across the table and grasped her chin with his fingers, lifting her face. "Believe me, no matter what, I would have given you a hell of a lot more than a second glance." The rough timbre in his voice sent shivers running across her spine and heat coiling deep in her stomach.

"Careful, Detective," she whispered. "This park is family oriented, and you're straying a bit beyond the boundaries."

He smiled. "Then it will just give you something to think about, won't it?"

Determined to return her pulse rate to normal, Elise kept one eye on Becky and Kim, who were busy chattering as they dawdled over the last of their hamburgers, and the other on the ladies' room door where people streamed in and out. But two familiar figures hadn't come out yet. Each time the wrong people left the ladies' room, her irritation rose.

"What's taking them so long?" Becky moaned, fidgeting in her seat.

"Good question." Elise frowned at the door. "In about two seconds I'm going in there and dragging those girls out by their immaculately combed hair."

The tingling along the back of Dean's neck suddenly intensified. *The son of a bitch was here! Close. So close Dean could almost smell him!* He pushed back his chair so violently it fell over as he stood up. "We're going now." he headed for the rest rooms.

"What are you doing? Oh, no!" A horrified Elise sensed his intent and dreaded the consequences. "Dean, you can't."

He ignored her as he walked over to the ladies' room door and pounded on it. "Keri, Susan, out now! Your hair must have been brushed at least five hundred times by now, and if you put any more of that eye stuff on, you'll look like damn raccoons!"

"Oh, no!" Elise moaned, covering her face with her hands. Maybe if she stayed in that position, no one would associate her with this madman.

Keri and Susan scuttled out of the restroom looking at Dean as if he were demented.

"I have never been so embarrassed in my life!" Keri yelped.

"Sure wish I had the nerve to do that to my daughter, buddy," one man told Dean as he passed them.

"I can't believe you did that." Elise pushed them all in the direction of the gift shops. She shot Dean a look fit to kill. "There was no call for that."

He clenched his jaw tightly. "It got them out, didn't it?" During the time he ushered them toward the gift shops to pick up the other girls, he kept scanning the area, looking for anything out of place. He silently cursed himself for allowing this trip at all. He should have guessed! His warning signal had gone off loud and clear when they arrived. Why hadn't he listened to it?

Elise was so angry with him, she didn't dare look at him, because if she did she knew she would hit him. Her fury blinded her to his agitation and to the idea that there might have been an excellent reason for his hurrying the girls out of there. "No wonder you're not a father. No woman in her right mind would dare mix her genes with yours." She already dreaded the drive home, with Keri and Susan acting like typical teen martyrs convinced their lives were over. She knew she would see humor in the situation later on, but right now she preferred to remain angry with Dean.

"Dean!" Becky and Kim ran up to him with anxious expression marring their tiny faces.

He crouched down, balancing himself on his toes. "What's up, cherubs?"

Kim giggled at the nickname. "Becky said we should tell you about the strange man that talked to us."

His interest sharpened. "What man?"

Becky held out a folded piece of paper. "He gave us this for you and a candy bar for each of us." She also held out the candy, which Elise snatched from her hand and Kim's.

"What did the man look like?" Dean asked, masking his rage. He couldn't believe he hadn't seen the two girls lag behind for a minute!

"He had black hair, all kind of spiky, and really weird eyes," Becky replied. She wrinkled her nose in disgust. "And a picture on his arm of a skull with a snake coming out of its mouth. And a scar like the one on my knee from when I cut it on that fence last year. He said Mom operated on him once, but I told him she only operates on animals. But he said she operated on him once." Her eyes dimmed with worry. "I wanted to get away from him, but he held my hand real tight, and I was afraid to call out to you."

Elise's hand covered her mouth, muffling a cry of alarm.

Dean slowly opened the piece of paper and scanned the one word scrawled across it. He clamped down on the pithy curse rolling around in his head. The two small girls were nervous enough without his adding to their worry. Not to mention the shock darkening Elise's eyes.

"Is it...?" She couldn't say the name.

He held up the paper so she could read the single word. A tiny moan escaped her lips as it penetrated her brain. *Gotcha.*

Chapter Nine

"The bastard was right there in the park. He was so close to us I should have been able to catch him!" Dean paced back and forth in front of Detective Santee's desk, one fist clenched tightly, the other holding a lit cigarette. He'd lost his battle with nicotine that morning when he stopped at a convenience store for a carton of cigarettes after driving the girls to school. "Instead of doing my job, I was rousting two teenage nymphets from the bathroom." He dropped into a chair. He rubbed his forehead with the hand holding the cigarette. "Damn."

"Why should I sit there and tell you what an idiot you are when you're doing such a great job of it yourself?" Santee said amiably. He settled back in his chair and propped his feet up on his desk. "Frankly, you've called yourself pretty much any name I might think up and a few I haven't."

Dean scowled at him. "You want to leave here in one piece?"

"Detective Cornell, what you're thinking of is illegal. Not to mention you're on my turf here."

"You never can tell. Your colleagues might thank me for it." Dean stubbed out his half-smoked cigarette in the ashtray Santee had set before him when he first entered. Within ten minutes it was filled with half-smoked cigarettes. "I hate eternally calm men," he muttered darkly.

"We're still checking out his old buddy, Bartlett. Maybe we'll get a lead there."

Dean glumly studied the toe of his boot. "Anderson isn't happy over Dietrich's not being caught yet." He winced, recalling his superior's screams of outrage earlier that morning when he talked to him on the phone. "He said if there isn't a viable lead within the next week, he wants me back. Although he didn't sound too eager about that, either."

The sheriff's detective shook his head. "What happened last week wasn't a viable lead to him?"

"Not if I didn't see the guy with my own baby-blues," he grumbled.

Santee chuckled. "Your eyes aren't blue."

"He doesn't care." Dean narrowed his eyes in thought as he stared at the other man. "I want to see this through."

"And you've got a week to do it."

He spoke slowly. "Unless I take my vacation." All along, Dean had feared time would run out before Dietrich was caught. And he knew, no matter what, he wasn't going to leave Elise and the girls alone on the property, no matter how many security alarms were activated, guard dogs on duty and loaded rifles in easy reach. The feminine foursome had come to mean a great deal to him, and he would do whatever was necessary to keep them safe from harm.

For a guy who'd always visualized himself as the perfect bachelor, he found himself settling into a homey routine all too easily. He knew it had something to do with Elise. Settling into any kind of routine would be easy where she was concerned. As it was, he discovered it was difficult to think about the time when he would have to return to L.A. Wouldn't the guys at the station have a good laugh over this. Dean Cornell, admirer of all women, was finally well on his way to falling really big for just one lady. Ah, but what a lady!

Santee shook his head. "Off duty means just that. You wouldn't have any authority."

Dean pounded his fist on the desk in frustration. "Yeah, but you can't have someone out there all the time. We both know if I leave, Dietrich will strike and disappear into some hole where we'll never find him."

Santee settled back in his chair. "It would be a good setup. A way to bring him out of hiding," he mused.

Dean shook his head. "No, that kind of trap is too dangerous."

Santee easily read his mind. "We could put her daughters in protective custody."

"Even with them gone it's dangerous, and you know it. By just talking to Dietrich's scum friends, we've learned he's a pretty sick guy. Right now he's fixated on Elise Carpenter, and he isn't going to stop until he gets her." He glanced at his watch and pushed himself out of his chair. "I've got to go. The doc is taking Keri and Becky to the dentist and shopping, and I'm looking after Lisa, who's in bed sick. I figured it would be a good time to wash and wax my truck."

Santee glanced out the window that overlooked the parking lot. A dusty blue pickup sat in solitary splendor near the building's entrance. "I don't think it'll help."

Dean laughed. "Probably not, but I do my best thinking when I'm scrubbing down that monster."

He nodded. "I'll call when I hear anything."

"Thanks."

Dean drove along the freeway, keeping an eye out for anything unusual but knowing it would be a miracle if he lucked out. At the same time, his brain reminded him, catching Dietrich meant his time in the Carpenter household would come to an end, and he wasn't ready for that. No, he wanted him and Elise to have a chance together. To really get to know each other and see where it would lead.

Right about now, if there was one thing he truly knew about the lady, it was that she was one of the most stubborn women he'd ever come across. Her agenda for that day was proof. He still wasn't comfortable with the idea of Elise going out by herself and voiced that concern at breakfast. But she'd had the perfect argument ready for him. If he tagged along with her, what about Lisa? It already appeared the dogs and watch geese were no match for a man like Dietrich. He had to admit that watching an abnormally quiet Lisa refuse breakfast and say she preferred to remain in bed, especially on a weekend, was unusual. So Dean was elected to baby-sit.

When he arrived back at the house, he watched a stone-faced Keri march past him, a wary Becky follow and an amused Elise on their heels as they prepared to leave.

"Keri has decided she will never talk to you again," Elise informed him as she opened the car door.

"Tell me about it. She's been so quiet around me all week, I began to wonder if she'd lost her voice. Okay, so I handled that scene at the park badly," he admitted, curling his hands over the top of the car door. "I'm not used to females."

With solemn eyes she studied him. "Considering your age and obvious experience, I'd think you've lived with your share of females." It was a question as much as a statement. Her low voice didn't carry farther than his ears.

He shook his head. "Not exactly. Probably something to do with my less than meticulous habits at home," he said honestly. "And boys like me didn't have a chance to learn much about teenage girls like Keri."

"I still can't picture you as the geek you claim to have been." She eyed the ratty T-shirt he now wore.

He looked down at his shirt. "Yeah, well, maybe I went too far overboard in changing my image. I never was one for the suit-and-tie routine."

Elise couldn't picture Dean in a suit. He was too comfortable and sexy in faded jeans and that torn navy T-shirt that proclaimed Cops Make Better Lovers. Hmm, that idea merited thought. But not right now. Not if she wanted to have a fairly sane day.

She'd finally come to realize it wasn't what a man wore that made him capable in his work, but what was inside. Her antagonism toward the police force had softened a great deal when she saw how hard Dean worked at keeping her and the girls safe.

"I didn't date very much myself," she admitted, "because I wanted to keep a 4.0 grade-point average and get into veterinary school. As women in veterinary schools are still somewhat rare, I had to work even harder there. Sometimes I think the main reason I dated Steve was because he was always there. He shared my passion for veterinary medicine, and he understood the pressure I was under. Not that we didn't share other things as well. But that was what I considered most important at that time." She looked off toward the hills, her gaze tracking the clouds obscuring the mountaintops.

"Don't get too maudlin, Doc, or I'll have to do something about it. Like throw you over my shoulder and carry you off to some romantic hideaway."

She arched an eyebrow. "And have your wicked way with me?"

"Naturally. Having my wicked way with beautiful women is what I do best." He lowered his voice to a husky purr. "As much as I admire your mind, Doc, I'd like to have a chance to admire your body, too."

How tempting he made it sound! "Careful, Detective, you'd probably run for the hills if I threw myself into your arms and begged you to take me away from all this."

"Try me."

Elise decided this was the right time to back down—before things got too heated up. She already sensed Dean would be an excellent lover. He'd certainly pushed all the right buttons with her that night in her office. The memory had given her plenty of sleepless nights since. Yet in so many ways he was ignorant about women. Not that he was callous; he simply didn't always know how to act around them. Although, she was the first to admit, when it came to teenage girls, it wasn't easy.

"We'll take this under consideration later. As for now, Keri wants to do some shopping afterward," she told him. "So don't worry if we're not back for a few hours."

He nodded, suddenly edgy for a brand-new reason as he realized Elise would be out of touch for a while. "What if— ah—Lisa starts feeling worse?"

"She's sleeping right now and may just do that for the rest of the afternoon. She'll call out if she needs anything."

Dean shifted uneasily from one foot to the other. "Are you sure it's safe?" he asked.

She immediately guessed the reason for his hesitation. "Safe for me to go or safe for you to handle Lisa? Dean, if I'm not worried, you shouldn't be either. I promise I'll watch for anyone showing too much interest in us. I just don't want to leave Lisa alone when she isn't feeling well."

"I guess if you feel comfortable about it, I should, too. Have fun." He tried to look as cheerful as possible.

She arched an eyebrow. "Fun at the dentist? Fun walking through who knows how many stores until my eldest finds exactly what she's looking for? If you'd prefer, we can change places."

"Mom!" Keri's wail of dismay was loud and clear.

"I'll stay home with Lisa," he said promptly.

Elise smiled. "I thought you would."

The moment Dean watched the Pathfinder roll down the driveway, he felt uneasy. He slowly turned and stared down the white goose watching him with what he was certain was malice in its beady eyes.

"I bet you'd taste great with orange sauce ladled over you," he told her.

Frances honked and ran toward him, wings flapping. Dean stood his ground for all of ten seconds before he jumped onto the porch.

"Why didn't you do this the night Dietrich showed up?" he muttered, entering the house.

He quickly changed into shorts and a fresh T-shirt and stopped by Lisa's room. The girl was wide-awake, huddled under the covers with her knees drawn up to her chin.

"You okay, kiddo?" he asked softly.

"Uh-huh," she mumbled.

"Would you like something to drink or eat?"

She shook her head.

He glanced at the small portable television Elise had evidently left on the dresser before she left. "Maybe the remote control for the TV?"

She didn't look at him. "Mom put it on my nightstand for me."

He couldn't remember ever feeling so helpless. "I'm going to wash my truck. If you need anything, you give a holler, okay? I'll be where I can hear you."

Still not looking at him, Lisa nodded.

Dean walked outside. He positioned his truck near Lisa's window before he went in search of a bucket and sponges. He also kept a sharp eye on Frances, who watched him from a short distance, her beak snapping open and closed as she muttered short, vicious honks.

"You are something else," he told the goose as he turned the faucet on and picked up the hose.

As he ran water over the truck, he could hear the dogs snuffling around the yard, the two geese playing their own games and Baby telling the world to "fud up." He laughed aloud.

"Quiet, dammit!" the macaw finally screamed, by now frustrated that no one was listening to her orders.

"Bet I know where you heard that," he murmured, running a soapy rag over the hood. He was just finishing rinsing it off when the ringing phone caught his attention. He quickly turned off the water and ran for the back door.

"Yeah?"

"Hey, buddy, Stacy gave me a beautiful daughter at 4:02 yesterday morning," Mac said without preamble. "Jennifer Anne McConnell."

Dean whooped. "That's great! You must be on top of the world!"

"Yeah, especially since she looks just like her mother. In fact, everything went so well that we all just got home. It appears hospitals don't keep new mothers any longer than necessary." He sounded as if he strongly disagreed with that idea.

Dean tightened his grip on the receiver. He couldn't explain the jolt to his gut at this announcement. He always thought Mac was going to be the last holdout in the marriage market. Then Stacy came along and swept the gruff detective off his feet, even resorting to kidnapping him in the end! And in the two years they'd been together, Mac had looked happier than Dean had ever thought he could be. Dean found himself jealous of his friend's luck and, for the first time, hungered for that same kind of future.

"I'm really glad for you, Mac," he said quietly, sincerity ringing in his voice. "If anyone deserves it, you do. How's Stacy doing?"

"She said she's happy she doesn't look like she's swallowed a basketball any longer." His voice sobered. "How's it going there? Found out anything new?"

Dean had already filled him in on the scare at the Wild Animal Park.

"Not one damn thing," he said, disgusted. "It's as if Dietrich disappeared into thin air. I questioned people there, but no one remembered seeing him. All we have to go on is Becky and her friend. Now Becky looks at me as if I was the bad guy, Keri considers me an embarrassment to the human race and Lisa's been moping around the house all week. My luck with the opposite sex has been absolute zero."

"You didn't say what the lovely doc thinks of you."

Dean hadn't told Mac about the kiss in Elise's home office, but his friend knew well enough that something must have happened—just by how much Dean *hadn't* told him about Elise.

"She just wants Dietrich caught," he said finally.

After Mac rang off, Dean stared at the receiver for a moment before finally settling it in the cradle. He frowned when he heard faint whimpering sounds from the rear of the house. He headed down the hallway.

"Lisa?" He stood in the open doorway of her room. "Are you all right?"

She lay in a fetal position, her back to the door. "Fine."

He walked slowly into the room and sat gingerly on the side of the bed. His hand hovered over her huddled body. "Can I get you something?"

She shook her head. "When's Mom going to be back?" Her voice was scratchy with unshed tears.

"She wasn't sure. Is it something I can help you with?"

She shook her head again. "Can you call Myrna for me? Please?" She buried her face in her pillow.

"Okay. I'll call her right now."

Dean called Myrna's house. No answer. He looked through Elise's address book and even tried Donna and Cheryl. As he heard Donna's answering machine click on, he suddenly remembered her talking eagerly the day before about a date with the new man in her life. And Cheryl's line just continued ringing. He even tried the dentist's office, just in case Elise was still there, only to be told Dr. Carpenter and her daughters had left there more than an hour ago.

"I'm sorry, sweetheart, I guess it's just you and me," he told her when he returned to the bedroom.

Lisa's now-choking sobs left him feeling helpless as he stood there fervently wishing he knew what to do to make her feel better.

"You can't help me. You're a man!" she cried. "You don't understand anything about this. I just want do die!"

Dean then remembered someone he could call. He quickly left the room and headed for Elise's bedroom, snatching up the phone and punching out the numbers. He sighed with relief when Stacy answered, sounding somewhat groggy.

"Hi, there, little mother," he greeted her, hoping he sounded calmer than he felt.

"Hi, yourself."

"How are you and the newest McConnell doing?"

"Just fine, but something tells me you didn't call to ask about us," she told him with her usual insight.

"Okay, you caught me. And believe me, I wouldn't disturb you if it wasn't important. I've got a huge problem that I don't feel qualified to solve," he announced before plunging in with the few details he could give her. Stacy's gurgle of soft laughter didn't leave him feeling reassured.

"You're right. You would have trouble solving it, because you're a man," she told him.

"Funny, that's just what Lisa said," he said sarcastically. "Come on, Stacy, give me a hint!"

"Without talking to Lisa, whom I'm sure would not be happy talking to a strange woman, I can't be sure, but I'd say she's just entered womanhood."

Dean frowned. "Give it to me in English."

"Dean, it sounds as if she's having her first period," she said gently.

"Oh, boy," he muttered. Now he was lost. "Should I take her to a doctor? I mean, is she all right, or should she have medical attention?" He'd never felt so far out of his depth as now.

"No, but fixing her a cup of hot tea and finding a heating pad to help her with her cramps wouldn't hurt. I'm sure she's taken care of the necessities herself, since girls are usually prepared for this in advance, but what she needs now is lots of TLC."

"Elise is going to blame me for this," he muttered.

"I don't think so. Look, if there's any more problems, call me, and if she's willing, I'll talk to her, okay?"

"Okay." He felt lost the moment he hung up the phone. "I can handle this," he told himself. "I can handle this." His chant didn't make him feel the least bit secure.

Taking Stacy's advice to heart, he searched through the linen closet and bathrooms until he found a heating pad. A hunt through the medicine chest provided him with a bottle of Midol, and he headed for the kitchen to heat a cup of tea in the microwave.

"Lisa, maybe this will make you feel better," he said softly, returning to her room. He plugged in the heating pad and placed it over her covered body. "I also brought you some tea."

She looked up, startled at the array of items before her. She could read in his face that he knew what was wrong with her, and her face turned bright red.

"I'm the first to admit I know more about being a boy than being a girl, but there is one thing I can tell you. I think girls are a lot more special than boys," he said conversationally, placing the mug of tea on the nightstand next to the bottle of Midol. "And more complicated. We guys only grow up worrying if we'll make the football team or if we'll be able to grow a decent mustache or beard, while you girls have to worry about makeup, hairstyles, prom gowns, jerky guys—you name it. Although, come to think of it, I wasn't too sure whether the girl I wanted to ask to my senior prom would say yes or just break down in laughter."

She scooted backward until she rested her shoulders against her bunched-up pillows. "It's not fair," she mumbled, deliberately ignoring the pill bottle. "They don't tell you the truth about all this. The school shows you this dumb cartoon about how your body is changing, and they hand out booklets and say all the same dumb stuff about how wonderful it is. But they never tell you how you're really going to feel."

"Like what?"

She squirmed, clearly uncomfortable discussing this with a man. "Just that you feel sick and you hurt. They never talk about that. What's so good about hurting?" She stared down at her fingers plucking at the edge of her comforter. "All Keri could talk about was buying a dumb bra. She even bragged about it to her friends! She never talked about how it aches and feels funny."

Dean knew right away he was out of his depth. He sensed if he said one wrong word, he could create one very large emotional mess that Elise would not appreciate having to clean up. He felt as if he were tiptoeing through a mine field that could blow up in his face at any moment if he wasn't careful.

"Yeah, well, it means you're growing up," he said slowly. "You'll be viewing the world a little differently from now on."

"You mean I'll start acting stuck-up like Keri?" Lisa unconsciously snuggled closer to him.

"Not necessarily." He slid an arm around her shoulders. "Keri's her own person, just as you are your own. You don't have to follow any special rules. Just continue to be yourself. This is all new to you, and because your body is changing, you do have aches now and then." He frantically searched his brain for the right words. "Look at it this way. You can do something we guys can't."

"What's that?"

"Have babies. Not that you should consider that right now," he hastily added. "That's something to think about a long time from now. A *long* time," he stressed. "But Lisa, just remember this, even with all these new and wonderful things going on inside of your body, you're still the same Lisa. And that won't change."

Lisa smiled wanly. "It really does make me special, doesn't it?"

He nodded. "You got it, sweetheart."

When Dean finally left her watching television, he felt as if he could handle the toughest problem that came along. After all, he'd helped Lisa realize that her feminine turning point wasn't so bad after all. Still, it didn't stop him from looking out the windows for the next two hours until the Pathfinder appeared at the end of the driveway.

"At last," he breathed in relief, hurrying outside.

Elise looked surprised at Dean practically running to the truck. "Was it that bad a day?" she teased. Then she noted the concern etched on his face. "Is it Lisa? Is she all right?"

"Yeah, but..." He paused, staring up at the sky as if he'd find the answer there. "How do I say this? Lisa's stomachache is because she . . ." He frowned. Exactly how could he word this?

"Because she what?" Elise demanded, now fearing the worst. "Dean, is she all right or not?" She moved to rush past him.

"She's fine," he assured her, grabbing her arm. "Elise, Lisa feels kind of emotional right now. I may only be a guy who doesn't have a great sense of tact where your girls are concerned, but I'd say she just entered a new phase in her life, and she's not entirely sure how to handle it."

Elise's eyes widened as the pieces fell into place. "You mean . . . ?"

He nodded. "I got out the heating pad, gave her some Midol and fixed her some tea."

"I have to see her." This time she did escape his grasp and ran inside the house.

"I had no cavities," Becky proudly informed Dean.

He crouched down. "Hey, that's great, sprite."

"Keri didn't, either," she confided. "But all she cared about was finding a new sweater."

Dean looked up at the teenager carrying bags into the house. After his successful mission with Lisa, he felt on top of the world. As if he could handle any obstacles that came his way. Including repairing things with Keri. "Keri, I know I handled things wrong last week. I'd like to try again," he said softly.

She paused and turned around. "You don't understand, do you? We don't need you here. We were fine before you showed up, and we'll be fine when you leave. *You're* the one making Mom afraid of that man. Besides, you haven't exactly done anything while you've been here except act like some macho cop. Why can't you just go back to where you belong and let us get on with our lives!"

"Keri!"

At her mother's sharp voice, the girl turned around. "I won't apologize for speaking the truth." She displayed her mother's stubbornness. "They say we need protection, but protection from what? A man giving Becky a note and a candy bar? A few phone calls? There's no proof that it's even the same man doing all this!"

Elise's face tightened with anger. "That man killed your father and your baby brother," she said tautly. "Nothing goes smoothly, and we're all feeling the stress of waiting, but if Detective Cornell is willing to wait this man out, the least we can do is be patient, too."

Tears sparkled in Keri's eyes. Without saying another word, she ran into the house.

"It's always hard on people who feel they've lost control of their lives," Dean said quietly. "It's even harder on kids."

"She still didn't have the right to say that to you after all you've done for us. I can't imagine any of this is easy on you either, even if it is what you do for a living. Don't worry about Keri. She'll come around. After all, that lethal Cornell charm hasn't failed yet," she teased lightly, placing her hand on his arm. "I want to thank you for helping Lisa. She was feeling frightened because there wasn't a woman around to help her through this, and from what little she'd said, you handled it beautifully. I thank you for that." Her eyes were warm sincerity.

He grinned. "I'll be honest with you. I was scared to death I'd blow it. Something like that is more than a little out of my league. That kind of problem was never handled at the police academy or in the Boy Scout handbook."

"Then you showed remarkable common sense for a usually less than tactful cop."

Looking away, Elise chewed on her lower lip. "I meant what I said, though, Dean. I want Dietrich brought out in the open. We can't remain in this limbo much longer."

Now he knew he had to tell her. "My captain is only allowing me to stay another week. If nothing happens by then, I have to return to L.A."

Fear flashed briefly through her eyes. Just as quickly, she masked all emotion. After all, she was used to having to handle things on her own. Having Dean there to count on was new to her. Still, in such a short time, Dean had become an integral part of the family, and Elise found herself unable to imagine what it would be like without him around. And, no matter what she said, she did fear the day Carl Dietrich might display his ultimate revenge.

"I guess you didn't think you'd ever hear this from me, but I'll miss you."

An admission of that kind from Elise *was* surprising. Dean couldn't imagine hearing better words from the lady. Except maybe...

To cover his sudden upsurge of emotion, he opted for humor. He ducked his head until his chin grazed her ear. "Will you miss me 'cause I'm such a great kisser?"

She bit her lip to halt her smile. "Myrna will miss cooking for you."

"She won't miss yelling at me to pick up my stuff. And I have to admit, I won't miss that tortoise snoring under my bed." His breath warmed her skin. "So tell me, does anyone snore under your bed? Or *in* your bed?"

She knew if she turned her head the slightest bit his mouth would be very close to hers. As it was, his beard brushed her skin. Tempting as it was, she continued concentrating on staring at the front of the house, idly wondering if it was time to paint the exterior again. It was definitely safer than thinking about the intense male standing next to her.

"Perhaps I should take the Fifth," she murmured demurely. "So I won't have to lie."

"Hey, you can lie all you want. I am one of the most comfortable people in the world to lie on," he told her.

"You paint an interesting picture, Detective," she drawled. "But all you've done so far is talk."

He leaned even closer over her. "Lady, you want action, you've got action." His eyes glittered.

"If I catch you in my room one more time, I will make you sorry you're alive!" Keri's scream was loud enough to shatter eardrums.

Dean stilled. "Back to reality," he said with a sigh.

Elise's smile drooped a bit at the edges. "In many ways."

He dipped his head, dropping a kiss that was definitely a promise of more to come. "We'll take up this discussion later—when reality is sound asleep." He walked off with that loose-hipped gait that sent Elise's imagination soaring with possibilities.

"Yes, we shall."

Chapter Ten

Feeling as if she'd scream if she stayed inside a moment longer, Elise sought the privacy of the front porch. She knew Dean wouldn't be happy to find her out here, but she was temporarily safe from his wrath since he was busy on the phone. She settled herself on the top step, greeting Bailey and Duke and Kola as each of the dogs came up for a hug and a pat on the head.

She looked off into the darkness, seeing the dim outline of the clinic. Memories swamped her mind. The busy hours involved in setting up a new practice, getting the girls settled in a new home and schools. Dealing with a grief that visited her at odd times, usually late at night when there was nothing else to occupy her mind. She was grateful those days and nights were over and she had gone on with her life.

Even though that same life had taken an abrupt turn lately, Dean's unusual entrance into her life wasn't something she'd care to change. She found herself unable to stop smiling. Dean had made a lot of changes in the way she viewed things. And he had given her a new outlook on men.

Thinking about Dean forced her to think about Carl Dietrich and the changes that man had made in her life. She couldn't help wondering if things would ever be the same again. To be honest, she wasn't sure if she wanted them to be. She did know one thing: she didn't want to hide anymore and felt there were few options open to her.

"Are you hiding?" Dean hunkered down next to her and passed her one of the coffee mugs he held.

She accepted the mug and sipped the rich brew. "Thanks. In a way, I guess I am. I looked around and felt as if the walls were closing in on me. During the summer, I come out here a lot after the girls are asleep. It's always peaceful and gives me a chance to think things over."

He sat next to her, their thighs brushing. "So what are you thinking about tonight?"

She took a deep breath. "I've been thinking about our situation."

"Good. Tell me more."

Elise looked away. She already knew what his reaction would be. "I think I should set myself up as bait to bring Dietrich out into the open."

"No." His reply was swift and emphatic. "It's too dangerous, Elise."

"It's already been established that he's watching us. All we'd have to do is get the girls off the property and let him think I'm here alone."

Dean swore under his breath. "He's not dumb, Elise. He'd smell a trap, which could set him off. And if he got past us, he'd take it out on you. There's other ways."

"Tell me one," she demanded. "Tell me one idea that you feel is foolproof that wouldn't require my participation. The girls are starting to grow afraid of their own shadows, and there's even nights when I'm tempted to look under the bed to see if he could be hiding there. This can't go on!" She also knew she couldn't go on with the knowledge that Dean would be gone in a short time and that if she didn't watch herself, she'd be nursing a broken heart long after he left.

Dean sighed. "Let me talk to Santee first. See what alternatives there are."

"All right." She bit her bottom lip. "I was so smug five years ago. I thought we would be safe here, that the girls would grow up happy and have normal lives. Yet, tonight, for all we know a madman could be watching us through binoculars, watching and waiting for the right time. He's hurt this family enough. I don't intend to see him hurt us anymore."

He slipped his arms around her shoulders and pulled her against his side. "Neither do I, love. No matter what, I don't intend to leave you here alone. We're in this together."

She rested her cheek against his shoulder, enjoying the warmth of his sweatshirt, the musky scent of his skin and the comfort of knowing he was there for her.

"Mind answering a personal question?"

He dropped a kiss on her forehead. "Go for it. My life is an open book."

She shot him a wry look. "And if I ask about women?"

He winced. "I'll take the Fifth."

"I thought so. Then I'll ask something a great deal safer for both of us. Do you have any brothers or sisters?"

He shook his head. "Just me. My mom said I was more than enough to handle." He easily read her inquiring expression. "She wasn't too certain who my dad was. He was either an aluminum-siding salesman or the guy who used to work on her car. She said it didn't matter because I was so much like her she felt as if she'd conceived me without anyone else's help. Still, I can't complain. She didn't drop me off on church steps or something equally depressing. She worked in a bar whose owner let me use the office for my homework or sleep on the couch until it was time to go home."

"She was a cocktail waitress?" she asked softly.

He smiled and shook his head. "No, she was a stripper. And a pretty good one, according to the customers. Her stage name was Mona the Minx. She said it sounded classier than Phoebe. I used to wonder if Cornell was our real last name or if she picked it out of a phone book. But that didn't matter much, either. Mom was hot for me to get an education. The first time she found out I ditched school she whipped my butt good, then she sat down and put her arms around me and cried." He stared pensively into his mug. "She said she didn't want me to grow up to be a numbers runner or bagman. She felt I was smart enough to do better than that. She said if she had anything to do about it, she wasn't going to spend her last days visiting me in prison. You know, I never skipped another day of school after that," he murmured. "It wasn't the whipping as much as never wanting to see her cry again that made me stay in school."

Elise tried to imagine Dean's childhood but couldn't. A childhood of strippers, bartenders and small-time hoods. Hers had been filled with loving parents, her sister, friends and a lot of pets.

"What does she think of your being a detective?"

"She hoped I'd become a lawyer, but she said if I ever took a bribe or turned the other way, she'd whip my butt again, and this time she wouldn't cry about it. She owns a tavern up in Lake Arrowhead now. She still has her figure and the best legs in town," he reflected. "She even has a couple of guys vying for her hand, but she thinks she's too old to get married. I hope one of them can change her mind."

"My dad was a purchasing manager for a medical manufacturing firm until he retired," Elise said quietly. "And my mom was the local Tupperware dealer. Very successful at it, too. Right now they're doing what they've wanted to do for years. They're taking a cruise around the world and having the time of their lives.''

"So you grew up in a two-story house with a white picket fence, a collie, roses in the backyard, and your dad home by five-thirty and your mother baking brownies in the kitchen.''

Elise chuckled. "Our house was one-story, my mother is allergic to roses, my dad never made it home before six and my sister and I did all the baking. But we did have two dogs, four cats and six hamsters. When my mother gave us each a hamster for Easter, she had no idea mine was pregnant. Kris eloped with her high school boyfriend when she turned eighteen and later divorced him. And while Mom and Dad hoped I'd become a doctor, I surprised them by going to veterinary school instead. So you see, there's no such thing as a perfect family. To me, what matters is having parents who love you no matter what.''

Dean sipped his whiskey-laced coffee. "Mom would like you.''

She smiled, warmed by his words. "Because I can keep you in line?''

"Because with all that's happened in your life, you never forgot your sense of family. You didn't crawl into a hole and wallow in self-pity. You went on with your life.''

"I wanted to crawl into that hole,'' she murmured. "I wanted to go off somewhere and scream out my anger at the world, but I realized I couldn't. Not when I had three children who didn't understand why their daddy wasn't coming home anymore or why they weren't going to have a baby brother after all. They were my link to sanity.''

Dean turned his head in her direction, looking at her with those dark eyes that could either say so much or nothing at all. This time they were speaking loud and clear.

Elise kept her eyes on his face as she slowly leaned forward, setting her mug on the coffee table. She opened her mouth to speak when the shrill ring of the phone broke the silence. For a moment she hesitated.

"Go ahead," he told her. "I'll listen in, just in case."

She didn't release her breath until the quavering elderly voice apologized for interrupting her evening.

"That's quite all right, Miss Turner," Elise soothed. "How can I help you?" She grabbed a notepad and scribbled across the surface. "Miss Turner, could you bring Tweetie in tonight? No, I'm sure it's nothing serious. But let's not take any chances, shall we? Yes, I'll meet you at the clinic in fifteen minutes." She hung up.

"Do you usually meet patients after hours?" Dean asked.

She shook her head. "Only Miss Turner. Tweetie is a budgie and her pride and joy." She grabbed a sweatshirt and pulled it on over her plaid cotton shirt. "I shouldn't be gone long."

"I don't like this. I'll come with you."

"No, Dean, you stay here with the girls." She flipped on the floodlights that illuminated the yard all the way down to the clinic's back door. "See? You can watch me." She grimaced when she saw his look of exasperation. "Look, I'll call as soon as I know something, okay?"

He knew he had to settle for that. "Every half hour."

Elise rolled her eyes. "I'll try" was all she could promise.

Dean remained in the doorway, watching Elise walk down to the clinic. He saw her unlock the door and close it behind her.

"You'd better have locked it," he muttered. He snagged the receiver the moment the phone rang.

"Just so you don't worry, I locked the back door," Elise informed him just before she disconnected the line.

He grinned. "She's improving."

Dean continued his vigil at the door until headlights swept across the end of the driveway and stopped in front of the building. Since Elise had floodlights around the clinic, he could see a tiny woman climb out of a car straight out of a fifties movie and walk slowly around the car to the passenger door. After retrieving a small cage from the front seat, she walked to the front door.

Dean didn't relax the first half hour until Elise called and tersely explained it would take a while. Before he could question her further, she ended the call.

"Damn fool woman," he muttered, glaring at the clinic.

Another half hour passed before he watched the woman leave, this time without the cage, and slowly drive away. By the time another hour passed, he was ready to chew nails. When an additional half hour ticked away, he considered dragging Elise out of there by her hair. With his limited patience now dissipated, he checked the sleeping girls and stalked out of the house, making sure he had a key before locking the door behind him. During the short walk to the clinic he issued dire threats on an unsuspecting Elise's head.

"All right, Elise, time to go home!" He pounded on the back door. "Dammit, Elise, let me in before I break the door down!"

He heard the snick of the dead bolt, but the door didn't open. He tried the knob and found it turning easily under his hand. He entered the storage area and headed for the only lit room. When he entered he found Elise sitting beside a glass cage where a tiny blue-and-white budgie lay on a thick towel. She leaned over, adjusting the thermostat to her satisfaction, then continued her vigil over the small bird.

"He has cancer," she said abruptly. "It will be a miracle if he's still alive in the morning."

Dean crouched down beside her. He stared into the heated cage, watching the bird's chest rise and fall in labored breaths.

"I didn't realize birds could get cancer."

"Oh, yes, they can get many human diseases." She pressed her fingertips against her forehead and rubbed them in a circular motion. She suddenly looked very tired.

He touched the glass with his fingertips, not surprised to find it warm to the touch. "What can you do for him?"

She shook her head. "Not as much as I'd like. Basically, all I can do is make him as comfortable as possible and let him know he isn't alone."

Dean turned his head, not missing the sorrow darkening her eyes. "Didn't the owner want to stay?"

Elise shook her head. "I sent her away. I didn't want her to see this," she said softly. "Miss Turner is eighty-three, and Tweetie is all the family she has. It would kill her if she watched him die."

They remained together in silence, watching the small bird struggle for each breath it took. When the end grew close, Elise gently took him out of the cage and kept him cupped in her palm as she crooned to him and stroked his feathers. Dean watched her comfort the dying bird to its last breath.

"This is always the hardest," she whispered, placing the lifeless bird on a towel.

Dean stroked his beard in thought. "Is there a way to replace the bird without her knowing it's not the same one?" he asked finally. "I mean, I know the idea is crazy...." He could feel the tips of his ears turning red. "I'll pay for the bird."

Elise's head snapped up. "No, it's not crazy," she murmured. "In fact, I think it would work." She turned around and reached for the phone. She punched out a number and waited a few minutes. "Hi, Marilyn, it's Elise. Yes, I know what time it is. No, I won't apologize for waking you up because I have an excellent reason. Do you have a pale blue-and-white male budgie? No, not a baby, an older one, about two or three years old. Miss.Turner's Tweetie just died." Her face lit up. "You do? Wonderful. Could we get it in the morning? Great. I'll see you then."

Dean watched her replace the phone. "Success?"

"Yes, and it's all due to you." Elise bustled around, cleaning up her supplies.

"And she'll never be able to tell the difference?"

She shook her head. "I don't think so. Miss Turner's eyesight isn't what it used to be. I think she'll be so happy her bird is healthy, she won't think to question it." She closed and locked cabinet doors. "Miss Turner is one of the kindest, most generous people I know. I'm glad you thought of this."

Dean smiled. "I bet you don't charge her your regular fees either, do you?"

She flushed. "She's on a fixed income."

Dean draped his arms over her shoulders. "Doc, you're a regular softie."

"Look who's talking about having a soft heart. Just don't let it get out. I have enough problem keeping the girls in line as it is."

"Come on. It's after two, and I need my beauty sleep." Keeping one arm around her shoulders, he guided her toward the back door. He took her keys out of her hand and secured the dead bolt, shaking the knob to make sure before they walked up the driveway to the house.

Elise curled an arm around his waist. "You're a very nice man, Detective Cornell."

"Does that mean you'll jump on my bones and have your wicked way with me?"

"I just might," she said archly.

Dean halted and turned her around to face him. "Don't tease me about this, Elise," he said seriously. "Anything else, fine, but not this. You know how badly I want you. I've sure shown you enough times how I feel."

She tipped her head back, her features backlit by the floodlights. "I'm not teasing, Dean. I admit I was happy in my insulated world. I had my work and my girls, and I didn't think I needed anything else," she said softly. "Then this cop crashed into my life and turned it upside down. Nothing's been the same for me since. You've made me come alive again. I see life a whole new way, and what I've seen about the new me, I like."

His fingers stroked circles against her nape. "Since meeting you, mine hasn't been so calm either. In fact, you're the best thing to come along for me in a very long time."

"I'll be honest. Your being a cop still makes me a bit nervous."

"And I don't like having a tortoise snoring under my bed. The thing is, that's not what's been interfering with my sleep since I came here."

She didn't have to ask the question, but she wanted to. She wanted to hear him say the words. "What is?"

"You. Wondering whether you sleep on the right side of the bed or the left, what you sleep in, if you put goo on your face before you go to bed." His lips curved slightly. "If you snore."

"The left side, shortie pajamas, I only use a lightweight moisturizer and no."

"I also sleep on the left, I sleep raw, I don't put anything on my face and I don't snore."

Her faint smile mirrored his. "Yes, you do."

His eyes twinkled, but instead of looking amused he looked positively wicked. "You been spying on me, Doc?"

"I was the one to rescue you from the couch, remember?" Her fingers curled upward, halting his from another sweeping caress of her arm.

"You gonna rescue me again?"

"You're not asleep."

"I could arrange to be."

"I think I prefer you awake."

"And?" he prompted.

"I think I could arrange to find you a bed that doesn't have a snoring tortoise under it."

"Where?"

Her eyes didn't waver from his intent gaze. "In my room."

Dean drew back, his arms at his side as he allowed Elise to precede him into the house. Once inside, he kept one hand against the small of her back as she walked down the hallway.

When they reached her bedroom, she paused long enough to close and lock her door. She remained still, her hand on the doorknob. "You have to understand this is somewhat new to me," she said in a low voice. "There's only been one other man in my bed, Dean, and he was my husband."

He knew better than to touch her at that moment. It was still up to her how far they would go. "Elise, if you want to change your mind, it's all right. I'm not going to force you into something you're not ready for."

Her head shot up. "You wouldn't get angry?"

"Frustrated as hell, yes," he said ruefully. "Angry, no. This has to be your decision. I want to make love with you, but I don't want it to be just for me. I want you to want me as badly as I want you."

She turned around, leaning back against the door. "I do want you. I wanted you that first night you kissed me, but I didn't know if I was ready then. Oh, I've gotten over

Steve's death, and I want you to know I don't see you as a substitute for him," she hastily explained.

His smile warmed her all the way through. Not the kind of heat that leaves one wanting, but the kind of slow warmth one seeks on a cold winter morning.

"I had hoped so, but hearing you say it makes it even better." Dean exhaled a rough breath. Could he honestly give this woman all that she deserved? He was sure going to give it his best try. He moved forward until she was trapped between the door and his body. He rested his forearms against the wood.

"Oh, lady, I want you so badly, but I want to make it special for you," he groaned.

She toyed with his shirt. "I already feel special. Just seeing the way you look at me lets me know how wonderful we'll be together." One hand ventured southward until it rested against his jeans zipper.

He drew in a sharp breath. "Damn." He found it harder to speak as he heard the hiss of the zipper being lowered and several daring fingers dipping past the metal teeth. "You're making me crazy, Elise."

Her fingers found their way past the cotton briefs. She idly wondered what color he wore as she encountered smooth hot skin that pulsed under her touch. "Please, let me have my way."

"Elise, if you keep that up, I won't last more than ten seconds," Dean said in a rough voice.

She trailed her mouth across the taut skin covering his collarbone, hearing his sharp breaths as he held on to what little control he had left. "You taste so good," she murmured.

He hissed between his teeth. "More than one can play this game." Deciding turnabout was fair play, he slipped one hand under her sweatshirt until he could find bare skin. He was grateful to find her bra had a front closure and easily released the tiny catch. Her nipples hardened instantly under his touch. He caught her gasp with his open mouth as it covered her parted lips.

After being married for close to twelve years, Elise thought she understood lovemaking, but she quickly learned that there were many aspects she wasn't aware of. Dean's caressing hand on her breast alternately kneaded and teased. His lips and tongue first swept through her mouth, then darted along her lower lip in feather-light touches. She released him long enough to raise her arms and allow him to pull her sweatshirt over her head, then helped him dispense with his. She fumbled with his belt buckle until he took pity on her and quickly released it, leaving it hanging as she flipped open his jeans. During this time, their mouths continued to seek out each other, hungry for yet another taste, then another, then another.

"As much as I'd like to just make love to you right here, I'm afraid I might be a little too old for these crazy positions," he said hoarsely.

By then Elise didn't care where they were. They fell onto the bed and quickly pulled off the rest of their clothing. Dean admired her ecru lace bikini panties, while Elise discovered Dean wore purple briefs.

"I would look at you in the morning and wonder what color you were wearing," she murmured, smoothing them down his hips and pushing them off the bed.

"I would look at you in the morning and wonder if you were wearing a bra." He inspected the scant piece of lace that matched her panties and tossed it over his shoulder. "You know, for a prissy doc, you wear some pretty sexy underwear."

She delighted in the fur covering his chest and arrowing down past his waist to surround his pulsing erection. "I bet you were the kind of kid who peeked in the girls' locker room." She tongued his nipple, pleased when he moaned under the feathery touches.

"Not only peeked but got caught for it, too. I got a month's detention." Dean wasn't sure how much he could take before he would explode, so he decided it was time to take matters into his own hands.

Elise laughed when he flipped her onto her back and moved over her, cradling his hips against hers. Her laughter quickly turned into a moan when he found the nub that sent shock waves racing throughout her body.

"Dean!" she keened, throwing her head back, her neck arched in a graceful curve. Her eyes were closed and her lips parted as she panted short breaths.

"Just keep saying my name, sweetheart." He found it harder to breathe as he realized just how ready she was for him. He parted her legs with his knee and moved down and in, entering her slowly as he felt her soft walls grip him tightly. No matter how aroused he was, he wasn't going to allow her one second of discomfort. Even if moving so slowly *was* driving him out of his mind.

Elise's eyes opened. Dean felt as if he were drowning in the brilliant turquoise depths with no chance of being saved. By the time he felt he was going down for the third time, he knew he was surely lost, because he knew he had fallen in love with her. He groaned and captured her mouth with his as their bodies moved into a rhythm that could have only one ending.

Elise couldn't believe the feelings coursing through her veins, the sensations washing over her body as Dean would shift his position just a bit and send himself deeper into her. Not content to simply hang on, she moved with him, faster and faster, until they both exploded. Her tiny scream of joy was swallowed by his mouth upon hers as they soared to completion.

Dean moved slightly to relieve her of his weight but kept his arms around her, reluctant to be parted from her.

"I had no idea," Elise whispered. "I never..." Her eyes clouded.

He understood immediately. She felt guilty because she'd felt more with him this first time than she obviously had all the years of her marriage.

"Don't forget that we've been engaging in foreplay for quite a few days," he whispered, rolling onto his back and pulling her against him, cradling her head in the crook of his shoulder. "In another minute I would have taken you against that door no matter how precarious our position might have been."

She turned her head and pressed a kiss against his damp skin. A thank-you kiss for understanding her feelings.

"I wish we could stay locked up in here forever," she murmured. "I don't want to return to the real world."

He turned, sweeping her under him. His thumbs caressed her cheeks as his fingers combed back her damp hair. "Then I suggest we make the most of it."

She smiled and shook her head at his knowing expression. "My darling, my medical specialty might be animals, but even I know that recovery time is—" Her eyes widened in surprise at the insistent bulge resting against her thigh. She laughed throatily as she linked her arms around his neck and pulled his face down to hers. "But then, medical science has been known to experience a miracle now and then."

MORE THAN ANYTHING, Elise wanted to ignore her insistent alarm beeping away and disturbing much-needed sleep. She heard a muttered curse, then a slapping sound before the alarm was abruptly silenced. Her next observation was that she was cold. It only took one open eye to realize why. She was minus her electric blanket. Turning over showed her that Dean was warmly covered from chin to toe under *her* blanket!

"Give that back!" she muttered, pulling on the blanket. She ignored his muttered protests and continued savagely tugging on the covers.

"It's cold!" he argued, gripping the sheet and blanket.

"No kidding, you hog." Elise dipped one cold foot under the blankets until she found a hair-roughened thigh.

"Aagh!" Dean almost shot out of bed. "Do you realize how close you were to freezing a certain part of my anatomy near and dear to me?"

"Not close enough." She pulled the loosened covers around her shoulders. "You took the whole blanket."

He leaned over her, planting one hand on either side of her head. "Then why didn't you ask for it nicely?"

"Because that never seems to work with you."

He dipped his head, brushing his nose across hers before covering her mouth with his for a good-morning kiss that rapidly escalated into something more intimate.

She sighed regretfully. "Dean, we can't."

He drew back. "Why not?" His expression turned instantly to concern. "I'm sorry, are you sore? I knew we were pretty active last night."

His regard for her was something Elise knew she wouldn't forget for a long time to come. Not to mention the night they'd just experienced. Medical science would have been very surprised indeed.

"You have to be out of here before the girls are up and around. It has nothing to do with you personally. I just don't want them to see you coming from my room, because they'll naturally assume one thing, and right now they're very fragile. Besides, I don't want there to be any awkward explanations." Her eyes silently pleaded for his understanding.

His immediate smile reassured her. "Think we'd have time for a shower together?"

She glanced at the clock and grimaced as she realized what time it was. "Not if we want to get clean, too. And I have to get that budgie for Miss Turner before she shows up at the clinic."

Dean kissed her slowly, but avoiding too much passion that might overwhelm them. "Okay, Myrna can take the girls to school, and I'll go with you to get the bird," he breathed against her mouth.

She was stunned by his easy capitulation. "You're not angry that..."

Dean wondered if there might have been times Steve Carpenter hadn't appreciated having to put off some loving because the hour might not have been convenient. While he wasn't familiar with having an intimate relationship with a woman with children, he knew well enough that what happened between him and Elise was private. At least, for the time being. "Not when you explain it so logically." After one last kiss, he rolled out of bed and hunted for his briefs.

Elise remained under the covers, enjoying the sight of a naked man walking around her room, picking up briefs here, socks there and jeans that had been flung in a corner. She didn't have to guess the origin of the round, puckered scar on his shoulder or several white lines across one thigh. The idea of his being wounded cut through her. But she had already come to terms with one thing. He was a cop. And danger was part of the job description.

"Dean," she said softly.

His head whipped up, his expression wary, as if he feared hearing something he didn't want to.

She sat up in bed, allowing the covers to drop to her waist. Longtime experience told her the girls weren't early risers and would sleep past the alarm unless someone routed them out of bed. Maybe they had enough time after all. "I've come to the conclusion that cops aren't so bad if you put them in their proper place."

His teeth gleamed in a broad grin. It wasn't difficult to read her intent. "And I suppose you know that proper place for guys like me?"

"Intimately."

"And you're willing to share it with me?"

"Absolutely."

"Right now?"

"Most definitely."

Chapter Eleven

"Come on, Dean, just try it. This won't hurt a bit," Elise crooned.

The mutinous expression on his face reminded her of a little boy. A little boy who could grow up within a heartbeat into a devastating man.

"Yes, it will."

"Just grasp her behind her head and stroke downward slowly. She loves it when people do that." Her voice lowered to a sexy purr. "Just the way I do."

He didn't look convinced. "Yeah, but you don't bite."

"I don't? Where's that big macho cop who made love to me all last night?"

"You turned him into a shadow of his former self." Dean grinned as he watched the wash of color creep up Elise's throat. "You started it, sweetheart."

She held the python up in front of her. "And you promised you would meet Althea. She's a sweet little snake."

He eyed the eight-foot reptile with a cautious eye. "You call that little?"

Elise shook her head, amused by the brawny man in front of her so unsettled by a snake most boys would kill to own. The same man who had wooed her into bed after the three girls were sound asleep and proceeded to show her an interesting version of a strip search.

In the past four days he'd turned her life even more upside down. By day he was the professional cop, talking to his partner, driving in to the sheriff's station and consulting with officers there, tracking down the slimmest lead in hopes it would take him to Carl Dietrich. By late afternoon, he turned into a playmate for the girls, urging them into a Frisbee match one day, snagging Elise into playing on the other team. She even thought he might be making a bit of headway with Keri, who still remained aloof in his presence. At least the girl didn't seem to snarl at him so much.

And late at night, he turned into *her* playmate, indulging in delicious necking on the living room couch before leading her down the hallway to her room, where the door was closed and locked against the outside world until dawn. He conquered her complaints about hogging all the covers by pulling her up against his heated body before they slept, and he even told her that, on her, flannel nightgowns were as sexy as silk and lace. That was when she knew the man was first-class trouble for her, because it was getting too easy to fall in love with him.

He even worked harder at keeping his room neater, much to Myrna's surprise, although the housekeeper's sly comments prompted Elise to think the older woman guessed his bed was only mussed in the morning for propriety's sake. The topper was when Dean made friends with Baby and Frances. Frances still chased him around the yard, but it wasn't with the malicious glee the goose usually displayed toward him. Now it was more an act of playfulness, as if the goose finally accepted him as part of the family.

She looked at him, admiring his forthright nature, desiring the man and finding herself falling in love. The idea that these beautiful moments could come to an end was something she preferred not to think about.

"Dean, are you afraid of Althea?" she asked gently, easily reading the expression on his face. If he thought he could hide behind his beard, he soon learned it didn't work with her. Already she knew him so well. But that didn't stop her from feeling eager to learn even more. "Wary of snakes in general?"

"Of course not," he said huffily, backing off another few steps.

"She's very affectionate," she assured him.

"Yeah, I saw that the first day when she tried to turn you into a human hot dog." He looked around the room, where a land tortoise dozed inside one hospital cage, and a cockatoo minus chest feathers watched him with suspicious dark eyes and frantically hopped back and forth on the perch while sending ear-splitting screeches into the air. He decided the only animal he felt comfortable with was the lopeared rabbit chomping on his food while ensconced in a large animal carrier.

Elise watched him somberly. "Didn't you *ever* have any kind of pet, Dean?"

"Our apartment was barely big enough for the two of us," he admitted, wishing he hadn't given in that night and talked about his past. It wasn't something he did easily. Hell, even Mac didn't know all that Elise did. "There wouldn't have been room for a gerbil."

"Gerbils are illegal in California," she pointed out with a smile. "They're considered a harmful rodent to farmers." She shrugged. "Sorry, I tend to lecture at times."

Elise placed Althea back in her carrier, making sure the top was closed securely. Past experience had taught the clinic staff that the python loved to escape and roam the halls, much to the other clients' dismay when they encountered the friendly reptile slithering along the tile floor, eager to make new friends along the way.

"Are you ready to go now?" Dean asked, edging toward the back door.

"Not just yet, boss lady," Donna said airily, entering the room. "You lost the coin toss, remember?"

Elise groaned. "I was hoping you'd forget."

"Fat chance." Donna pulled her purse out of a locked cabinet and slung the strap over her shoulder.

Elise looked at Dean expectantly. "Dean," she cooed, "would you like to do a favor for me?"

He was instantly suspicious. "What?"

"Just like a cop," she tsked. "Always expecting the worst."

Donna burst into laughter. "Come on, Elise, he can't even look at Althea without turning green. How do you expect him to feed her?"

Dean could feel the green wash over his face. "Feed?"

"Just mice," Donna explained. "No biggie. It's just that none of us are really all that happy doing it, so we take turns feeding Althea when she boards here. Cheryl and I were very relieved it wasn't our turn."

He swallowed as he watched Elise pick up a mouse. "You're kidding, aren't you?"

She shook her head.

Dean suddenly found the ceiling very interesting. "Snakes that squeeze people and eat mice. Lizards bigger than your arm. Hell, the rabbits probably have teeth bigger than a cougar's. I'll go out and secure the front gate after Donna leaves. Another hot date?" He knew he couldn't bear to watch Elise's grisly task.

"You got it. It's refreshing to date a guy who doesn't talk about himself all the time. He's interested in me, too," Donna told him as they walked outside.

"Coward!" Elise called after him.

"With a capital *C*, sweetheart!" he called back.

"You know, you're good for her," Donna commented as they walked outside. "Elise tends to forget that she's supposed to have a life of her own."

"Yeah, well, I think she's pretty special, too," he admitted.

Donna opened her car door and slid into the driver's seat. "Catch this creep, Dean," she insisted. "I'm so afraid he's really going to hurt her. She's been through enough without all this happening to her, too."

"That's what I intend to do."

She managed a smile. "I know. It's just that it's left all of us on edge. You don't know who to trust anymore. Well, I'd better get going. See you tomorrow." With a wave of the hand, she was off.

By the time Dean swung the front gate closed and secured it with a lock, Elise was walking outside. He stopped for a second, enjoying the sight of her with wisps of hair springing free from her braid, her clothes rumpled from her work and several suspicious green stains on her jeans. The same kind of stains he encountered on his own clothing after handling Baby. What really punched him in the stomach was her smile as she walked toward him.

For too many years women had enjoyed being with him because he was a cop; therefore, he must be dangerously hot in bed. He was grateful Elise didn't see him that way. She'd probably be happier if he did something safe, like selling cars or insurance. So when she smiled at him or touched him with those delicate fingers, it was because of him—Dean, the man, not Detective Cornell, who had to wear a gun. He liked that. He liked it a lot.

"Think the girls will go to bed right after dinner?" He leered at her as he looped an arm around her waist and brought her up against his hip.

"Not without a major argument." She brushed her cheek against his shoulder. Her voice softened. "You're going to have to return to L.A. this weekend, aren't you?"

His jaw tightened. "Not if I can help it."

"But your boss will demand it, and you can't ignore orders."

"I have plenty of vacation time due me, Elise. I'm not leaving you until this is settled."

"What if it's never settled?" Her soft voice washed over him. "What if he's gone far away?"

"Do you believe he has?"

"No, but I hope he has. Then we could have a normal life again."

Yeah, with me in L.A. and you here. That doesn't sound all that normal to me. His gut wrenched at the thought of leaving Elise. For many years all that had mattered was his work. For the first time, he found himself willing to toss it down the tubes if it meant he didn't have to leave this woman, if he could persuade her to let him into her life.

"We'll talk about it when the time comes, okay?" His voice sounded hoarse.

She opened her mouth as if to say something more, then changed her mind. "Okay."

At the same time they saw the package lying innocently on the front porch. As Elise reached out to pick it up, Dean gripped her hand and roughly pulled her back.

"Don't touch it," he ordered.

She looked up, startled by his vehemence. "But, Dean..."

"No." He pushed her up the stairs, away from the package. "Go in and call Santee. Tell him to get some men out here, pronto. Tell him what we've found."

Elise looked at the package, then at Dean's stone-carved features. "Do you think...?" she whispered, horror washing over her face.

"Just go now, and keep the kids inside."

She fled.

Dean could hear the girls chattering their questions and Elise's voice trying to calm them. He wasn't about to leave the porch with its supposedly innocuous package lying there. He knew it hadn't been there when he walked down to the clinic fifteen minutes ago to get Elise for dinner. And he hadn't heard anyone come through the front gate.

"Dammit, what is it with those dogs and geese?" he muttered darkly. "Frances, you're not worth anything more than acting as the main course for Sunday dinner."

For the next few hours, Elise watched the commotion in her front yard from her front window. Dean had insisted she remain inside and keep up a semblance of normalcy by feeding the girls dinner. As if she could act normal with what looked like half the sheriff's department in her front yard. She had tried to eat, even forcing several bites of dinner down her throat until her stomach started to rebel. Now she just stood there, watching them, wondering when it would all be over. Wondering if her life would ever be her own again. It didn't take an expert to guess that a bomb squad had been brought out to inspect the package.

"What are they doing?" Becky demanded.

"Mom, why can't we go out and watch?" Lisa whined. "This is just like on *Police Story!*"

"Mom, what is going on?" Keri asked, her face taut with fear.

"All of you be quiet," Elise insisted, rubbing her fingertips against her forehead. Their constant questions didn't help her throbbing headaches one bit. "Keri, would you get me some aspirin please?" The girl nodded and disappeared into the bathroom. "Lisa, you and Becky load the dishwasher," Elise went on. "Then go to your rooms and finish your homework."

"I finished mine already," Lisa argued. "Can't we watch TV?"

Elise's lips tightened. "You'll have to watch it in my room. And get that damn bird to shut up!" she practically shouted.

Baby's most recent "fud up" halted in midsyllable.

Keri handed her mother two aspirin and a glass of water.

"They think it's a bomb, don't they?" Keri whispered, although the other two girls had disappeared into the kitchen and only their squabbling could be heard.

"I don't know what they think." Elise swallowed the tablets and wrapped her arms around her body. She couldn't remember the last time she'd felt so cold. Had she felt this chilled and alone when she knew Steve was truly dead?

"Mom, Dean isn't going to let anything happen to us," Keri assured her.

Elise looked down at her oldest with surprise. "I thought he was your least favorite person."

She flushed. "Well, he is a bit obnoxious at times." Elise swallowed her chuckle at that. "But, as you said, he's only doing his job. And in his own weird way, he does care for us. I know I've been a beast to him, but it's because I was so scared. I didn't want to lose you, either."

Elise wrapped her daughter in a strong hug. "You aren't going to lose me that easily," she whispered, dropping a kiss onto her brow. "Now, would you mind making sure they don't break anything and herd them into the other room?"

Keri hugged her tightly for a second, then nodded.

Elise was left alone to watch. Officers dressed in special protective suits, inspecting the package before they gingerly picked it up. Dean and Detective Santee standing off to one side, both looking grim as death. She swallowed a sob as the description hit her mind. It was something she didn't want to speculate on.

She had no idea how much time passed before a member of the bomb squad nodded and handed the package to another man, who appeared to be dusting the package for fingerprints. When he finished his part of the job, he handed it to Detective Santee. He and Dean turned their backs to the house as they inspected it. Within a few minutes, they came inside.

"We want to borrow the VCR for a minute, Elise." The grim expression on Dean's face hadn't disappeared as he looked at the videotape case Detective Santee held.

She nodded and gestured toward the television set.

"Why don't you go back with the girls." It was an order, not a suggestion.

There would have been a time when Elise's ruffled feathers would have sent her stomping down the hallway. This time she nodded and escaped, but only as far as the doorway. She knew Dean was trying to protect her from whatever was on the video cassette, but she had to know its contents.

"Maybe we should play this at the station." Santee's murmur barely reached her straining ears.

"Maybe you can wait, but I can't." Dean inserted the tape into the machine and pushed the play button.

Air hissed between his teeth when the picture first rolled, then settled into a close-up of a decidedly homey scene. Laughter was heard as Keri flipped the bright red Frisbee into the air and jumped up squealing when it sailed over Dean's head. For long seconds, the two men viewed the game as the camera panned on each participant in the game until it zeroed back in on a laughing Keri.

"Cute kid, lady doc," a low voice intruded on the scene. "A lot like you, but I bet she'd be easier to control. Maybe I'll save her for last. As for the cop boyfriend..." The camera swung past the others until it centered on Dean, who was involved in a tug-of-war with one of the dogs who'd decided the Frisbee was his. A crude target was drawn over his face. "Well, I'm sure you can guess what I intend to do to him."

Elise's hands flew to her mouth, muffling her cry, but Dean heard it anyway. He turned his head. The dark expression on his face frightened her nearly as much as the video had.

"Get out of here, Elise," he growled.

Eyes wide with fear, vocal chords paralyzed, she could only shake her head.

"Dammit, Elise, get out now!"

The picture crackled and darkened, turning their attention back to the screen. At first, only shadowy shapes were discernible, then soft sounds, muffled moans and whispers.

"Hey, cop, you really know how to protect a lady," the voice on the tape cackled. "I just bet your buddies would love a copy of this. If I'd known being a cop came with fringe benefits like this, I might have switched over to the other side."

Dean looked as if he wanted to kick the television screen in. A string of curses fell from his lips as he quickly switched off the tape and ejected it from the machine.

"How?" Elise cried out, walking into the room with jerky steps. "How could anyone do such a terrible thing!"

Detective Santee stood off to one side. It hadn't been difficult for him to guess the last images were of Elise and Dean making love. The shock on her face and the murder written on his said it all. He plucked the cassette from the machine and pushed it back into the case before slipping it into his jacket pocket.

"What are you doing?" Elise asked, watching his every move.

"It's evidence, Dr. Carpenter." Seeing the stunned hurt in her eyes, he wanted nothing more than to apologize for putting her through this. No wonder Cornell had fallen for the lady, even if both men knew it was most unprofessional. That was a piece of information he'd keep to himself. What Cornell did could lose him his badge. But, hell, who could predict when you'd fall in love? She was just what the doctor ordered for a battered cop who needed love. He felt the need to tack on, "Although we couldn't find any prints on the case or tape, we have his voice to go on. There's no guarantee that will be enough, but it's something."

"But..." She dipped her head, searching for words. "It shows..." She sounded close to tears.

Dean ground his teeth. He didn't want that tape passed around the sheriff's station any more than she did, but he was aware of procedure. Right now, that procedure sucked. The fact that it showed him in a very compromising position wasn't what worried him. What bothered him was the raw pain on Elise's face. She didn't deserve this.

"I'm going to keep this locked up in my files," Santee said quietly, easily reading Dean's mind.

Dean breathed deeply several times, struggling to contain his anger. The bastard had been close enough to peer into Elise's bedroom! How often had he stood there watching them? Damn! Why hadn't Dean thought to close the drapes no matter how much Elise enjoyed having them open to catch the morning sun!

"Thanks."

"You want to call Anderson or shall I?"

Dean read his meaning loud and clear. This was the best reason for him to remain here. "I'll do it, but I wouldn't mind if you backed it up with an additional call tomorrow."

"My pleasure." Santee looked at Elise with compassion. She hadn't moved, still too stunned to comprehend what she'd seen. "Dr. Carpenter." He left the house.

Elise could only stand there staring at Dean. She tried to swallow the bile rising in her throat but found her muscles frozen. With a muffled cry, she spun around and ran down the hall.

Her frenzied retreat galvanized him to action. "Elise!" He took off after her.

Dean entered Elise's bedroom to find the bathroom door closed and three frightened girls huddled on the bed. The comedy playing on the television was incongruous with the scene playing out before him.

"What's wrong?" Becky cried, tears streaming down her face.

He picked her up and carried her into her room, all the while assuring her everything would be all right. After suggesting she put on her nightgown and he'd be in later, and ensuring the other girls were in their rooms, he returned to Elise's room. He found her crouched in the bathroom, her head hanging over the porcelain bowl.

"Oh, baby," he murmured, wetting a washcloth and filling a glass with water and mouthwash. He squatted down next to her, wiping her forehead with the cloth and letting her know he was there for her. Afterward, he helped her to her feet and urged her to rinse her mouth.

"He made it seem so dirty." Her voice trembled as she allowed him to strip her clothes off and drop a nightgown over her head. "He took something beautiful and made it cheap and filthy."

"No, he didn't, sweetheart. He just wanted you to feel that way," he told her, steering her toward the bed. He pulled the covers around her and turned on the electric blanket before settling on the edge of the bed. "Listen, I'm going to check on the girls. You really scared the hell out of them. Then I'm coming back here. You'll be okay for a few minutes?" His voice sharpened when she didn't reply. "Elise!"

She nodded jerkily. "Yes." Her voice was dull and life-less.

Dean checked on Becky first. He was relieved to find her in bed with all her favorite stuffed animals arranged around her.

"Is that man going to hurt Mommy the way he hurt Daddy?" the little girl asked.

"Not if I can help it," he vowed, giving her a quick hug.

Her chin wobbled. "Can I have my night-light on, please? And the door open?"

"Sure." Dean stopped in the doorway. "Becky, if you wake up scared, you just holler and I'll come running, okay?"

She nodded, watching him with the same wide eyes as her mother.

Lisa was just as frightened, although she tried not to show it. "You gonna start sleeping with your gun?" she asked, sitting cross-legged on top of her bed. "You'll shoot the guy if he shows up, won't you?"

"Only if I have to. I like to talk first and shoot second," he told her.

"Yeah, but he's making Mom scared, and she never gets scared," she explained. "When Dad died, she used to stay up a lot of nights, walking around the house and coming into our rooms as if making sure we were still here, but she wasn't scared, just sad."

Dean rested a hand on her strawberry-blond curls. "Lisa, my love, you're growing up too fast," he said gruffly.

"Yeah, but I still like softball more than I like boys."

"Thank God for small favors," he intoned, walking out of the room and starting to pull the door closed after him.

"Can you leave it open please?"

If he didn't feel so much like crying, he would have laughed. Lisa hadn't grown up so much after all.

Dean found Elise's sixteen-year-old replica sitting up in bed, a textbook propped against her knees. When she looked up, he saw Elise's eyes looking at him gravely.

"There was something bad on that tape, wasn't there?" she asked. "Something about us kids."

How could he lie to this child-woman? "He videotaped us during a Frisbee game," he said baldly.

Keri's swift indrawn breath gave away her reaction. "Then he's in the hills behind us."

"He could be anywhere. A zoom lens can eat up a lot of distance."

She shook her head. "The closest house to us is that horse ranch, but there's guard dogs patrolling the area, and they're really mean, so he couldn't sneak in that way. And old Mr. Myer lives on the other side, and he hates people so much he'll go after someone with a shotgun if they stand too close to his fence. It has to be the hills. Especially if the house was in the background."

Dean considered this. "That's very good deductive reasoning, Keri. I'll pass it on to Detective Santee."

She watched him closely. "If you'd like, I'll check on Lisa and Becky for you, so you can keep the bedroom door locked like you always do."

Dean, who'd never thought he had an embarrassed bone in his body before he came to the Carpenter household, found himself blushing in front of this girl who apparently knew a great deal too much.

"Oh, it's all right," she rushed to reassure him. "I don't feel traumatized or anything. I mean, it's not as if I think that because Mom is sleeping with a man I have to run out and do the same thing. It's just that for a while after Dad's death, Becky used to have nightmares and would crawl into bed with Mom. If she calls out, I'll bring her in here." She grimaced. "Although she kicks in her sleep and takes all the covers."

For a minute, Dean looked at her, unsure whether to laugh or cry. He opted for leaning over and pressing a kiss to her forehead. "If I wasn't in love with your mother, I'd wait for you to grow up."

She wrinkled her nose. "No offense, but you're more than a little too old for me."

Dean grinned. "Thanks for the kick in the ego. Don't stay up too late studying," he cautioned as he left. "And if you hear anything, yell."

"Did you mean it, Dean?" Her question stopped him. "That you love Mom?"

He nodded. "Does that bother you?"

She considered his reply. "Not as much as I thought it would. But can I make one request for the future?"

"What?"

"When I start dating, please don't see if my dates have a police record or act like a cop around them. That kind of thing could kill my social life before it even got started."

The future. That was something Dean hadn't dared to think about. He had a hunch that a future with Elise and the girls would rapidly turn his hair gray. But, yeah, he could live with that.

"Honey, if you grow up to be a fraction of your mother, I'll lock you in your room until you're thirty," he gravely promised.

Keri's smile was enough to warm Dean's heart.

He made a detour to the kitchen before returning to Elise's bedroom. He wasn't surprised to find her with the covers pulled up to her chin. Nor to find the drapes pulled tightly across the window. He felt saddened at the thought of not seeing the morning sun spill across the bed to highlight her hair and face. At the same time, he felt anger that Elise had to fear having the drapes open.

"Here." He held a filled wineglass out to her.

"I don't want any."

"Yes, you do."

Recognizing his do-as-I-say look, she grabbed the glass and downed the wine like water. She coughed when she finished and defiantly handed the empty glass back.

"Well, that was a waste of a good vintage," Dean said dryly, pulling his sweatshirt over his head and tossing it onto a chair. His jeans, socks and briefs soon followed.

Elise watched his movements with suspicion. "What do you think you're doing?"

"Getting ready for bed." He padded into the bathroom, where Elise could hear water running while he brushed his teeth. When he walked back into the bedroom, she could see a fleck of toothpaste on a corner of his mouth. The last time she'd found one she'd licked it off.

She licked her lips. "I think you should sleep in your own room tonight." She didn't flinch under his glower. "Tonight frightened the girls. Becky might have a nightmare and need me."

"Keri already said she'd take care of Becky if she woke up." He pulled up the covers on the left side of the bed and climbed in, nudging her with his hip. "Move over, Doc."

Having no choice, she moved a few inches. "Keri? You mean, she knows about...?" Hadn't she had enough shocks for one night?

"About her mother having a sex life? Yes." He picked up his wineglass and sipped it. "I'll share if you won't chug-a-lug it." He held out the glass.

She grabbed it and swallowed a mouthful. "I can't handle this."

Dean retrieved the glass and set it back on the nightstand. "No kidding." He pulled her into his arms and held on tightly as she struggled. "Ellie."

"I can't!" she cried. "Not after that bastard..." She couldn't bear to finish her tortured thought.

"Yes, you can," he said firmly, rolling over onto his side, keeping her close to him. "Don't let him win this round. What we have is beautiful and very special. No one can ruin it as long as we don't allow him to."

"Maybe you're used to this kind of filth, but I'm not!"

His eyes darkened. "And neither am I. Elise, you are the best thing that's happened to me, and I'm not going to let that creep influence what we have. Dammit, woman, I love you!" he roared.

Elise's eyes turned into saucers. "You do?" she breathed. It was amazing: it only took three words to break through her shock.

He looked as if he was afraid Althea might be hiding under the covers. "Yes," he admitted grudgingly. "And since Keri already gave us her blessing, you can't back away from allowing us to find out just what we could have together."

Disjointed thoughts ran through Elise's mind. She tentatively lifted her hands and traced the muscular arm draped across her waist. "Maybe it's just sex," she whispered, more than a little fearfully.

He muttered a pithy curse. "Trust me, it's more than sex if I can look at you wearing that truly ugly nightgown and still want to make love with you."

"You do?"

He nodded.

Elise suddenly knew that was what she needed, too. She needed Dean's possession to cleanse her of the night's memories, to make what they had pure again. She stared into his eyes, watching the dark irises widen with his arousal. The same arousal she felt brushing her belly.

"I don't need a gentle lover tonight," she whispered. "I need to forget, to be swept away until I can't think."

He raised himself up over her. "Then I suggest we get rid of something first." He gripped the neckline of her nightgown and easily ripped it down to the hem.

His kiss threatened to devour her, his lips nipping and biting her, silently urging her to follow his lead. Elise didn't need a second invitation. She turned into a streak of fire in his arms as she returned every rough caress with one of her own. She nipped his ear until he growled, and invited his thrusting entrances with her hips arching upward.

Time stood still for the lovers. Elise lost track of the world around her as Dean swept her away into a climax so shattering that she was positive the world exploded around her. She fell into a sleep so deep she didn't move a muscle all night. But Dean remained awake until dawn, listening to every sound in the house. When Becky's tiny cry intruded on the charged silence, he started to get up, until he heard soft noises from Keri's room and her whispers assuring her younger sister that everything was all right. Then it was quiet again. Which was fine with him, as long as he could hold Elise in his arms and consider her all his.

Chapter Twelve

Elise understood the expression "easier said than done" when she tried to wake up. She found herself much too comfortable under the warm covers to want to wake up and face the world. If she did that, she'd have to remember last night. Last night. Well, not all of it was bad.

"You're smiling, so I know you're awake."

"No, I'm not."

"I've got coffee."

The heavenly scent reached her nostrils. She opened one eye. "You know all my weak spots, don't you?"

Dean grinned the grin of a wolf holding on to its favorite sheep. "I sure do. But I noticed you found a few of mine along the way, so I guess we're even."

She sat up, accepting the coffee cup he held out. She drank the dark brew, savoring the caffeine racing through her veins.

Dean leaned forward and brushed his lips against hers. "I'm afraid it's later than usual, though, and we're going to have to face the real world."

Elise looked at the clock and grimaced. "You're right." She cradled the coffee cup between her palms. "You're going to have to call your captain about last night, aren't you?"

He nodded.

She appeared to pick and choose her words. "Are you going to tell him about the tape?"

He didn't want to answer that. "I have to."

Her expressive eyes seared his soul. "Everything?"

"It's procedure, Elise," he said reluctantly.

She slowly nodded. She slipped out of bed and headed for the bathroom. "I'd better shower and dress. Would you please tell Myrna I won't have time for breakfast." The door closed after her with a decided click.

Dean swore under his breath and pounded the bedclothes. Did she think he liked this any better than she did? In a mood to commit murder, he stomped out of the room and quickly showered and dressed, reaching the kitchen before Elise. The girls were grouped around the table, finishing their breakfast, and Myrna stood at the stove.

"That Detective Santee called," the housekeeper announced, setting a plate in front of him. "Said you weren't to bother calling your captain until you came down to see him, and you should make it a conference call."

For once Dean felt no appetite when he looked at the food. "Thanks," he muttered. "Elise said she won't have time for any breakfast." He drank his coffee but couldn't bring himself to touch the golden-brown waffles.

Myrna looked at him with shock. "You're not eating?"

"I'm not hungry."

"Now I've seen everything," she clucked, taking the plate away.

Dean ignored her. "You girls almost ready?" he asked in a subdued voice.

The three nodded in tandem.

He pushed his chair back and stood up. "Okay, let's roll."

The ride to the schools was made in silence. When Dean stopped the truck in front of Becky's school, she started to climb out, then turned and threw her arms around his neck.

"I love you, Dean," she told him, kissing him on the cheek before climbing out.

He sat there, watching her race for the front door, where she stopped to talk to friends.

"Oh, boy," he said, sighing. "I'm caught, hook, line and sinker."

When he reached the sheriff's station, he found Detective Santee sitting at his desk, looking as if he'd had little sleep.

"Considering your superior's attitude, I figured a little backup wouldn't hurt," the man greeted him after handing him a mug of coffee that looked like black ink.

"Yeah, he's a real charmer," Dean said ruefully, grimacing after his first sip of the coffee. "Used a new brand of battery acid this morning, didn't you? This is almost drinkable."

Detective Santee punched out a phone number and tapped on the speaker phone. Within seconds, he was connected with Captain Anderson. Using as few words as possible, the sheriff's detective related the previous night's events.

"What's on the videotape?" the police captain demanded before Santee finished speaking.

Santee didn't even look at Dean. "He filmed a Frisbee game going on between your detective and Dr. Carpenter's daughters," he said crisply. Dean shot him a look filled with surprise.

The other man sputtered out curses on Dean's head. "What does that idiot think he's down there for? He's supposed to catch an escaped criminal, not run around playing kids' games!"

"Captain Anderson, there was a threat made on the older Carpenter girl, and a target drawn on the tape over Detective Cornell's face." His voice hardened. "If I were you, I'd worry more about this man taking potshots at an innocent girl or one of your men than what they happen to be doing. The way I understood it, Detective Cornell was sent down here to work with us, and that means protecting Dr. Carpenter and her daughters. He can't keep them inside all the time, and if that means he has to participate in one of their games, I'm all for it."

The silence on the phone spoke loud and clear. "I want a copy of the tape."

"It's already made and on its way to you. Do you care to say anything to Detective Cornell? He's right here."

"Only that he'd better get on the ball and do his job before he finds himself pounding a beat," the man snarled.

"Since you obviously sent your man, I don't know why you're so worried. Unless your head is also on the line regarding this case," Santee said mildly.

"Who the hell do you think you are to talk to me that way?" the man roared.

"Easy. I'm the man in charge of this station. If you have any complaints about me, I suggest you—" His reply was the buzz of a disconnected line. Santee gave Dean a rueful look. "Your captain is very impolite."

"I told you he was a charmer." Dean shifted in his chair. "You already sent a copy of the tape?"

Santee nodded. "Sure. It's only a Frisbee game, right?"

Dean carefully set his coffee cup on the desktop. "I realize what happened was unprofessional and can cost me my badge but..." How could he explain something to someone else when he couldn't truly understand it himself?

"I'd say Anderson would like nothing better than to get something on you that would throw you out on your butt," Santee said. "I've had to deal with his kind for more years than I like to remember. Dr. Carpenter is a nice lady, and she doesn't deserve having him use that small piece of tape as ammunition just because he seems to carry a personal grudge against you."

Dean heard Santee's implicit message. *That small piece of tape*—which could be easily edited out. He was grateful to the man.

"You're dead right. Anderson would have spouted regulations loud and clear right before he kicked me out," Dean replied. "Especially since my partner married a woman who was once a suspect in a series of robberies. She proved to be innocent of all charges, but she had a fairly long juvenile record, and Anderson still feels she wriggled out of something she was guilty of. There's no shades of gray in his world."

Santee shook his head. "I don't think I'd care to meet the man."

"There's days when I wish I hadn't wanted out of vice." Dean leaned back in his chair. "I'm forty-two years old, and some days I feel a hundred and forty-two. I quit smoking a few years ago, and I started up again."

"Why don't you take your pension and get out?"

"It's beginning to sound better all the time." He stretched his arms over his head. "Just as soon as I figure out what else I can do with my life."

"You thinking of relocating out of L.A.? Maybe somewhere hereabouts?"

"Could be."

"I wouldn't blame you. It's a nice area, fairly smog-free. Nice people." Santee stressed the last word.

"If I did, would you be willing to tell me your first name?"

He smiled. "I doubt it."

Dean sobered. "I have a hunch Dietrich is stepping up his campaign, and the videotape is just the beginning."

Santee nodded his agreement. "I just wish we had more information on the man."

"Yeah." Dean sighed. "All we know is he likes his drugs and he puts the fear of God into his so-called friends so they're afraid to talk about him too much. What little Mac learned was only because he was able to put more fear into the guy than he felt for Dietrich. This guy is one mean individual. Right now, he's using scare tactics against the doc, making her afraid for her kids more than for her own life. I don't want to think of the day he makes his move."

Fear for Elise cut through his body like a knife. What if he wasn't able to protect her? It wasn't his job he was worried about. That didn't matter one bit. What mattered was Elise. How could he put into words how he worried when he was away from the house? Even if a patrol car drove by more often than usual. It wasn't enough. He knew it. Santee knew it. But they were all powerless in one way or another, and Dietrich seemed to know that. The man was playing a dangerous game, and Dean could only hope to remain one step ahead of him.

"Time's running out." Santee spoke Dean's thoughts out loud.

"Yeah, but what will be his plan? What move will he make next? Will it be against one of us personally or another mind game?" Dean muttered curses under his breath. "The bastard doesn't have a pattern. That's why he's eluding us so easily."

"Maybe there is a pattern and we just haven't figured it out yet."

Dean considered his suggestion. "Maybe," he mused. "Okay, let's look over what's happened so far."

More than three hours later, Dean's stomach burned from too much coffee and no food and from frustration at not finding anything revealing a pattern. Even looking into Carl Dietrich's past didn't give them any ideas.

"If nothing else, he's an equal-opportunity criminal," Dean concluded. "Robbery, murder, rape, drug possession. This guy has his fingers in a lot of pies." He snapped his fingers. "That's it!"

Santee looked up. "What?"

"He deliberately doesn't have a pattern."

"Tell me something we don't already know."

"No, this is how he plays his games. By not finding a pattern in any past crime, we can't figure him out, and he knows it. This way he figures we'll be running all over the place. So we don't," Dean said softly. "We just sit back and wait for him."

Santee's interest sharpened. "Set a trap?"

Dean shook his head. "Not exactly. He'll expect a trap."

"Now you've lost me."

"If my ears weren't deceiving me, he was sounding a little strung out on that videotape. If he's getting low on his favorite mind benders, he'll be looking to make a drug buy soon. If you keep your ears open, maybe you'll hear about it. And we can pick him up then."

Santee slowly nodded. "It might work."

Dean looked grim. "We can hope so."

He kept that thought for the rest of the day. Dinner that evening was more subdued than usual, and he noticed Elise didn't have to voice her suggestion about homework more than once to the girls. Even she looked weary, as if it were all finally getting to her. She had demanded the not-very-hopeful truth about his meeting with Santee, and he'd given it to her. Now she looked as if she regretted asking.

While he sat in a chair with a bottle of beer in one hand, she curled up in a corner of the couch, not even pretending to watch the blaring television.

"I keep wondering what he's going to do next," she said quietly.

He didn't bother to ask who she meant. "Worrying will only give you ulcers."

She studied her hands lying clenched in her lap. "What did your captain say about the tape?"

Now he understood part of the reason behind her tension. "Santee talked to him this morning about Dietrich catching the Frisbee game on tape and told him he'd sent a copy."

Elise's head snapped up. "That was all?"

Dean nodded. "Yeah."

"If—" She swallowed. "If he knew about the other, you could lose your job, couldn't you?"

"They'd consider my behavior on the case unprofessional" was all he said.

She appeared vastly interested in her fingers, which now plucked at a loose thread in her sweater. "I won't have you get in trouble because of me."

"Hey, where's that fire-eater I first met?" Dean demanded. "The one who looked down her nose at me that day in the bank."

A smile reluctantly tugged at the corners of her mouth. "Your watch is still forty-five seconds slow," she murmured. "You still dress deplorably, and you desperately need a haircut."

He felt relieved to see her smile. "I wouldn't know how to act if I had an accurate watch, dressed decently more than twice a year and had my hair cut on a regular basis. Ellie, you can't worry about everything," he said quietly. "What's between us is nobody else's business, and Santee was nice enough to keep it that way. The fact that he doesn't like Anderson any better than I do helped a lot."

"What if Dietrich tries to hurt me through you? If he can catch you on videotape, he can catch you just as easily with a rifle, can't he?" Her eyes pleaded with him for the truth. "He could hide out there and pick us off one by one. What's stopping him from doing that?"

"Nothing, except he's still having his fun playing mind games."

"But it could end at any time," she pressed.

He saw no reason to lie. "Yeah, it could."

She drew in a deep breath. "Then we're all powerless. We're just pawns waiting for his next move!" Frustration laced her voice. She pounded her fist against the arm of the couch.

"Elise, you can't lose it now!" He spoke sharply. "You have to remain strong."

Her eyes blazed with more fire than he'd seen in the past few days. "I want the man dead, Dean. I want to know he'll never bother us again." With that, she stood up and left the living room. A moment later, Dean heard her bedroom door close.

He took his time making sure all the doors were locked and windows secured. Baby glared at him and squawked when he pulled the covers over her cage, but a walnut seemed to soothe her irritation.

When Dean settled on his bed in the guest room, he wearily listened to the soft snores coming from under the bed.

"I didn't miss you one bit," he informed the sleeping tortoise. "But something tells me she would not welcome my company tonight, and I don't deal real well with rejection."

AFTER A SLEEPLESS NIGHT, Elise didn't look forward to a full day at the clinic. She left the house early, intent on looking over her schedule before her staff arrived. Not to mention she didn't want to see Dean just yet. She'd spent most of the night thinking about him. About what would happen when the case was finally over and he was back in L.A. Would that be the end of it? Would he dismiss her as a fond memory and return to his former life?

One part of her argued that Dean wasn't the kind of man to tell a woman he was in love with her, then just take off. But this wasn't a normal courtship, and she was feeling unsettled about so many things that she was afraid to believe in anything just now. Afraid she might be wrong. Afraid she might lose Dean before she truly had him.

She unlocked the back door and walked inside, stopping a few paces inside the door. Something was wrong. For a moment, she wasn't sure whether to continue into the building or run back to the house yelling at the top of her lungs for Dean. She opted for the former, all the while telling herself the door had been locked and everything appeared to be in its place. Except the animals were agitated, which fed her unease.

"Hey, guys." She comforted a screaming cockatoo, who hopped around his cage, before moving on to check an African Gray, who looked wild-eyed. "Everything's fine. Honest."

But it wasn't, some sixth sense insisted loud and clear. Something was very wrong. Pulling her sleeve down over her hand, she carefully opened cabinets and eyed the rows of medicines, then checked the refrigerator, where other medications were kept. Nothing looked out of place, but something still didn't feel right to her. Keeping her sleeve over her hand, she gingerly picked up the phone to call the house.

"Myrna, please have Dean come down here right away," she said without preamble.

While Elise waited, she walked through the rest of the clinic, looking at supplies and office equipment in hopes she would find something, anything, that didn't look right, but still she couldn't find anything amiss. She knew her calm exterior hid a very frightened woman when Dean tore through the back door, the expression on his face unnerving her even more. He looked like a man ready to do battle.

"What's wrong?" he demanded.

She shook her head. "I don't know, but something is."

Dean's intuition had saved his life too many times to question hers. "You'll have to close the clinic for the day."

"I assumed you'd say that. I got the names and numbers of today's appointments, so they can be contacted," she replied.

Dean looked around. "Let's lock up until a lab team can come out. You can call everyone from the house. I knew I shouldn't have let you talk me out of a security system for this place."

"There's no guarantee someone was here," she argued.

"What makes you think someone broke in?"

"The animals are upset, and I just feel it."

"That's good enough for me." He dragged her outside and locked the door.

During the short walk back to the house, Dean quizzed Elise on her every move from the time she entered the clinic until she called him. The fact that she could only give him a bad feeling for a reason didn't bother him one whit, and he sensed it wouldn't faze Santee, either. After he called the sheriff's detective, he left Elise to phone her staff and give them the day off, then contact her patients, using the excuse that there was an electrical malfunction in the building, causing it to be closed until further notice. She didn't promise to be open the next day, just in case.

"How up-to-date is your inventory?" Dean asked her when she finished her calls.

"Every day we track everything used on an inventory sheet to make sure we never run short of anything important," she explained.

"Where is it kept?"

"On the inside of the cabinet doors, and that's updated in our computer on a weekly basis. I'm a real stickler for accurate records." Elise ruefully noted the arrival of the crime-scene van. "I guess by now they can find their way here with their eyes closed." She watched Dean head for the door. "I know, stay inside."

"Just until we make sure there's nothing wrong," he told her. "I'd still like to know how he's getting past the dogs and geese."

"Maybe because they're not true guard dogs," she admitted. "Their size puts off most people, but they'd rather lick strangers to death than attack them."

"Oh, that's great!" he exploded. "Why didn't you say anything sooner?"

"Because I knew you'd react just the way you are right now." Elise didn't bat an eyelash under his fury. "They often bark at strangers, but if someone tells them to be quiet, they'll usually settle down without too much argument. Besides, the first time he drugged them. I didn't think he'd try to enter the property again."

Dean rolled his eyes. He strode to the door and suddenly spun around, pointing his finger at her. "You need a full-time keeper." With that pronouncement, he walked out, slamming the door behind him so hard the windows rattled.

"I wonder if he's volunteering for the job," Myrna commented.

"I don't think he meant it as a compliment," Elise countered, watching him cross the yard in ground-eating strides.

"Do you want him to stay?" she persisted.

Elise's quiet reply floated through the air. "Yes, but what matters most is whether he wants to stay."

DEAN STOOD inside the clinic, watching the lab technicians dust for fingerprints, take a random sampling of medications and anything else in boxes or bottles and even leaf through the shelves of file folders for anything that looked out of place.

"How does she work with all this?" Santee asked, wincing as an Amazon parrot kept asking everyone if they wanted a cup of tea.

"Meow, I'm a cat, I'm a cat," an African Gray parrot insisted.

"Hey, buddy, you're a bird," one of the police technicians informed the parrot.

The African Gray snapped his beak at the man. "I'm a cat!" he shrieked. "Meow."

"Okay, you're a catbird." The man shrugged his shoulders at one of his colleagues, who chuckled at the scene.

The bird dipped his head, looking coy. "I'm a bird," he cooed.

"That's Oscar," Dean explained. "He did that to me, too. He's boarding here while his owners are on vacation."

Santee looked around. "My idea of an exotic pet was a lizard or a king snake, but now it seems like anything goes. At least snakes don't talk back to you."

"If you catch this guy, he'll probably get put away in the state hospital." The head technician approached Santee.

"Does this mean I'm not going to like what I'm about to hear?"

The lab man nodded. "I won't be able to tell you more until I can run some full tests, but what I've been able to check out here isn't good."

Dean didn't need to see his grim expression to guess that. "Meaning?" he asked.

"Meaning this guy has a very nasty sense of humor. So far, we've found traces of hydrochloric acid in the soap dispenser in the bathroom, a hallucinogen in the drinking water dispenser and we even found ground glass in the Kleenex box.

He paused, then continued carefully. "Not all of the medication bottles were touched, just enough to make trouble. They were played with by an expert. If you weren't looking for something out of the ordinary, you wouldn't find anything wrong with them. He seemed to pick them at random. Something was put in them, we're not sure what, but I won't be surprised to find some kind of poison. According to the inventory records, a box of latex examination gloves was taken, along with about fifty hypodermic syringes. He probably used a pair of the gloves but didn't leave them behind. Everything's clean as a whistle. We couldn't even find prints of the regular staff on anything, much less anyone else's. The guy is thorough."

Dean and Santee shared a long look.

"She's not going to be happy about this," Dean said finally. "She could go over the edge."

"Which he'd enjoy," Santee finished.

"That's not all." The technician spoke again up. "There's no sign of forced entry. One of the men is checking this out further."

Dean looked ready to explode. "I don't like any of this."

"Tell me about it." The young man sounded reluctant. "This guy had a lot of fun while he was here. He even changed the message on the answering machine. I think you'll want to hear this for yourself."

He led the way to the front of the office, where another technician had just finished dusting the desk and files for prints. Dean and Santee stood behind the reception desk, watching the man depress the announcement button on the answering machine.

"I'm sorry, but Dr. Carpenter's clinic is closed indefinitely due to a death in the family." Dietrich's voice was unmistakable.

Dean spun around. He felt so furious that he doubted even putting a fist through the wall would dissipate his rage. He'd never *wanted* to kill before, but he wanted to see Dietrich dead, and he'd be more than happy to do the honors.

"How?" he roared. "How is he doing all this without leaving one damned clue?"

Santee looked grim. "I don't know, but more than ever I want this guy caught. He's getting way too brazen. I don't want to think what he'll try next."

Dean breathed deeply to contain his fury. "Elise has already called her clients and explained the clinic was closed until further notice. He's going to know this and realize he has one less place to hit again. If nothing else, we're narrowing his playground for him. If necessary, we'll send the girls off somewhere and narrow it even more. I want to piss him off enough that he'll realize I'm the one behind it, and he'll start coming after me. I want this fight."

"Just remember one thing." Santee stepped in as the sensible one here.

Dean was past thinking sensibly. "What?"

"He might decide to piss you off more by going after her."

Dean found it painful to draw air into his lungs. "Yeah, I know. That's another thing I'm afraid of."

The technician was called away by one of the other workers, and the two conferred in low tones. He returned to Dean and Santee with an unhappy look on his face. "One of the guys just discovered something that's not going to make you two happy."

Dean closed his eyes. What could possibly make this situation any worse? "What?"

"There's no sign of a break-in for an excellent reason."

Dean and Santee looked at each other. They knew the answer before they heard it.

"It looks like he used a key."

Chapter Thirteen

"How comforting to know he used a key instead of breaking a window or smashing in a door to enter my clinic." Elise's eyes spat out turquoise fire as she paced the length of the kitchen. "I'm sure the insurance company will be so happy to know they won't have that additional cost."

Dean didn't say a word. He just straddled a chair, resting his arms across the back. He looked over at Santee, who sat in another chair, his own expression shuttered. "I've discovered it's safer to remain out of the line of fire," he muttered to the sheriff's detective.

Elise rounded on him. "You—you cop you!"

Undaunted by her temper, he grinned up at her. "I love it when you talk macho to me."

Incredibly, her face turned a bright rose color, but she visibly tamped down that emotion and worked on bringing back her anger. "That man invaded my clinic. He tampered with my equipment, poisoned the drinking water and left a disgusting message on my answering machine. I'm only grateful he didn't harm any of the animals! And now you're telling me he barely left any trace of a physical presence other than his sick idea of a practical joke!" She looked at them as if they were complete idiots.

"Dr. Carpenter, my boys combed that place for clues, but this man is very clever," Santee told her in his low voice. "He's a world-class games player."

She stood there, her arms crossed over her chest, her very posture indicating she wasn't buying any excuses, no matter how logically the detective presented his case.

Dean simply remained in his seat, admiring the picture before him. In deference to the warm day, Elise had changed into yellow shorts and a yellow-and-white-striped tailored shirt. Her outfit, coupled with yellow socks and white running shoes, left her looking as young as one of her daughters.

His stomach tightened as he watched her. He'd never felt such an intense need for a woman. But the more he was with Elise, the more he wanted of her. There was only one problem. No matter how much he wanted to think about the future, he couldn't as long as he had a job to do. He was only here as long as Santee deemed him necessary.

Dietrich should have been caught long ago. He looked up at the one thing that made this whole miserable scenario bearable. At least it kept him close to Elise. But he could see the strain she was under. Shadows under her eyes, testifying to the nightmares that didn't fully awaken her but left her listless and out of sorts most mornings. And now one of the few places she thought safe had been invaded.

He couldn't blame her for being angry. He could only blame himself for not having seen this coming. He rested his chin against the wood, only half listening to Elise rant and rave to Santee. She was usually so cool and controlled that most people would assume she was ice clear through. He knew better, and he'd liked being the only one to see both sides of Elise Carpenter. Santee, he knew, would probably steer clear of Elise after this.

"Maybe there is a pattern after all," he mused.

Elise stopped her tirade in midstream and turned toward him at the same time Santee did. Dean shifted his gaze in their direction.

"He has to know how important her home is, so the first step he took was to invade her property with the kind of tactics a bunch of kids would use. You have to admit, it's a great way to throw off the police—make them think it was a bunch of kids pulling a sick joke. Except you didn't believe it. And I came down, so Dietrich knew *we knew* he was around.

"Then there was the episode with Becky at the Wild Animal Park. Still keeping a little distance, so to speak, but getting more personal. Then came the videotape—up close and personal and meant to show us that he was very close and in control, that he could take any of us out any time he wanted to.

"The clinic would be his next step, because he knew that invading it and polluting it the ways he did would be almost like violating her." Dean had stated his thoughts as reasonably as he could. Now he waited for feedback.

Santee closed his eyes, obviously mulling over Dean's words. "You could be right. He's slowly invading her territory by first showing he could get on her property without any problem, approach her kids in public without anyone noticing anything wrong, spy on the household and now invading her workplace. He's working on her bit by bit, each time coming just a little bit closer, trying to break her down."

Dean smiled at Elise. "Trouble is, he doesn't know the doc has a spine made out of tempered steel. She doesn't break easily."

She bowed her head. "If necessary, I'll pull the girls out of school and send them away," she murmured. "I can't take the chance of something happening to them."

"If you'd like, I can arrange for an officer to drive them to school and pick them up," Santee offered. "I'll be honest with you, Dr. Carpenter, I don't think you should be left without protection from now on. He's getting too close."

Elise sighed. She knew she looked as defeated as she felt. Her earlier fury had left her drained of any more emotion. "Yes, whatever," she murmured, turning away. She walked out of the kitchen without another word.

"What can I do to help?" Myrna spoke up. She had refused Elise's suggestion to go on home, instead saying she intended to remain close by.

Dean stood up and pushed the chair under the table. "Just be here," he told the housekeeper.

Santee also got up and headed for the door. "I'll call you later if we find out anything else," he told Dean as he left.

"I only hope we do," he murmured, intent now on finding Elise.

He didn't have much trouble. He found her curled up on her bed, the pillows propped up behind her as she stared at something braced against her knees. Dean sat down by her feet. He picked up the picture frame she held and studied the family photograph. Elise, smiling at the camera with a tall man standing beside her: a younger Keri, with braces glinting on her teeth; Lisa, her face a bit plumper than now; and a tiny Becky perched in her mother's lap, a broad grin on her face. For a brief second, Dean hated the man in the picture. Hated him because he feared that when he made love to Elise, she might be thinking of her dead husband, comparing them.

"He's in my heart because we had twelve good years and he gave me three beautiful children, and he's gone, Dean," Elise said softly, reading the thoughts etched on his grim features. "I've never needed to pretend you were Steve."

She reached forward, plucked the frame out of his hands and laid it to one side. She grasped his hands between hers, rubbing them in a circular motion. "Steven and I had a good marriage, but I suspect he put the clinic even before me. His work was his life, and his greatest joy was in coming up with new surgical techniques and writing papers about them. By all rights, we shouldn't even have been in the clinic that night, but Steve took the call and assured the owner we would take care of his bird right away."

She stared down at their hands, absently noticing how callused his finger pads and palms were. "I was tired. That pregnancy was more difficult than the others, and I wanted nothing more than to go home and put up my feet, but I let Steven talk me into staying to help him."

Her brow creased in thought. "There are so many things I don't remember about that night, and so many things I wish I could forget. The sound of the bullet hitting Steve, that maniac's laughter, then his curses as he realized we didn't have the kind of drugs he wanted. I don't really remember any pain when he beat me, probably because I was in so much shock over Steven being shot. I have no memory of picking up the scalpel and cutting him."

She trailed off for a few moments, then continued with quiet vehemence. "I just wish I had connected with his throat instead of his arm. Do you know I even welcomed the pain from my miscarriage because it told me I was still alive? In the space of a few hours I lost my husband and my baby, but I couldn't cry over either of them," she whispered, lifting her head. She looked at Dean with eyes filled with such agony it hurt him to look at her. "The doctor said it was shock, but I knew what it was. I couldn't cry because, to me, it wasn't over. It can't be over until that man is tried and convicted for his crimes. And even that didn't happen." Her voice choked. "Dean, I feel as if something is eating away at me inside, and I can't stop it."

He reached for her, pulling her onto his lap and cradling her against his chest. "I wish I had a ready answer for you,

Elise, but I don't think there is one. It was left unresolved five years ago because Dietrich had to be freed. You saw your chance when he was arrested again, only to have it snatched away when he escaped. Now you have to sit and wait, again a victim. And due to what's been going on, you're more the prisoner than he was when he was in jail. It's all built up inside you, and you haven't been able to let it out."

"I hate smart men," she muttered against his chest.

He grinned. This was the woman he knew best. "No, you don't."

"Yes I do."

He pulled her shirttail out of her shorts and ran his hands over her back. "Hmm, I thought you weren't wearing a bra." He nipped her earlobe. "Lady, you should be ashamed of yourself for going around half-naked in front of Santee."

"He didn't notice."

"The hell he didn't. I saw the way he looked at you."

"And I noticed the way *you* looked at me. Those kind of looks are almost as obscene as those shirts you wear." She plucked at the soft cotton of his navy T-shirt. "I hate to think what kind of influence you've been on the girls."

"I haven't seen any signs of trauma."

Elise's chest rose and fell with a heavy sigh. "You've stopped rubbing my back."

"I'm still rubbing."

"Yes, but that isn't my back." She tipped her head in order to look at him. "Sex can't settle everything, Dean."

He laid her down and leaned over her, his hands braced by her shoulders. "No, it doesn't, but I feel the need to touch and love you," he said seriously.

Elise studied his face and saw something new there. No hint of his usual teasing manner, no light quips, just a man who needed her as much as she knew she needed him.

"It's the middle of the day." It was more a statement than a protest.

"I can close the drapes."

"Myrna might need one of us."

"We both know she's happier when we stay out of her way. If you're worried, I can lock the door." He didn't move a muscle as he waited for her decision.

She moved her hands upward until she could lace her fingers through his. "When this is all over I want you to take me out on a real date," she murmured. "I'm talking calling and asking me out, flowers and candy, you wearing a suit with a shirt and tie, dinner reservations at a nice restaurant, then dancing." With each word she spoke, Dean's head lowered until his mouth hovered just above hers.

"Shouldn't that be my idea?"

"Considering the way you dress, I thought you might need some assistance in that area. I have a feeling your idea of a fancy restaurant is the kind with a drive-through window."

"What happens after the dancing?" he breathed.

The corners of her lips tipped upward. "I'm sure you can think of something."

He released one of her hands and began unbuttoning her blouse. "Yes, I'm sure I'll have no problem there."

"I FEEL AS IF I could sleep for days," Elise murmured, burrowing in closer against Dean's side. She felt boneless and thoroughly loved.

"Considering all the nights you haven't been sleeping well, I'm not surprised." He yawned.

She rolled over until she could prop herself on his chest. "I have something to say, and I don't want to hear a word from you until I finish," she said quietly.

"Okay."

She chewed on her lower lip. "Carl Dietrich is either remarkably clever or totally insane, and if he decides to truly come after me, I might not survive. I need to know that the girls will be taken care of. I realize what I'm saying might be presumptuous, but if something does happen to me, I want you to have guardianship of the girls."

Dean wasn't sure whether to feel horrified or awed by her trust in him. "Ellie, I'm not going to allow anything to happen to you."

"What we want might not come into it in the long run," she argued. "We've both already seen that by what's happened so far. He seems to appear out of thin air, then vanish just as easily. How can we stop someone who doesn't seem to exist? I need to know the girls will be taken care of. There's more than enough insurance for their material needs, but I need to know their emotional needs will be taken care of as well."

He still couldn't take it all in. "What about your sister, or your parents, or even your in-laws?"

"I love my sister dearly, but her patience with children is next to nonexistent. She's best as the aunt they see on special occasions. And my parents are getting older, and they've earned some time for themselves. As for the in-laws..." Long-buried pain surfaced in her gaze. "Steven was an only child, and the only way his parents could deal with his death was to blame me. They felt that I was the one who forced him to work in the clinic that night, and I somehow enraged Dietrich into shooting him. They haven't had anything to do with any of us since the funeral."

Dean could only wrap his arms around her and hold on tight. "They gave up so much," he murmured. "And here my mom would be ecstatic to have grandkids to spoil."

"Then you won't argue with my idea, because I want to make it legal and binding." She rubbed her cheek against the coarse hair on his chest.

"There's no reason to, Ellie."

"For my peace of mind?"

With her cheek resting on his chest, she could hear his chuckle rumble under her ear. "Are you sure you want this tactless guy who's a slob at heart, wears obscene T-shirts, not to mention is a cop, to be a role model for your daughters?"

She turned her face enough to kiss a dark brown nipple embedded among the coarse curls. "With luck, *they'll* influence *you* and turn you into a model citizen."

Dean grasped her arms and pulled her upright. "When this is all over, we're going to have a long talk," he said hoarsely. "And I do mean *we,* because I don't intend for anything to happen to you. Do you understand me, Doc?"

She rubbed her thigh against his. "Before, during or after that dinner date you'll take me on?"

He was past teasing. "I'm not going to lose you, Ellie." He couldn't remember feeling as serious about any subject as he felt right then. "I'll fight the very devil to keep you."

She didn't smile. "I think you're already fighting the devil."

DEAN DIDN'T HAVE much of an appetite. Myrna puttered around the kitchen, muttering about how a person's chicken and dumplings weren't appreciated anymore and she might as well throw out that blueberry cobbler she'd slaved over. Even the girls were quieter than usual, without the usual dinnertime squabbles over whose turn it was to clear the table or who had the best or worst day at school.

While Dean had roamed the house, furious with his inability to nail down one man, and spent time on the phone arranging for a security system to be installed, Elise had spent the afternoon on the telephone arranging for a colleague to take over her patients until further notice. Since she hadn't wanted too many people to know her troubles, she merely said that her clinic had to be reoutfitted before she could reopen for business. A sheriff's deputy had picked up the girls and deposited them at the front door with a few words to Dean and a brief smile at Elise. Elise sat them down and explained the situation and then quickly left the room before she broke down in the tears she had repressed for so long.

"How about a game of Frisbee?" Dean had asked, hoping to divert the girl's attention. "I bet Kola and Bailey and Duke would be happy to join in."

"Maybe we should try something else so Dietrich doesn't get bored taping us doing the same thing." Keri spoke up, her delicate face furrowed with worry.

Daunted by the grim reminder, they had all chosen to remain inside.

"Dean, will you watch movies with us after dinner?" Becky asked now, touching his hand as the group sat around the table, picking at their food.

He managed a smile. It wasn't difficult to guess they needed reassurance. "Sure. I'll even help with the dishes."

"Wait a minute—*I* want to get a picture of that," Myrna jibed.

Dean shot her a dirty look. "Hey, you have to admit the guest bedroom is a lot neater these days."

She looked down her nose. "Yes, and we know why, don't we?"

"You'd better behave or you'll find a snoring tortoise under *your* bed," he threatened.

"I'm worried, I'm worried."

ELISE SAT behind her desk, lost in stormy thoughts over the invasion of her clinic. Dean had arranged for someone to come out that very afternoon to install a security system.

As she sat there, she stared at the floor-to-ceiling bookshelves filled with veterinary medicine textbooks and journals Steven and she had accumulated over the years.

She had already given up one practice because of Carl Dietrich, and she refused to lose another. And there was another consideration in her life now: Dean. How ironic that the man she'd fall in love with would be a police officer. A cop.

Not to mention that his job was seventy miles away, and her work was here. She couldn't ask him to give his up, but could she really think of starting over again? She laughed without humor. As if Dean had even brought it up. All he mentioned was having a long talk when this was over. That could mean any number of things. She was finding it difficult to think positively after everything that had happened lately.

She had no idea how long she sat there, reliving the past few weeks that she doubted she would ever recover from.

"You going to stay in here all night?" Dean stuck his head around the door.

She turned. "I thought you were watching TV with the girls."

He groaned. "I have been. We had a *Star Wars* marathon. Becky fell asleep halfway through the second movie, and Lisa barely made it through the third. I just carried Becky into her room, and Keri's getting her into a nightgown." He flexed his shoulder muscles. "Either I'm getting old or your youngest isn't as lightweight as she looks. I'm just glad I was able to prod Lisa to her feet. Carrying her might have given me a hernia."

She smiled. "You didn't know? A sleeping child automatically gains twenty pounds." She was shocked when she glanced at her small desk clock. "I must have lost track of the time. How could you let them stay up so late?" She shot out of her chair and headed for the door.

He grasped her by the shoulders. "One, there's no school tomorrow, so I figured you wouldn't mind. Two, it helped get their minds off things." He didn't need to elaborate on what things they might be worried about.

"Even considering what happened to their father, I hoped they'd never have to deal with the darker side of life." Elise sighed. "I should have known it wouldn't be possible. How can Keri indulge in worrying about whether the boy she has a crush on will invite her to the winter dance when she has to think about a madman out there stalking her mother? Or Lisa—how can she think about all the changes going on in her body and the new emotions she's feeling? And Becky, who's entering the mainstream of school and friends. It isn't right," she bit out. "It isn't right that they can't laugh and not worry about anything more pressing than what to wear to school the next day or how they'll spend their weekend. It just isn't right!"

His hands dug into her shoulders. "Elise, you're letting it affect you more than it's affecting them."

She raised her chin in that obstinate gesture he already knew so well. "Really? Do you know Becky used to sing to herself almost all the time? Keri and Lisa complained constantly because they said she sang tunes that stuck in their minds whether they wanted them to or not. I can't remember the last time I heard her even hum a tune, much less sing. Have you heard her sing?" She barely waited for him to shake his head. "And Lisa never stayed in the house if she could be outdoors, even if it was to just play ball with the dogs. Keri thought the only decent television channel was MTV and danced around the living room. They had friends running in and out of the house at all times, and either Keri or Lisa tied up the phone constantly with their friends. Have you seen them doing that or heard me yelling at them to get off the phone?" she demanded.

"No," he had to ruefully admit. "No, I haven't seen or heard any of that." He shifted uncomfortably under her direct gaze. "Dammit, Elise, you're making *me* feel guilty," he grumbled. "What is it with you women? Is this some trait that comes out at puberty, or what?"

She bit down on her lower lip. "Dean Cornell, no man has ever made me as angry as you have. But what I hate the most is when I get mad at you, you have a talent for making me want to laugh at the same time." She covered his hands on her shoulders with hers, squeezing them gently. "Now that I see what time it is, I think I'd better check on the girls and make sure they're in bed and not reading or listening to the radio."

"I'm going down to the clinic to check out the security system," he told her. "I'll be back in a few minutes."

Elise dropped her hands until they rested lightly on his waist. She frowned, sensing something wasn't quite right. Before Dean could guess her intent and move away, her hand slipped around to his back and encountered a lump under his sweater. She quickly slid her fingers under the hem and found smooth leather and hard steel. She snatched her hand away as if it had been burned.

"You're wearing your gun," she said woodenly.

"You know I've been wearing it when I go outside the house," he reminded her.

"Yes, but . . ." How could she explain that it had finally sunk in *why* he had to wear it.

"I've kept it out of the girls' reach when it's not on me," Dean sought to assure her.

She shook her head. "Funny, it took until now for me to finally see why you wear your gun and why it's so necessary. As if it's been nothing more than a bad dream I'll wake up from soon." She stepped to one side. "I'm sorry, Dean, I'm probably not making much sense. You go on and check the clinic. I think I'll take a shower before bed."

Sensing she needed some distance, he merely nodded and walked away.

Elise checked the bedrooms and found Becky sound asleep under the covers with her favorite stuffed bear, Lisa sleeping with her pillow partially covering her head, and Keri reading a teen magazine. As Elise moved through the house, she could hear the dogs' joyful yips diminish. She guessed they'd probably followed Dean down the driveway.

Before she headed for her bathroom, she stopped at the locked cabinet that held her rifle and a handgun. She quickly unlocked it, took out the gun and loaded it.

"If Carl Dietrich dares to enter this house and Dean doesn't get him, I will," she vowed under her breath as she slid the gun under her mattress.

Instead of a shower, Elise opted for a bath, scenting the hot water with her favorite bath oil. She stretched out in the tub with the water covering her to her chin. By closing her eyes, she could almost forget about the real world and transport herself back to simpler times. The tension in her muscles slowly eased.

"Now there's decadence for you."

She opened her eyes. Dean stood in that doorway, holding a glass filled with Baileys Irish Cream and an open beer bottle. He sat down on the commode and held out the glass.

"Thank you. I decided a shower wouldn't relax me as much as a bath would." She sipped the drink.

Dean lifted his head and sniffed the air. "Smells real sexy in here."

Elise arched an eyebrow. "Do you equate everything with sex?"

"Only where you're concerned." He rolled the bottle between his palms.

Elise set her glass on the side of the tub. "So much has happened, Dean, that I wonder if what's gone on between us is because of the situation and, therefore, not real."

"No!" He shot to his feet, towering over her and looking more angry than she'd ever seen him. "What we have is about as real as you can get, and don't you dare try to deny it!"

"But how do we know?" Elise persisted, a part of her knowing she was pushing even when she shouldn't.

He put the bottle to one side and hauled her up out of the water.

"Dean!" She struggled to keep her balance.

His dark visage should have frightened her, but it didn't. She knew she was the reason for his anger. She'd tried to dismiss what they had, tried to say it wasn't real, when all she wanted was to hold what they shared close to her.

"Elise Carpenter, you're the best thing that's ever happened to me," Dean said, his voice raw with emotion. "And I'm not giving you up for anything or anyone. Understand?"

She stared deep into his dark eyes. "Yes," she whispered.

They remained in their precarious position, Dean uncaring that suds smeared his clothes and Elise not feeling the chill.

"Everything will work out just fine," he told her. "Everything." He hooked an arm under her knees and picked her up. "Just remember that."

She slid an arm around his neck. "I don't think you're going to let me forget."

HE REMAINED in his crouched position among the rocks overlooking the darkened house. The small lit window—the bathroom, no doubt—went out, and no light went on in the bedroom.

Damn. No lights, and the drapes remained closed. He knew he shouldn't have sent that tape of them rolling around in bed. Now the drapes were closed all the time, taking away his fun.

He ran his fingers down his arm, feeling the scar tissue marring the tattoo he'd gotten when he was stationed in the Philippines. He'd never hated anyone as much as he hated that bitch when she cut him up with that scalpel. She'd 'bout near took his damn arm off! His lean features tightened.

He'd sat up there that morning watching the fool cops run all over the place. He wondered if they found all his little clues. They didn't worry him. Only that bastard who was there all the time was trouble. But Carl Dietrich had known trouble before, and he wasn't afraid of it.

"Soon, lady vet," he murmured. "Soon it will be just you and me. And payback time."

Chapter Fourteen

"What were you trying to prove with this dumb stunt?"

Elise didn't falter under Dean's low-voiced rage, nor did she look at the gun he held in his hand. "I'd be careful with that if if I were you. It's loaded."

He took several deep breaths to contain his anger. "Naturally, that was the first thing I checked, and now it's unloaded. What were you thinking, putting it under your mattress?"

"You must be like the princess and the pea."

"A pea this size would hard to miss," he informed her. "That was a crazy stunt, Elise. Or didn't you think I could protect you properly?"

She lifted her chin. "I thought it best to hedge all my bets."

With an expression of distaste, Dean tossed the gun onto the bed. "Do you realize how many people are killed by their own guns?"

"That lecture won't work. It used to be my own argument against having a gun in the house." She poked her forefinger against his chest. "And I hate that damn shirt!"

Puzzled, he looked downward. "What's wrong with it?"

"Feel Safe Tonight—Sleep With A Cop," she snapped. "Why can't you wear plain shirts like most adults?"

He didn't seem angry with her insult, but he didn't appear happy with her, either. "I'll wear what I please. But what you're trying to do here is change the subject, and I'm not going to allow that."

She dropped onto the bed and buried her face in her hands. "I'm tired, Dean." Her voice was muffled. "I'm tired of hiding out, of not even being able to go into work, of having to allow my answering service to pick up my calls and know anything suspicious is being traced. And I'm so afraid that our next step will be to take the girls out of school and send them away."

"Those five cups of coffee you've already had this morning haven't helped either," he said dryly.

Elise held out a hand, palm down. He was right: she had the jitters. "Good thing I'm not performing any surgery," she said sardonically.

"Right about now I wouldn't even ask you to remove a splinter."

She looked up. "How do you handle this? This constant waiting for something to happen. How can you do this every day without going insane?"

He crouched down in front of her, placing his hands on her knees. "For one thing, it doesn't happen every day. Some days we sit in the station and do nothing but type up reports."

She allowed herself the briefest of smiles. "It only takes you that long because you're such a rotten typist."

"That, too," he agreed, relieved to see a bit of her spirit returning.

Elise stared over Dean's shoulder, lost in thought. "He's narrowing the battlefield. He doesn't want anyone to escape the trap when he finally springs it. I know someone who trains guard dogs. I should have asked him if I could borrow a few for the yard. There's nothing like a Doberman going for a man's throat to make him think twice."

Dean shook his head. "This guy wouldn't think twice about shooting a dog. That tranquilizer-dart business the last time was just part of his game."

"Dobies don't give up easily." She needed to keep talking, just to know she was looking at every angle, if nothing else. "Dean, I am so frightened," she whispered. "Not for myself, but about what could happen if he decided to go after one of the girls to get back at me."

"I won't let him," he insisted fiercely. "You know that."

She covered his hands with hers, pressing down tightly. "But you can't watch all of us twenty-four hours a day! I'm not immune to the tension building up every day. You and I are snapping at each other like junkyard dogs!"

He allowed himself a grin. "Pretty good description, Doc, although I would think you'd describe us more as mauling macaws or leaping lop-ears or—"

"Enough!" She held up a hand. "I hate it when you make me laugh!"

"It's better to laugh than to cry. And in this business, we learn early to indulge in gallows humor. Now, come on." He jumped to his feet and pulled her. "We're going to coax the girls into going to the movies, where I can hold your hand in the dark and steal your popcorn."

She shot him a dry look. "Dean, girls of certain ages refuse to be caught dead going to the movies with a parent."

"Keri?"

"Keri *and* Lisa. They would insist on walking in a different door, pretending they don't even know us and, if possible, even sitting in a different theater. In fact, Keri would probably refuse to sit in the same theater as Lisa. Not exactly what you want us to do, is it? Since you prefer to keep an eye on all of us and can't manage to be in more than one place at a time."

Dean grimaced. "Teen years are hell."

"And they won't get any better in a hurry." A part of her wanted to warn him now. After all, if there was a way for them to make it together, Dean had to learn just how difficult the next few years would be. By the time Lisa left her teen years, Becky would be in the midst of hers. The idea was daunting even to Elise. She hugged him briefly, savoring the clean, soapy smell of his skin. "You never wear any kind of after-shave or cologne."

"When I'm crawling around on bank floors, I don't want anyone to smell me first," he explained.

"And you say the robbery detail is easy?"

"Easier than vice or narcotics," he told her. "Come on, let's find something to get our minds off what's going on."

"You said I could wear it!" Lisa shrieked.

"I never said any such thing! And now you've ruined it, you little idiot!" Keri's voice was shrill with anger.

Elise and Dean barely stepped out into the hall before they heard the sounds of war coming from the family room.

"Fud up! Fud up!" Baby screamed, joining in.

Elise sighed. "When I was seventeen I thought it would be wonderful to have eight children. I'm so glad I wised up in time." She hurried down the hall. "All right, what's going on here?" She had to shout to be heard above the girls' screams of outrage.

Dean stood on the outskirts, watching Elise deal with both sides of the heated argument. "I wonder what Robert Young would do here," he murmured, crossing his arms over his chest and leaning against the doorjamb. He decided it was much safer to remain a spectator. He wanted to tell Elise the girls' fighting was an outlet for the tension permeating the house but sensed this wasn't a good time to offer any such *Father Knows Best* opinion.

"She took my new sweater, and look what she's done!" Keri glared at her younger sister. "It's ruined, Mom, and I never even had a chance to wear it."

"She said I could wear it!" Lisa argued. "I wouldn't have spilled anything on it if she hadn't grabbed my arm."

The two began speaking so rapidly that Elise just stood there for a moment, taking in the verbal volleyball as Keri, Lisa *and* Baby kept on screaming.

"Enough!" She breathed deeply, grateful for the brief spate of silence. She looked at the once pale green crewneck sweater Lisa wore. The sweater Keri had begged Elise for for more than two weeks. The sweater that hung on Lisa's bony shoulders and now sported a large ink stain in front.

"I'm not saying you're lying, Lisa, but I do know that Keri would never have allowed you to borrow this particular sweater," she said slowly.

"She said I could borrow some of her ciothes!"

Elise placed her hand over her middle daughter's mouth. "Don't dig your hole any deeper, Lisa. You will not receive any allowance until the sweater is paid for." She held up her hand to forestall further arguments. "You will have kitchen duty for the next month, and no television for two weeks."

Lisa opened her mouth, then quickly closed it, recognizing the look on her mother's face. If she voiced a protest, the punishment would only be harder.

"You wanted the sweater, Lisa. It is now yours."

Lisa looked down. "But it's dirty."

"You know where the washer and the stain remover is. I suggest you try it." Elise turned to Keri. "Why don't you call the store and see if they have another sweater you liked," she suggested, easily reading her daughter's expression. "Don't worry, I realize you won't necessarily want the same one."

By the time Elise left the family room, she felt as if she'd lived five lifetimes.

"Very good," Dean applauded. "But how did you know Keri wouldn't want the same sweater she loved so much?"

"I have a sister, too," she replied. "Our bloodiest battle dealt with a favorite blouse of mine she wore on a date and spilled pizza sauce on." She paused. "The scary part is, Dean, this is only the beginning. It has to get worse before it gets better."

"I guess the idea of going to the movies is out, huh?"

Elise nodded. "You got it. Unfortunately, we'll all have to suffer right along with Lisa." She looked him square in the eye. "I told you the tension was getting to all of us."

He nodded. "One time I was lucky enough to baby-sit an important witness to a gangland killing. This guy thought room service was designed just for him, he cheated at poker and he snored worse than your tortoise."

"You snore almost as bad."

"No, I don't."

"Yes, you do. I'll tape-record you just to prove it."

"Mom! The washer is making funny noises!"

Elise closed her eyes and swore under her breath. She quickly opened them and glared at Dean when he chuckled.

"This is not going to be a fun day," she predicted.

DEAN QUICKLY REALIZED Elise's prediction was on the mark. The girls didn't want to do anything or go anywhere. Elise refereed arguments all day and finally sent all of them to their rooms until they reached the age of twenty-one. By bedtime, Elise fought a raging headache that even aspirin and a neck rub from Dean didn't help.

"Wave the white flag," she murmured. "Tell him we give up."

"No, you don't. Everything will be fine in the morning," he assured her, digging his thumbs into her tense neck muscles. "Sunday will be great. You'll see."

"Ha! You weren't the one to hear the washer repairman say he can't come out for two weeks, nor were you the one to listen to Becky scream bloody murder because she couldn't find her pink sweat shirt. Or Keri realizing she'd left her French notebook in her locker at school, or Lisa suddenly remembering she has a science project due on Monday. Tomorrow will be even worse."

"Only if you let it."

Elise knew better but didn't try to persuade Dean differently. Once they were under the covers and he wrapped his arms around her, she should have been ready to succumb to blessed sleep. Instead, she lay wide-awake.

"Not sleepy?" Dean rumbled in her ear.

"Just thinking."

"About what?"

"Wishing things were different. Wishing we'd met under other circumstances."

"If I'd hit on you and asked you for a date, would you have said yes after you learned I was a cop?"

She hated his logic. "Maybe," she opted.

"Maybe no. You don't like cops, remember?"

She lazily traced a finger around his beard. She'd never thought of beards as being soft and sexy until she knew Dean's. "You're beginning to change my mind."

"Yeah, I figured I did that once I didn't have to sleep with that tortoise anymore." He yawned broadly. "Now, be a good girl and go to sleep. I need my beauty rest."

As Elise listened to Dean's deep-breathing slumber, she only wished she could find the same.

THE NEXT DAY was a repeat of the one before, with tempers rising steadily until Elise threatened corporal punish-

ment, not one of her usual choices, and banished
everyone—including Dean, for trying to calm her down—
to their rooms. Dean was smart enough to hide out in the
guest room until things cooled down.

He wished he could break the thick cloud of tension
hovering over the house. He wanted nothing more than to
let the Carpenter women return to life as usual, but he knew
better. He knew time was running out and Dietrich could
strike at any moment. He wanted it over just as much as
Elise did, because then he could talk to her about a subject
that was growing more important every day. He figured his
best argument would be that Elise wouldn't have to change
her initials.

Elise spent Sunday night and the early hours into Monday walking the floors, looking in on her girls and staring
at the drawn curtains. She jumped each time she heard the
dogs moving about, and she peered out through the curtains but saw nothing other than the yellow floodlights illuminating the yard. As far as she was concerned, it was
much too quiet. She had no idea as she wandered through
the house that Dean lay awake listening to her footsteps,
wishing he could make things all better, and knowing, as
she did, that time was running out.

SIGHING IN RELIEF, Elise watched the sheriff's deputy drive
off with the girls. She enjoyed the idea of savoring a leisurely breakfast with Dean as they talked about anything
that came to mind except for the problem that refused to go
away. She had just finished loading the dishwasher when
she turned around to find Dean shrug on a denim jacket.

"I'm going in to see Santee so we can make our usual
idiotic call to Anderson," he told her. "Want to come with
me?"

She shook her head. "I think I'll take advantage of the
peace and quiet and read one of the books I've been mean-

ing to read for the past year. And, no offense, but police stations aren't my idea of fun.''

"Mine either. Okay, then do me a favor and stick close to the house." He looked around. "I won't be gone long."

"Dean?" She waited until he looked at her. "No offense, but I'll be very happy to have some time to myself. That's why I told Myrna not to bother coming in today."

He hesitated. "There's a patrol car parked near the front gate."

Elise smiled. "Stop fussing like a mother hen, Dean. I know the routine. If I even hear a leaf rattling, I'll holler good and loud. I promise." She kissed him for effect.

"As much as I'd like to pursue that kiss, duty rears its head." He sighed with regret. "I'll be back as soon as I can."

"I know."

She watched the blue truck rattle down the driveway and make its way out of sight.

"Enjoy the quiet, Elise, it won't be for long," she murmured, turning away.

It took her less than a half hour to realize none of her books looked interesting, and even the idea of cleaning out her closet wasn't appealing. She ended up in the kitchen, thinking about baking brownies, when the phone rang, making her jump.

"Dr. Carpenter, this is the answering service," a cheerful voice trilled in her ear. "I'm sorry to disturb you, but the gentleman insists it's an emergency with his bird."

"That's all right, I'll take the call." She waited for the telltale clicks indicating the call was being put through.

"Hey, lady doctor."

Elise felt the hairs on the back of her neck stand on end. "What do you want?"

"No, I think it's more what *you* want, and that would be your littlest bird," he jeered. "A great touch with your answering service, don't you agree? Your big bad cop lover is gone, so it's between you and me now. And I'm going to talk fast just in case this call is being traced."

She looked down and quickly pushed a button on the answering machine.

"I got your kid, lady, and if you don't want anything to happen to her, you'll get out of there without that cop near your house following you."

"I don't believe you." Except she did.

"Mom?" Becky's tearful voice tore through her bluff.

"Is that enough?" Dietrich jeered. "You meet with me, and the kid stays in one piece. And don't try any tricks, or she'll be the loser. I want this to be strictly between us. The kid is my insurance that you'll behave yourself."

Elise blanked her mind to all but the instructions given to her. By the time she hung up the phone, she felt ice-cold. All thought processes were on automatic as she headed for the locked cabinet. She knew exactly what she wanted and wasted no time getting it.

"What?" Dean exploded the minute the news was relayed to him.

Santee looked grim. "Rebecca Carpenter's school just called us to say that she didn't return to her classroom after morning recess. The principal was under orders to contact us immediately if something like this happened."

"It's Elise he wants, and he's using Becky to get her." He grabbed the phone and dialed Elise's number. After dealing with the answering service and listening to the distant ringing, he slammed down the phone. "I'm heading back to see what's happened. And when I find that son of a bitch, I'm killing him," he vowed.

"You call in!" Santee yelled after him.

"Go to hell! I promised Elise we wouldn't screw up this time, and I mean to keep that promise." He stormed out of the station,.

ELISE HAD NO TROUBLE leaving the property after summoning a cheerful smile and informing the officer outside that she was only heading for the nearby grocery store for some brownie ingredients. He hesitated, suggesting it might be better if she waited for Detective Cornell to return, but she overrode his objections by insisting she was only traveling a mile and wouldn't be gone for more than ten minutes. She wasn't surprised when the young man finally backed down. She purposely kept her speed level until she was out of sight. Then she floored the accelerator.

As she drove, she only hoped Dean picked up the message she'd left behind. She wouldn't be surprised if Dietrich was somehow watching her leave, and she intended to make sure Becky wouldn't be harmed. As she drove up the winding road into the hills, her expression grew more grim. She was glad she remembered Dean's habit of snuggling a gun against his spine and only hoped her jacket would hide the bulge that dug painfully into her back.

"This time, you bastard, you won't get away," she vowed, pressing down on the accelerator and sending the Pathfinder racing at a death-defying speed. "I'll make sure of that."

ELISE PULLED her truck off the road and slowly climbed out, swiveling her neck from left to right as she scanned the area. Nothing looked out of the ordinary, but she had learned the hard way that that didn't mean danger might not be right around the corner. She took several deep breaths as she headed for the footpath that led to the outlook point Dietrich had told her about. As she walked up the steep path, her ears strained for any sound from Becky.

With each step her rage grew, until it turned dark and cold and endlessly bitter. She was determined that not one ounce of emotion would hinder her intention of destroying the man who had made her family's life such hell. She had just stepped over the rise when she found Carl Dietrich standing a short distance away, holding a sobbing Becky against him.

"All right, I'm here. Now let her go," Elise called out. She drew deeply upon that cold, dark part of herself, the part that wouldn't allow emotions to confuse her. She already knew any sign of fear would automatically sign her and Becky's death warrants.

He laughed and shook his head. "Not so fast, baby. How do I know you didn't call the cops?"

"Mom!" Becky shrieked, starting forward, only to be jerked back by Dietrich's arm wrapped painfully around her throat.

Elise wanted nothing more than to claw the man's eyes out. Instead, she forced herself to remain calm. If she showed the least bit of weakness, she would lose. "You know I didn't call the cops because you have my daughter. Now let her go. I'm the one you want, not her. Although I have no idea why you're going to all this trouble. You'd be a lot better off if you'd just leave the state."

"Lady, no bitch cuts me up and gets away with it," he snarled, ignoring Becky's distress.

Elise looked into his wild eyes and saw his jerky movements and knew it would take all her wits to get her and Becky away alive. Carl Dietrich's heavy drug use had finally caught up with him, and there would be no reasoning with him; he was caught up in some bizarre world of his own making.

"That happened five years ago," she said carefully. "Why are you coming after me now? Because I recognized you at the bank?"

But he wasn't listening as he ranted about past sins that had nothing to do with Elise.

"I want all of you dead!" he screamed, waving a knife close to Becky's terror-stricken face. "I'm going to start with this kid and work my way through the family and your cop lover. You're never going to bother me again!"

"No!" Elise screamed, reaching behind her at the same time Dietrich's knife hovered too closely to Becky's face. She didn't have to think about what she was going to do. All she knew was that her baby was going to be killed if she didn't do something first. She swept the gun out and fired with deadly accuracy.

"No!" Dean also screamed, running up the path as fast as he could, his gun drawn. He skidded to a stop, finding Becky in Elise's arms as Dietrich lay on the ground, screaming curses at the world. It only took a glance to see blood streaming down Dietrich's arm and a quick kick to knock the knife out his reach. After making sure the man had no other weapons on him, he grasped Dietrich's shirt-front in both hands and pulled him partially upright.

"You slimy son of a bitch, I ought to finish the job here and now!" Dean snarled, savagely twisting the fabric between his fingers.

"Hey, man, I didn't hurt them!" Dietrich blubbered, recognizing the murderous glint in the detective's eyes.

"Dean, let him go," Elise called, also aware of what might happen. "He's not worth it."

Dean stared down at the wounded man for another minute, breathing heavily, concentrating on regaining his sanity.

"If you'd harmed one hair on either one of their heads, you would have been dead meat, Dietrich," he said tightly. "And I would have made it the most painful way to die I could find." He let go of him as if he were the vilest creature he'd ever encountered.

Dean turned and headed for Elise and Becky, wrapping his arms around both of them. "I was so scared," he muttered, raining kisses on them.

"I wanted to kill him for all he'd done to us. But I was also afraid I might hit Becky, so I aimed for a shoulder," Elise babbled, holding Dean tightly with one arm while keeping the other wrapped around Becky.

Dean scrambled to pick up Becky in one arm and wrap the other around Elise's shoulders. "I know, honey, I know. You did great." He laughed shakily when he heard sirens. "Sounds like the cavalry's a bit late in arriving again."

She wiped her tearful face against his T-shirt. "You guys better do it right this time, Cornell, because next time I promise I won't just wing him."

"Hey, you know the old saying, 'third time's the charm.'" He stood there feeling more than a little tearful himself, wondering how a seasoned cop like himself could even think about crying. Then he looked down at the woman he'd almost lost and the little girl talking a mile a minute about how Mom had rescued her. No wonder there was moisture in his eyes.

"SHE OUGHT TO BE in here begging me not to go," Dean grumbled, gathering neatly folded T-shirts and underwear out of a dresser drawer and tossing them onto the bed. "Can't she see I'm exactly what she needs? I can't imagine anyone else putting up with that temper of hers." He kept on mumbling to himself as he stuffed his duffel bag, heedless of whatever mess he was making.

In the past twenty-four hours he'd been busy writing up reports and giving statements. The best part was seeing Carl Dietrich kept under close guard. This time, there would be no escape for the man.

Except now, Dean had no further reason to remain. Oh, he had plenty of personal reasons, but he wasn't sure Elise was ready to hear them yet. While he was good with flippant retorts, something from the heart was a lot more difficult to phrase.

"Can't she see how much I love her and don't want to leave her? Damn woman, we're good together! She can't be so blind she can't see it," he groused, closing the zipper so savagely he almost took off a finger. He grabbed the bag by the handle and turned around, stopping short when he found Elise standing in the open doorway. Her face was paper white, her lips trembling.

"All packed?" she asked quietly.

He nodded jerkily. If he could say all the right words a couple of minutes ago, why the hell wouldn't they come out now?

Elise opened her mouth as if to say something but quickly closed it again. Dean hoped she was going to ask him to stay. At the same time, why should he expect *her* to say the words? Why couldn't he? Why couldn't they say them at the same time?

"Well, I guess this is it." Dean shifted from one foot to the other as he looked at Elise.

She kept her eyes downcast as she stepped back to allow him to leave the room. Was he so eager to leave that he barely finished writing all his reports and he was off? Tears pricked at her eyelids, but she exerted all her willpower to keep them at bay. After all, she still had her pride. If Dean wanted to leave so badly, she wasn't about to ask him to stay. Although the idea of placing Althea in the doorway to keep him from leaving the house *did* cross her mind.

Say something! her brain screamed. *Tell him how much you need him. Take a chance for once!*

Dean walked outside, telling himself to give her a little space, let her settle down a bit before he started honest-to-God courting procedures, beginning with that dinner and dancing she'd teased him about. Still, he couldn't believe she could stoically watch him pack up and could stand there and say nothing about their future! Hell, even the girls looked a little sad at his leaving! Why couldn't she?

Elise looked up at him with those brilliant eyes that could look, oh, so cool or oh, so warm. Now there was no expression. But she blinked a lot—as if she were trying to hold back tears?

"Thank you for all your help," she said in a low voice.

Dean bit down on a curse. He hated himself for not having the nerve to say the right words and hated her for not saying them, either. "Well, if you need anything, you know where I am," he said in a rough voice. "Bye, girls." He looked beyond Elise, who stood as still as statue.

"Bye, Dean." Becky's lower lip trembled.

"I'll miss you," Lisa mumbled.

Keri managed a small smile. "Me, too."

Dean started to turn away, then shook his head and muttered the curse he'd wanted to say a second ago. He grabbed Elise by the shoulders and hauled her into his arms. He kissed her so deeply he could feel her start to sag in his arms. Then he stepped back.

"See if you can forget that," he bit out, and he headed for his truck without a backward glance. "See you at the trial, Doc," he threw over his shoulder.

Elise stood there, stunned. How dare he leave after kissing her senseless? Only pride kept her from running after the truck that now roared down the driveway with the dogs barking after it. Pride kept her standing there, watching the man she loved drive out of her life as if she'd been nothing more than a job he'd finished successfully. Pride... She was about to say to hell with her pride and run after Dean when another idea came to mind.

"There is no way I'm going to allow him to leave this county, dammit," she vowed, running into the house.

Keri's head swiveled as she watched her mother streak past. "What's wrong, Mom?"

"Mom, you're swearing!" Lisa sounded delighted that her mother had indulged in a vice she wholeheartedly discouraged in her daughters.

"If this doesn't work, I'll be doing a lot more than that in a few minutes." Elise picked up the phone and quickly punched out the numbers printed on a card she held in one hand.

"DAMN CRAZY WOMAN," Dean muttered, shifting gears with a heavier hand than usual. "She could have told me she wanted me to stay. It wouldn't have hurt her to admit she needs and loves me. I made all the other moves first. It's her turn to get off that high horse of hers and admit the truth about us." He switched the radio on, listened to a song about hard-hearted women and quickly turned it off. "I'll show her. I won't call her for a month." He bobbed his head, pleased with his description, even though he was dying inside. "I'm not going to be the only one to suffer here."

Dean glanced over his shoulder and into the side-view mirror before changing lanes.

"Okay, maybe I'll only give her two weeks. And she'd better be grateful I'm going to call her at all. Not many men would put up with a snoring tortoise and a prissy woman like her." He swore loudly and slapped the steering wheel with his palm. "Damn her! Why couldn't she give me one little sign that she wanted me to stay?" He looked up to see a patrol car with its red-and-blue lights flashing. "Now what?'' He swore several more times just because it made him feel better, and he quickly pulled over to the side. He opened his door and hopped out of his truck. "Santee? Hey, you didn't have to come out here to say goodbye." He grinned. "I was going to stop off at the station and see you on my way out."

The man's face remained impassive as he stood a short distance away, his hand resting lightly on his gun. "I've got orders to bring you in, Cornell."

Dean was incredulous. "What? Okay, so maybe I was going sixty-eight in a sixty-five mile zone. What can I say?" He chuckled, thinking this was all a joke. "Last I heard, it wasn't a felony."

"No, but the crime you're accused of is." The handcuffs he dangled from one hand didn't look like a joke. "Turn around and spread 'em," he ordered.

"Wait a minute!" Dean found himself spinning against his truck and frisked before the handcuffs found their way around his wrists pulled behind his back. "What's this all about? What are the charges?"

"Grand theft." Santee pushed him toward the patrol car. "Don't worry about your truck. I'll arrange for someone to pick it up."

"Grand theft!" Dean yelped just before his head was pushed down as he was guided into the back seat of the patrol car. "Hey, watch it!"

By now Dean didn't see any humor in the situation, but none of his questions were answered other than by Santee quietly saying, "You'll find out soon enough."

Dean sputtered and cursed the entire drive, but the sheriff's detective ignored him. By the time he realized they were pulling in behind the Carpenter Avian and Exotic Animal Clinic to the house in the rear, he was hopping mad. He glared at Elise, who stood at the foot of the steps, while the three girls stood on the porch just outside the front door.

"What is this?" he demanded once he was taken out of the car.

"Grand theft," Santee repeated.

"Get these things off me so I can commit some bodily harm," he growled, vainly trying to wiggle his bound wrists as he advanced on Elise. "I didn't steal anything!" he yelled at her.

"You stole my heart, you jerk!" she yelled back. "And if you think you're going to get away with it, you've got another thing coming, mister!"

"You had me arrested!" Dean bellowed.

"You were going to leave me!" she shrieked, once and for all dashing the image of the cool, collected doctor.

"Only because you were so damn stubborn you didn't ask me to stay!"

"I didn't think I had to. I figured you had brains enough to figure out on your own that I wanted you to stay! Besides, you could have told me you didn't want to go! There's no reason you couldn't say the words! I should have known better! Cops only have brains enough to write a lousy parking ticket!" She stood toe to toe with him.

"It would have been nice to be asked. For all I knew, if I said I was staying, you might have decided to kick me out. I'm not real good with rejection."

Elise almost crumpled at his reluctant admission.

"I think it's time we went inside so they can talk privately," Keri murmured, herding the girls toward the door.

"Are you kidding?" Lisa argued, twisting her head one way, then the other. "Things are just starting to get good! This is even better than the movies!"

"In, Lisa."

"I think you two can handle it from here on," Santee said quietly, unlocking the handcuffs from Dean's wrists before heading back to his car.

Dean didn't move one inch from his position of towering over Elise, who didn't look one bit daunted. With her eyes blazing and her cheeks flushed, he decided she'd never looked more beautiful. "Okay, lady, you want it, you got it. But with a few revisions in your rules. I don't intend to be threatened with no meals if I don't pick my clothes up twenty-four hours a day. I like my beer, and I don't intend to apologize if I cuss a blue streak once in a blue moon. I can't cook worth a damn, I have a horrible temper, I hate reptiles of all kinds, especially snoring tortoises, and I don't remember my own birthday, much less anyone else's," he ground out. "As for you, you wear the ugliest nightgowns known to man, you're a bit prissy, though I intend to change that real quick, and you need to learn when not to argue with me about my choice in clothing or hairstyle, but, dammit, woman, you're never going to find another man who loves you and your girls as much as I do, and whether you like it or not, we're getting married as soon as possible!"

She smiled at his expression. "Anything you say, Detective."

He stopped and blinked. He looked a little wary, as if waiting for the other shoe to drop. "No arguments?"

Elise shook her head.

Dean took several deep breaths. "Then why did you stand there like an idiot and watch me pack? Why did you watch me drive out of here? And why did you have to drag Santee into this?"

"I hoped you'd change your mind," she said softly. "And since you didn't, I called Santee, who was only too happy to arrest you for the first charge that came to my mind."

For a moment, Dean felt as if he'd been outmaneuvered somehow. "I'll screen Keri's dates and do the same when it's Lisa and Becky's turns, and they'll hate me for it," he muttered.

"For a while, but they'll eventually learn you only do it because you love them." Elise's eyes warmed. "Besides, the time might come when you'll have more to worry about than their dates, when you're walking the floor with a colicky baby and learning to change messy diapers."

Hope slammed into his chest. "You mean you wouldn't mind having another baby?"

"Not as long as it's yours." Elise combed her fingers through the dark hair curling wildly around his ears. She knew nagging wouldn't prompt him to get regular haircuts, but that was all right. She decided she liked this man who dressed and acted like a thug most of the time, because he was *her* thug. And no matter how rough and gruff he got at times, she knew she'd be able to handle him. "But I don't want you to give up your work, Dean. It's too important to you."

Something else he didn't expect. "Santee said we might be able to work something out. Either way, I have other options. I just want you and the girls, Ellie. Nothing else matters."

She couldn't stop smiling. "Then I only have one request."

By then he was ready to give her the world. "Ask and it's yours."

She braced her hands on her hips in her old fighting manner. "No more crawling through bank windows to rescue hostages. I won't have you meeting other women that way!"

Dean drew her into his arms and picked her up. "Doc, you're more than enough woman for me." He glanced over her shoulder at the three hopeful faces peering out the window. "All right, give us some privacy here!" he yelled. "As your stepfather-to-be, I command you to go to your rooms and stay there until further notice!"

Three "Yeas!" sounded from inside as the faces disappeared.

"Why don't I ask Myrna to take them out to lunch and shopping. Then *we* would be the ones to go to our room and stay there until further notice," Elise murmured, linking her arms around his neck and nuzzling his chin with her lips.

Dean bumped the door open with his hip and carried her inside. "Doc, I do like the way you think."

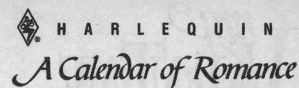

HARLEQUIN

A Calendar of Romance

Be a part of American Romance's year-long celebration of love and the holidays of 1992. Experience all the passion of falling in love during the excitement of each month's holiday. Some of your favorite authors will help you celebrate those special times of the year, like the romance of Valentine's Day, the magic of St. Patrick's Day, the joy of Easter.

Celebrate the romance of Valentine's Day with

#425 VALENTINE HEARTS AND FLOWERS
by Muriel Jensen

Read all the books in *A Calendar of Romance,* coming to you one each month, all year, from Harlequin American Romance. COR2

my VALENTINE 1992

Celebrate the most romantic day of the year with
MY VALENTINE 1992—a sexy new collection of four
romantic stories written by our famous Temptation
authors:

> GINA WILKINS
> KRISTINE ROLOFSON
> JOANN ROSS
> VICKI LEWIS THOMPSON

My Valentine 1992—an exquisite escape into a romantic
and sensuous world.

 Harlequin Books

VAL-92-R

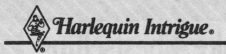

Harlequin Intrigue®

It looks like a charming old building near the Baltimore waterfront, but inside 43 Light Street lurks danger... and romance.

Labeled a "true master of intrigue" by *Rave Reviews*, bestselling author Rebecca York continues her exciting series with #179 ONLY SKIN DEEP, coming to you next month.

When her sister is found dead, Dr. Kathryn Martin, a 43 Light Street occupant, suddenly finds herself caught up in the glamorous world of a posh Washington, D.C., beauty salon. Not even former love Mac McQuade can believe the schemes Katie uncovers.

Watch for #179 ONLY SKIN DEEP in February, and all the upcoming 43 Light Street titles for top-notch suspense and romance.

LS92

Take 4 bestselling love stories FREE

Plus get a FREE surprise gift!

Harlequin Intrigue®

Trust No One...

When you are outwitting a cunning killer, confronting dark secrets or unmasking a devious imposter, it's hard to know whom to trust. Strong arms reach out to embrace you—but are they a safe harbor...or a tiger's den?

When you're on the run, do you dare to fall in love?

For heart-stopping suspense and heart-stirring romance, read Harlequin Intrigue. Two new titles each month.

HARLEQUIN INTRIGUE—where you can expect the unexpected.

HARLEQUIN
PROUDLY PRESENTS
A DAZZLING NEW CONCEPT IN ROMANCE FICTION

One small town—twelve terrific love stories

Welcome to Tyler, Wisconsin—a town full of people
you'll enjoy getting to know, memorable friends and
unforgettable lovers, and a long-buried secret that
lurks beneath its serene surface....

JOIN US FOR A YEAR IN THE LIFE OF TYLER

Each book set in Tyler is a self-contained love story;
together, the twelve novels stitch the fabric of a
community.

LOSE YOUR HEART TO TYLER!

The excitement begins in March 1992, with
WHIRLWIND, by Nancy Martin. When lively, brash
Liza Baron arrives home unexpectedly, she moves
into the old family lodge, where the silent and
mysterious Cliff Forrester has been living in seclusion
for years....

WATCH FOR ALL TWELVE BOOKS
OF THE TYLER SERIES
Available wherever Harlequin books are sold

TYLER-G